BRICK BRANNIGAN IS BURIED ALIVE ON THE FAROE ISLANDS!

BY ERIC BONKOWSKI

BRICK BRANNIGAN IS BURIED ALIVE ON THE FAROE ISLANDS!

CHAPTER 1: Buenos Dias Señor Del Toro, Gibraltar, and the New Leg of Our Journey (All Welcomed Over Suspicious Glasses of Sangria and a Sampling of Tapas)

Raúl Del Toro was sitting on a white brick storm wall, smoking a cigarette, watching the sun rise over the Mediterranean. It was nearly lunchtime, and despite skipping breakfast, he was not hungry, even if a ham and Manchego sandwich waited for him in the icebox.

A seagull landed beside him. Its two beady eyes locked on his.

"*Desaparece*," Raúl said morosely. "Be gone."

The bird just stared at him.

Señor Del Toro had been feeling despondent for far too long. Each morning he rose and went through his daily tasks, managing the squat red and white lighthouse sitting on the craggy bluffs of the Iberian Peninsula. He swept the floors and trimmed the wicks, wound the clockworks and polished the lenses. At the end of each day, he turned down his small cot and read the poetry of Antonio Machado over a glass of *Sangria* until sleep found him.

Everything was done in solitude.

November had arrived, and the temperatures were slowly dropping. The frightening politics he read in *El Correo de Andalucía* over his coffee each morning were not helping to ease his sense of hopelessness that had been plaguing him for some time.

And so, he smoked and watched the sea change beneath the golden Mediterranean sun.

"That is enough," he said, dropping his cigarette and turning away from the ocean.

He strode back to the lighthouse and opened the door, walking into the cramped keeper's quarters, scratching the two day growth of a beard on his chin.

In the kitchen, he stopped.

Something was not as it should have been.

His eyes moved over the icebox and the pantry, the empty kitchen table and cold oven. From the counter, he pulled a long silver blade from the knife block. After an unfortunate past event with a pair of seafaring ruffians, Del Toro had long since determined he would never again be robbed.

On the white tile floor of the kitchen, a streak of dirt heralded the entry of an uninvited individual.

"*Quien están aquí?*" he asked. "*Muéstrense.*"

The door to the pantry *creaked* open a fraction of an inch and the depressed lighthouse keeper threw the blade with the remarkable prowess you would not expect from an overweight fellow with an affinity for poetry.

End over end, the blade crossed the room almost as fast as a bullet from a gun.

THUNK.

"¡*Espere!*" a muffled voice called from within.

"¡*Salgan*! *Ahora!*"

The pantry door opened further and two figures emerged, an attractive woman and a nervous-looking young man. Both had their hands raised into the air.

"*¿Quién están ustedes?*" Del Toro asked. "*¿Y qué están haciendo aquí?*"

The woman turned to the boy and nudged him with her elbow. "Andrew..." she said.

The young man bit his lip, his brow furrowed. "Uhh..." he said. "*Somos...*"

"You speak English," Del Toro said.

The two strangers sighed, obviously relieved. "We do, yes," the woman said. "You are... fluent?"

Del Toro shook his head. "I speak enough," he said. "Many travelers have come by my lighthouse in the past. They speak many languages. I have learned enough."

"We are..." the woman stopped when Raúl turned and walked from the room. "Sir...?" she ventured.

A moment later, a *crackle* of a radio broke the silence.

"*Punto de Victoria al alguacil de Gibraltar...*"

"Wait!" a voice called from the kitchen. A moment later, the two strangers rushed into the radio room. "Wait," the woman said again.

Del Toro ignored them. Months spent alone had made him callous to the supplications of strangers.

"*Punto de Victoria al alguacil de Gibraltar...*"

"What is he saying, Andrew?" the woman asked.

"I believe... I believe he is calling someone. I think... the sheriff?" the young man said.

The woman brashly stepped forward and snatched the electrical cord from the radio. With nary a *hisss*, the great radio died quite suddenly.

"*Mujer tonta!*" Del Toro said. "Why did you do that?"

"I don't know your name, sir, and at the moment I don't care. If you are who I hope you are, you will help us. If not... well, I hope you will help us anyway. My name is Liliana Halifax and I am a close associate of Professor Hugo Brannigan. Does that name mean anything to you?"

Del Toro frowned. "Brannigan?" he said. He blinked his brown eyes and Dr. Halifax noted that it seemed as though he had just been hit in the head. "Brannigan, you say?" he asked again.

"Yes, Brannigan."

Del Toro removed his glasses and rolled up the sleeves to his woolen sweater. "Señorita," he said. "In situations like this, you will find... that you should begin with that word."

Lily frowned. "I'm sorry?"

"Brannigan," he said. "All you needed to say... was 'Brannigan.'" He smiled. "It is good to be among friends once again. It has been far too long. Welcome to Gibraltar, Miss Halifax."

***

Señor Del Toro was in the kitchen, pulling stuffed olives from a jar and cutting his Manchego cheese, leaving Lily and young Caine alone in a small sitting room, contemplating their fate.

"Are you sure this is wise, Doctor?"

"What do you mean, Andrew?"

"This... Cabal. They seem to have agents everywhere."

Lily nodded. "Yes, and?"

"How do we know this man is... not among their agents?"

"Hugo said he was close acquaintances with the keeper of this lighthouse."

Andrew nodded. "Yes, but are we certain it is *this* man?"

"You are implying..."

Andrew nodded again. "Perhaps this man is an impostor. Perhaps he's killed the true Del Toro. Or perhaps the true keeper is not named Del Toro at all. He was trying to use the radio, and I didn't understand everything he said. And there was a plane crash just now... why has he not mentioned it? How could he have missed the sight of that huge plane falling from the sky?"

Dr. Halifax opened her mouth to respond, but she was cut short when Señor Del Toro walked from the kitchen, three plates filling his hands.

"Sit, my friends," he said. "Please."

On a small round table, the keeper set down the three dishes. Despite Lily's growing fears, her stomach grumbled loudly at the sight of artichoke hearts, stuffed olives, mushrooms, Manchego slices, and chorizo.

Del Toro was smiling, until he looked into the faces of his new guests.

"What is wrong?" he asked. "You are... not hungry?"

"It's, um... not that, Señor," she smiled. "Please, sit."

Del Toro took a seat across from them. "You look afraid," he said, his elementary grasp on the language giving a particular candor to his words. "What bothers you?"

"How long have you known, Hugo?" Lily asked.

At the mention of the Professor's name, the keeper smiled. "Señor Brannigan I have known for years," he said. "He saved my life."

"When did you meet?"

The man squirmed. "I was... for a time, I was a hired soldier. I fought in the Cilicia War. I was mistaken to do so." The man pulled his sleeves down and then rolled them up once more. "It was because of the money that I did so."

"You are... a mercenary?" Andrew asked.

"No," Del Toro said, his voice sharp. "I am no mercenary."

"But... you were?"

Slowly, the man shook his head. "I did many bad things, but I was young. And stupid."

"And you met Hugo in the war?" Lily asked.

"He was also young. He was digging in Ammam. It was a dangerous place." Del Toro looked at his visitors. "I do not wish to talk about this." He rose abruptly and went back into the kitchen. Lily and Andrew looked at the food.

"Do you think it's safe?" Lily whispered to Andrew.

The young man blanched and dropped the slice of chorizo he was raising to his lips. "You think... it is *poison*?"

Lily could not get the image of the black worm from her mind's eye, the same worm that had taken control of her friend Nero, almost costing her her life. Her brazenness was shrinking, seeming to withdraw after the adrenaline rush of the crash faded. She took a deep breath, hoping her bravery could carry her through this strange confrontation. Without a doubt, it would only be the first of a great many before she found Hugo again.

"I don't know," she whispered. "You made me *paranoid*!"

In the kitchen, she could see Del Toro pull back the curtain to a small window and look out at the Mediterranean. He glanced back at her and caught her eye.

"Are you thirsty?" he called. "I will bring drink."

Lily looked at Andrew. "Is there a dock here?" she asked. "What's he looking at?"

The young man shrugged nervously. "Do you think a ship is docking?"

Now Lily shrugged.

From the kitchen, Del Toro returned with a jug of *Sangria* he had removed from the icebox. In his other hand were glasses. Only *two* glasses.

He set one down in front of Lily and one in front of Andrew.

"Drink," he said, pouring red liquid into each small juice glass. "You must be thirsty. Drink. Please."

Andrew remembered what Nero had told them about Jari, the Nigerian Cabal member who had held a pistol to Lily's head in Port Harcourt. "*He was no evil man,*" Nero had said. "*But he was forced into service of the Cabal on threat of death to his family.*"

"Do you... have a family, Señor?" Andrew asked, displaying a rather unsettling lack of discretion or subtlety. "*Una familia*?"

Del Toro stared down young Caine with two fierce dark eyes. "Why do you ask this?" he said. "*Mi familia es mi familia*. It is no business of you." He shook his head and looked at the *Sangria*. "You drink, no?" he nudged the glasses towards them.

Beside young Andrew, Lily was slipping her hand into Brannigan's satchel, fingers searching for the pistol she knew waited inside.

"I'm not thirsty, Señor," Andrew said. "*No tengo hambre*," he said.

"I understand," Del Toro said, frowning.

"I think I do, too," Lily said.

Quickly, she stood and pulled the pistol from her bag. "Get back," she said.

The Spanish man stood angrily. "*¿Qué haces, mujer?*" Del Toro asked. "*¿Estás loco?*"

"Sit down, Señor Del Toro," Lily said. Now standing, she could see out the small window in the kitchen. A black-sailed ship rose and fell with the tide just outside.

"Andrew," she said. "Let's go. This is a trap."

"Go?" the young man asked. "Go where?"

Lily racked her brain, trying to remember what Hugo had mentioned. The lighthouse had seemed so safe, and she was wrong. *Now what?*

"North," she said. "We need to get onto the mainland and get to a major city."

"You go to Sevilla, no?" Del Toro asked.

"Damn," Lily said. Foolish again, she realized, disclosing her plan. "You shouldn't have heard that!" she said. "I really need to work on this spy business."

"Spy?" Del Toro said, his eyebrows rising.

"Andrew," Lily said, ignoring the lighthouse keeper. "Get some rope."

Andrew turned to rummage a closet when a banging came at the lighthouse door. *KNOCK KNOCK.*

Everyone inside froze.

Lily whispered, "Who is–"

"*Herr Del Toro!*" an angry German voice shouted. "*Abra la puerta!*"

KNOCK KNOCK KNOCK.

"Escape?" Del Toro asked quietly. "I think you are too late, señorita..."

CHAPTER 2: Out of the Frying Pan, Into the Dark Pit; Out of the Dark Pit, Into the Frying Pan

There was silence–well, except for the persistent pounding on the door.

"Herr Del Toro! *Abra la puerta*!"

Andrew's eyes were wide. "What do we do?"

Lily turned to Del Toro. "Well, señor," she said. "Are you to turn us in?"

The lighthouse keeper frowned. He opened his mouth to speak when the officer of the Cabal interrupted once again.

"Herr Del Toro!" There was some muttering next, then, "*Break it down*."

The next impact was not the casual knocking of a guest, it was a ferocious pounding of a fascist shoulder with plenty of might behind it.

What now? Lily thought. *Run? Fight?* She hugged the leather bag close to her, feeling the shape of the Cipher of Dumuzid and the metal skull press against her body. She had to protect them from the clutches of the Cabal. But at what cost? *Damn it all*, she cursed herself. *Where is that adventuress blood now?*

While Lily pondered her doom and adventuress shortcomings (and Andrew grew paler by the second),

Señor Del Toro took action–thank goodness! Turning from the door, he knelt in the center of the small sitting room and pulled back the knit throw rug, revealing a square, wooden trapdoor. Seizing the small silver ring screwed to the door, he pulled, opening the door on a deep and dark space beyond.

A blast of sea air interrupted Lily's foreboding mental meanderings. "Uh, what are you–?" she said, returning to the moment. She turned to look down into the darkness.

Raúl Del Toro, still kneeling, looked up at her. "Give me your hand," he said.

"What? Why? What are you doing?" The most suspicious part of her was still, yes, suspicious, but this Del Toro man was perhaps not a villain after all.

"Your hand, señorita!" he said, his voice sharp. "Before the door comes down and they are upon us!"

Impacts still rained against the barrier protecting them from the agents of the Cabal, but thankfully the lighthouse door was built from more than mere balsa. The old wood held strong.

Lily tightened the satchel on her shoulder and quickly took a seat on the precipice of the trapdoor, her legs dangling. "Where does this go?" she asked in a hushed voice.

Del Toro smiled. "Señor Brannigan has used it more than once," he said. "It was an old sewer drainage from the guest cottage before it was knocked down. It leads down a sharp slope to the sea."

"*Sewer drainage*?" Andrew asked skeptically.

Lily ignored him. "Is it safe?"

The pounding on the door continued. A bookcase

against the same wall rattled, sending a few small volumes tumbling to the floor.

"Safer than here, señorita! Go!"

Without another thought, Lily jumped. Just a few paces behind her, the scrawny form of Andrew Caine followed, his arms pinwheeling.

Lily hit a jagged slope of rock and rolled down towards the water, shrouded in darkness. Above her, the square of dim light disappeared as Del Toro shut the trapdoor.

They were on their own.

Had the chilly tide of the Strait of Gibraltar not jarred her from her fears, she may have succumbed to those insecurities that had begun setting in. Grateful are we, dear reader, that even in the darkness, a good splash of cold water has a remarkably restorative quality.

"Andrew, get up!"

"What? What's going on?"

In the dim light, Lily could see Andrew shaking his head like a wet dog.

"We need to get out of here before–"

Gunfire from above interrupted her.

"Good lord," Lily said. "Mr. Del Toro..."

Making sure she still had Brannigan's bag–which she did, Lily grabbed Andrew's arm and led him across the rocky shore, boots slapping against the water's edge. In the dark culvert beneath the lighthouse, a column of sunlight shone from a barred drain at the far end of the space. It was toward this drain that Lily led young Caine.

In a hushed voice, Andrew said, "Do you think Señor Del Toro is–"

A second volley of gunfire interrupted our young

graduate assistant and froze our adventurers in their tracks.

"I don't know, Andrew," Lily said honestly. "I can only hope he is all right."

Wading waist-deep into the water, Lily approached the gated drain and slowed at the site of the black-sailed clippers that rose and fell in the tide just outside. She pulled Andrew back into the shadows as a pair of rifle-wielding Cabalists approached the nearest clipper's gunwale.

Andrew pointed. "Are those–"

"*Shhh*!" Lily said. "Stay back!"

The men on the clipper were smoking and talking, but over the sound of the ocean their words were lost. Above them, harsh words were being exchanged.

"What are they saying?" Lily asked Andrew.

"Up there?" he gestured above them. "I don't know. Can't hear well enough."

Somewhere above, glass shattered. An angry voice rose but was cut short. A moment later, the heavy sound of a body falling sounded through the floor of the light-house.

"We've got to do something," Lily said. "I can't just stand by, hiding, while–"

A single gunshot explode above them, making both our hidden adventurers flinch.

"That's enough," Lily said. "There must be another way out."

Withdrawing from the grated drain, she waded back into the shadows, a chill beginning to set in from the water.

"Andrew," she called softly. "What is this?"

In the corner, shrouded in darkness, the concrete wall of the sewer chamber held strange brackets bolted into the stone. She ran her hand across them as she shivered. "I can't see well enough in the dark, but there is definitely..."

She shivered again, realizing that she and Andrew certainly needed to get out of the water–to say nothing of help Mr. Del Toro.

Splashing indelicately through the water, Andrew crossed the space, crossing his arms over his chest and rubbing for warmth.

A few inches taller than Lily–and blessed with rather gangly arms–Andrew's greater reach afforded him a bit more information than Lily's.

"These used to hold... a ladder!"

"*Shhh*! Keep your voice down, Andrew!"

"I'm sorry," he said softly. "I just got excited. You see, up here..." In the darkness, he stretched and caught hold of something. "The ladder remains. The bottom portion must've broken off!"

With a grunt, the young man pulled himself upward, slowly, one rung at a time. In only moments, his dripping-wet boots were dangling above the water line.

"Is it a way out?" Lily asked.

Slowly, Andrew continued his ascent.

Where the ladder met the rough stone of the ceiling, a flat metal panel was fit into the concrete. Andrew pushed his ear against in and listened.

From below, Lily whispered as loudly as she dared, "What did you find?"

"I believe this is some sort of access panel," Andrew said. "I can't hear anything. It may be all right."

"Perhaps you should not—"

Before Lily finished her sentence, young Caine put the flat of his hand against the panel and pushed, raising it with a faint *groan*.

A pair of jackboots were facing his wide eyes—heel first, thankfully. The grate led outside, and in the bright sun, Andrew was forced to squint. Below him, Lily raised one hand to shield her eyes.

Other than the jackboots of a Nazi soldier, Andrew saw nothing but the minimal vegetation of a well-kept garden and a path following the sharp line of a seawall.

Perhaps I should do something, Andrew pondered. *Jump this fellow? Bludgeon him with my shoe?*

Andrew's proclivity towards risky behavior due to his desire to be heroic was a trait that Professor Brannigan appreciated. Professor Brannigan, however, was not there, and young Caine had not yet learned that caution was the new watchword.

In the glare of bright sunlight, Lily had discovered a rocky outcropping that afforded her the benefit of an extra foot or so, just enough to get hold of the ladder. With nary a word to young Caine, Lily hopped the ladder and began to climb.

Above, Andrew continued his dangerous line of thinking. *Perhaps give him a good wallop with my fist? The professor did say I have a respectable punch...*

Unbeknownst to both our adventurers, the old metal brackets that affixed the ladder to the wall began to fail. It started at the top where the first bolt pulled free from the masonry. Had young Caine's head been in the game, perhaps he would have noticed. At the moment, dear reader, he did not.

Lily continued to climb, her fast hand-over-hand motions a bit too quick to notice that the ladder had begun to move, a slight wiggle as it worked towards pulling the remaining bolts from the stone.

I've got this old pocket knife the Professor gave me, Andrew thought. *I could... stick him? No, certainly not. The Professor wouldn't dream of it!*

Lily reached Andrew just as the left-hand side of the ladder pulled free, halting Lily's meteoric climb and frightening Andrew enough to not only cease his schemings, but also enough to make him drop the panel he held open.

It fell with a *CLANG*.

Now, during her climb, truth be told Lily was meandering through many of the same thoughts young Caine was. She had not quite gotten to shoe bludgeoning yet, but it was not far off.

As I've said before and I promise I'll say again, dear reader, thank goodness for Lily's adventuress blood, perhaps the only thing that gets our adventurers out of situations like this one.

When the panel *CLANG*ed shut, Lily broke from her frozen (unclimbing) state and squeezed past Andrew–the two adventurers just *barely* fitting on the ladder at once–and slipped one hand into Brannigan's shoulder bag.

The panel lifted to the angry face of a Nazi soldier, a bolt action Karabiner 98K rifle barrel leveled at our adventurers' faces.

The blonde haired villain opened his mouth–either to speak or call for help, it mattered not which–when the butt end of a pistol swooped from the mouth of the dark space and *cracked* against his temple.

Eyes rolling back into his head, the soldier collapsed in a pile.

Andrew turned to Lily. "Cracker jack, Doc, how did you manage that!?"

Lily, eyes wide in her own shock, looked at Andrew and found herself smiling. "I've no idea, I–"

"You moved like lightning! I've only ever seen the Professor move like that! You were like a ninja with that gun and–"

"Andrew, we need to practice restraint, remember?" Lily interrupted him as he began making punching sounds not unlike those a child would make while playing with toys. "We are trying to move with stealth. Mr. Del Toro still needs our help."

Lips closed tightly, the young assistant only nodded eagerly.

Together, Lily and Andrew pushed open the metal panel and stepped into the sunlight.

They stood on an esplanade that wound down from the green hills to the rocky coastline. On our adventurers' right was the seawall, a white stone and stucco barrier that overlooked the cold and choppy seas (and the smattering of black-sailed cutters that still loomed ominously). The lighthouse rose to their right, candy-cane painted in red and white stripes.

Save for the unconscious Nazi at their feet, the path was clear.

"Now what?" Andrew said. "We make a run for it?"

Lily looked at him askance. "What do you mean? Leave this place?"

Andrew nodded. "Beat a path for–"

"Andrew!" Lily scolded. "And what about Mr. Del

Toro?"

"Oh, uh. Um." Andrew blushed and shrugged. "I didn't mean to leave him out, Doctor."

"I'd like to think not, Andrew. Mr. Del Toro saved our lives, and if possible I intend to return the favor."

Andrew–now red with shame–followed Lily as she crept to the outer door of the cottage at the base of the lighthouse, the very same cottage from which they had made their sewer escape.

Standing beside the door, Lily pressed her ear close and listened.

"Well?" Andrew asked.

"I hear... only muted voices," Lily said. "Accented... *German*."

"And Mr. Del Toro?"

Lily closed her eyes and listened, struggling to hear more than guttural mutterings and the crash of waves against the shore.

Finally, she shook her head. "No," she said.

Andrew, now dead set on proving himself, said, "We need to find another entrance!"

"What?"

He turned and began winding around the outer wall of the cottage, Lily hot at his heels.

He stopped at an open window looking into the cottage's kitchen. Curtains were pulled back, revealing the small kitchen in which Del Toro had prepared their tapas and *Sangria*–now empty. In the center of the floor was a mound of broken dishes and food crushed underfoot (not far from the original muddy footprint Lily herself had left when she and Andrew had first arrived).

There had been some struggle in the kitchen.

18

Lily cursed her doubt and suspicion, realizing far too late that Raúl Del Toro was no Cabal agent after all. It had all been a fear-induced fantasy, and there was far too good a chance now that he had paid dearly for his hospitality. Perhaps even with his life.

"Lift me up, Andrew," Lily whispered.

"*What*? You're going in there?"

"Of course I am. There is very little help I can offer from outside."

Lily slipped the pistol back into Brannigan's bag and put a booted foot into Andrew's interlocked fingers. With a grunt, he hoisted her up onto the window ledge. Carefully, ever so carefully, she slipped inside.

From the kitchen, the voices were louder. Fortunately, the fearsome goons were speaking English.

"Of course he is lying. Delacroix sent us here. From what I understand–"

"You understand nothing, Paul. Captain Von Faust said–"

"The Captain himself *works* with Black Fang. We can trust him."

"But this man is nothing. A lighthouse keeper, nothing more. The Captain said that Delacroix Frenchie has been making many mistakes–"

"Captain Von Faust did say that, but this bastard has *spy* written all over him. Isn't that right, keeper?"

The silence that followed did not raise Lily's spirits.

Nor did the soldier that appeared from the corner of the room. Nor did the pistol he raised and pressed flush to her temple.

"Drop your bag, fräulein," a brutish voice said. Lily looked to see a heavy-browed man with a terrible sneer gesture with a Luger. "Let's go," he said. To the men in the adjacent room he called, "I have got her. It seems Herr Delacroix was right this time, my friends!"

Lily scowled. "Oh, damn it all!"

CHAPTER 3: Andrew Earns His Keep & Our Adventurers are Introduced to Señor Aurelio Reyes

The sneering Nazi with the gorilla's brow bullied Lily from the kitchen into the quaint sitting room at gunpoint.

Standing over Mr. Del Toro, Lily saw two strapping young men in German military uniforms. With the gent behind her, the trio cut quite a menacing figure. On the floor in front of her was Raúl Del Toro, hands tied and mouth gagged. Blood smeared his face, running from a substantial cut across his head.

He had been beaten brutally, Lily recognized.

"You terrible ruffians," Lily said through gritted teeth. "Why did you assault this man? He has done nothing, nothing at all!"

"Shut up, woman," the curly-haired soldier said. Lily recognized his voice from earlier. He was *Paul*. "Your capture proves that he has done something. Hidden you!"

"Indeed," Paul's partner said. "We saw your parachutes come down. Where's your partner?"

Lily opened her mouth, preparing to say *I have no partner*, when she realized the lie was useless. They'd seen his parachute. She tried a different tact: "He was killed in the landing," she said. "Neck broken."

From a small end table, the oafishly browed gent at her back pointed to a collection of half-filled dishes. "Nice try, woman. Where is he? And I thought I told you to drop that bag?"

The barrel of the Luger jammed in to her ribs. Slowly she pulled the strap over her head and lowered the bag to the ground. "Mr. Del Toro," she said. "Are you all right?"

The bloodied Spaniard nodded shortly before a soldier kicked him in the stomach. "Don't you fret him, woman," Paul said. "You'll both be quite free of worry soon enough." Turning his gaze to the oafish man behind him, Paul said, "Check her bag, Rolf. The Captain said we need those relics. And you," he turned to the otherwise silent soldier to his right. "Get to their radio, Matthäus. Call the ship. Tell them we've got the scientist."

Behind her, Rolf knelt and opened her bag. "*Mein Gott*," he said. A moment later, he rose, the black disc of the Cipher of Dumuzid in his hand.

Lily said something softly, soft enough for the Nazi to miss it.

"What'd you say, love?" Paul said, leering in her direction.

"I said I'm not a scientist." She stared him down with every ounce of her adventuress blood. "I'm a professor."

Paul, apparently the ranking officer in the room, laughed. "Some distinction, you harpy. Now we have the relic. If I were you, I would speak. You've no secrets left but one. So where is your partner?"

A gunshot cracked through the small space like an

explosion, slicing through the curtains in the window and slamming into Paul's chest with a *THOOMP*. Blood flowed, but Lily did not afford herself the seconds to be shocked. Twisting, she cracked her elbow into Rolf's face, feeling the hardline of his jaw crack beneath the impact. He dropped the disc. Across from her, the soldier named Matthäus raised his rifle and fired.

Lily ducked, feeling the bullet pass over her head as she snatched the Cipher from the air before it hit the ground. Fortunately for Lily, the errant shot meant for her had found a new target. Behind her, Rolf fell to the ground, dead.

Glass broke as another gunshot tore through the room from outside. Matthäus turned and fired his rifle through the front wall of the cottage repeatedly, his right hand working the bolt of the rifle after each thunderous shot. Small framed pictures and wall hangings exploded as 8mm bullets ripped through them.

Kneeling, Lily turned and scuttled backwards, crawling to Rolf's Luger that was still clutched in his lifeless hand. She snatched the pistol just as Matthäus turned his attention back to her.

Rifle fire sent her skittering for cover as Matthäus emptied his Karabiner 98k in her direction. Lily heard wood cracking and glass breaking as she pulled herself through the doorway into the kitchen and fired a few errant Luger shots over her shoulder.

"Damn you, woman!" Matthäus shouted. "Come out! I've got a round with your–"

A *thump* silenced him. From her position in the kitchen, Lily heard the heavy sound of a body falling. Tentatively, she peeked out from her vantage in the kitchen.

Andrew stood in the center of the room, a long rifle in his arms. He opened his mouth to speak but was unable. A traumatized look seemed stained on his face as he took in the death and destruction around him. With an air of finality, he dropped the rifle to the floor.

***

"We both owe you our lives, Andrew," Lily said as she cut through the thick rope binding Del Toro's hands. "You did what you had to–"

"I *killed* that man," he said. "Shot him right through the chest."

He had, indeed. After Lily disappeared into the lighthouse cottage and been captured, Andrew had returned to the felled Nazi at the sewer access panel and retrieved his rifle. Then he had fired through the cottage's front window, killing Paul and saving the day.

But it was the killing part that was troubling the young man so.

"I know, Andrew. But it was necessary. If you hadn't, we would soon be dead and the Cipher of Dumuzid would be in the hands of the Cabal."

Andrew mulled this over. After a time, he nodded. "But I'm just... a graduate student. A graduate *assistant*. The Professor has me do the paperwork. I catalogue our findings. I pack the shipping crates. I–"

"Today, Andrew," Lily said, helping Mr. Del Toro to his feet, "you saved our lives. Today you are the hero."

This seemed to raise the young man's spirits, at least to some degree. "I don't want to do that again, Doctor," he said. His voice lowered. "Kill someone."

"Believe me, Andrew," she said. "I understand. I'm hoping neither of us will have to again." Even as she spoke, she saw the face of Abassi, the Nigerian Cabal agent, as he fell to his death in Port Harcourt, all because of Lily. She knew what it was like to take a life, even if it was to save another.

"How about you, Mr. Del Toro? Are you all right?"

Our brutalized lighthouse keeper had taken a seat on a bullet riddled chair and was wiping blood from his face with a linen napkin he'd taken from among the half-filled tapas dishes.

"I am... all right," he said finally. "But we need to move, señorita."

"Move? Why?"

"The ships, remember?" He pointed through the blown out kitchen window at the nearest clipper that rose and fell in the tide. "These men are not here alone."

Lily shook her head. "Of course. How could I forget?" She really needed to get her adventuress chops sorted out. "What should we do, Mr. Del Toro?"

With a labored sigh, the keeper stood. "I have an idea," he said.

***

"You need to get to a city, a *big* city, no?"

They were in a truck, a busted lorry with a cracked axle, trundling around the cape towards the sprawl of the city.

Lily sat on the passenger's side with Andrew squeezed in the middle. "Yes," she said, clutching Brannigan's bag close.

"What is your plan?" the Spaniard asked.

"I... I'll need some time to think about that part."

"Find the Professor," Andrew ventured.

"Exactly, Andrew, we just need to figure out *where*."

"I believe I can help," Del Toro said, shifting gears to the tune of *grinding*. "I know many people. As I said previously, you meet many strange people in my line of work."

"Who do you know who can help us, Mr. Del Toro?"

The Spaniard smiled. "An interesting fellow, señorita."

An interesting fellow the man was indeed. When Señor Del Toro steered the old lorry down into town, he led them not into Gibraltar proper, but instead towards the main harbor.

The Port of Gibraltar was a bustling harbor, crowded with ships both large and small, many waving the flag of the British Empire. As he drove, Del Toro explained its strategic importance as a shipping port, especially in the seventy years since the Suez Canal had opened.

"Many English ships stop here at Gibraltar prior to traveling further east and through the Suez on their way to India."

"But what does this have to do with us, Mr. Del Toro?" Lily asked impatiently.

"Well, nothing," the Spaniard said with a shrug. "I just find it interesting."

"Fine, fine," Lily said. "What is your plan for us?"

The lighthouse keeper smiled. "That," he pointed.

The rumbling lorry came to a stop before a small cutter that looked in worse disrepair than Del Toro's wretched truck. Stenciled on the bow were the words

Barco Jamón. A great, fat, bearded gent sat on the quay before the ship, smoking a pipe and scratching a mop of greasy hair on his head. He looked up when Del Toro killed the truck's engine.

"Aurelio!" Del Toro shouted. "*¿Cómo estás?*"

"What you want, Raúl?" the big man said in a gruff and gravelly voice, alternating his scratching from his head to his substantial paunch.

Del Toro smiled and stepped out of the truck, slamming the door behind him. "*Quiero cobrar una deuda, amigo.*"

A terrific string of obscenities escaped the fat man's mouth that managed to cross the language barrier, making both Lily and Andrew blush as they followed the lighthouse keeper.

Shrugging, Del Toro said, "I cannot help the timing. *Lo siento. Pero... Tengo algo para endulzar el trato.*"

Still frowning, the big man's curiosity was at least piqued. "And what is that?"

From his back pocket, Del Toro pulled his wallet. From inside the billfold, he removed a wad of *pesetas*.

The big man laughed. "Money?" he said skeptically.

Del Toro shrugged. "*El dinero siempre es suficiente*, Aurelio."

A fog horn sounded as a freighter began its slow and laborious departure from the port. Lily and Andrew waited, understanding very little of what was happening and only hoping for the best.

Finally, the big man said, "*Multa. Dámelo.*"

"*Primero... Estas de acuerdo en ayudar a mis amigos entrar en España.*"

"*Entrando en España?*" the big man laughed. *Es*

fácil!"

Easy as it may have been, the fat man snatched the money from Del Toro's hand nonetheless. "*Después de que llegue mi cargamento*." Without another word, he turned and stalked off down the pier, smoking and chuckling to himself.

"What is happening?" Lily asked.

Andrew cleared his throat. "The, uh, *large* man is going to help us get into Spain? Is that right, sir?"

"It is," Del Toro said. "His name is Aurelio Reyes and he is an exporter of *ibérico*. He makes much money doing it. He will get you into Spain without rousing any suspicion."

"*Ibérico*?" Lily asked.

Del Toro smiled. "It is a delicacy," he explained.

"It's ham," Andrew said dryly. Lily laughed.

"Do not laugh, it is no mere ham," Del Toro said. "Its worth is undeniable."

Lily shrugged. "Expensive ham or not, I'll do whatever need be to get this journey started!"

CHAPTER 4: The Journey Begins in Earnest! AKA Sailing the High Seas on the Appropriately–Albeit Ridiculously–Named *Barco Jamón* with the Wise Aurelio Reyes

Sea sickness gripped Dr. Liliana Halifax. The sun had set and she was hunched over the gunwale, expelling her–

Wait. I've gotten ahead of myself.

The *Barco Jamón* departed the Port of Gibraltar in the afternoon. After the departure of the mysterious Aurelio Reyes, Lily had shared a few words of apology and thanks with Raúl Del Toro before the keeper left our adventurers to return to his lighthouse and the trouble that awaited him. Were German soldiers awaiting him even now? Were agents of the Cabal? Soldiers had died in his lighthouse, and he would no doubt be held responsible.

As his lorry trundled away, Lily could not help but worry that her and Andrew's arrival had put the kindly Spaniard into trouble of his own, but when she brought it up with him, he'd only shaken his head.

"Señorita," he said. "I involved myself. I chose to become a part of this. What awaits me back at the lighthouse awaits me because of my choices." He patted her shoulder kindly. "Regret nothing. I do this for you and for Andrew and for Señor Brannigan."

When Señor Del Toro had gone, a skinny waif of a

man named Capo had helped Lily and Andrew board the *Barco Jamón*, handing them a pair of rolled hammocks and pointing out where they could be hung. At Lily's request, Andrew spoke with the small man.

"He says we're sailing for Cádiz," Andrew finally explained after a few laborious exchanges in Spanish.

"Cádiz?" Lily asked. She racked her brain. *Cádiz... Cádiz...* "And where is that?" she eventually asked.

Andrew smiled. "Um... in Spain?" he said with a shrug.

Ah, what to do with a pair of inexperienced adventurers, dear reader?

With the sun descending to the west over the water, Reyes returned, wheeling an empty dolly behind him.

"¡*Vámonos*!" Reyes said, leaping from the dock onto the deck of the *Barco Jamón*, causing the small cutter to rock in the water.

"Mr. Reyes," Lily said, handing her hammock to Andrew. "Can I have a–"

"No. Perhaps when we get moving, Señora," the big man interrupted before belching quite loudly. "But now I have more important things to do." Turning his back on her, he waved to Capo. "*Levante el ancla*," he said.

"What a rude and disgusting man," Lily said.

Not another word (or sound) was shared by Señor Reyes before nightfall.

As for Andrew and Lily, they too were relatively silent.

They sat on the cramped deck–Lily on a capstan and Andrew on a crate–as the small cutter left the Port and sailed due west, straight for the Atlantic. While Capo worked the sails and Reyes stood at the wheel, Lily and

Andrew were left to their own thoughts, a dangerous proposition, indeed.

Andrew thought about the Nazi named Paul who had died by his hand.

Lily thought about Brick and the danger she'd put Señor Del Toro into. *Some adventuress*, she lamented.

By the time the sun was down, the coastline had disappeared from view and the sea had grown choppier. It was now that Lily began to feel the first intimations of sea sickness.

"Are you all right, Dr. Halifax?" Andrew asked softly.

Lily nodded stiffly. "I feel a little... ill," she said.

"I do, too," Andrew admitted.

"Strangely, it doesn't help that I'm hungry," Lily said. "Not what you'd expect, of course, but it's true."

Andrew looked down at his shoes, lit dimly by a nearby oil lantern. "Do you think I was wrong, Doctor?"

Grimacing, Lily turned her attention to her young companion. "About what?"

"That man..." Andrew said. "The soldier. I think his name was Paul?"

Wise and sensitive as she was, Lily understood all too well what the young man was going through. She remembered the face he'd worn earlier when he dropped the rifle after saving their lives.

"You did what was necessary, Andrew," Lily said. "I understand the guilt you feel." She thought once more of Abassi plunging from the roof back in Port Harcourt–a thought she would gladly throw overboard and watch sink in the blue sea if she could. "Honestly, Andrew, I cannot forget the man that I killed." She shook her head.

"I have hoped that he will fade, and perhaps it will, but it has not yet. I have to believe that I did was what I had to do to save Hugo."

"What did you do?"

Lily realized Andrew had not been with them on the roofs that night. "I... I used a pistol to shoot a man," she said softly. "He was about to murder Hugo and I knew that I could not stand by. I shot him and he fell from a rooftop. He died instantly."

"He fell?" Andrew asked.

Lily nodded. "I have not been able to forget it."

Andrew sighed. "I am afraid I will be the same way."

"Do you know what I have learned, Andrew? It's all right, this remembering. That memory will be a reminder of what was done and the possibility of the person we could become if we forget how precious life is. I do not want to kill again, and I hope I never will. Do you want to forget that?"

He shook his head.

"Neither do I. After what I've seen since beginning this adventure, I can think of no greater crime than becoming complacent with life. It is a precious and beautiful thing."

The young man nodded.

"Do you know what I do regret?" Lily asked.

"What?"

"Not trusting Mr. Del Toro. We believed him to be an agent of the Cabal," Lily said. "We nearly attacked him in his own home. If we had, we most likely would have been seized by the Nazis. He offered kindness, and we doubted him."

"But we didn't know," Andrew said. "He could have

been–"

"I know, Andrew," Lily interrupted. "But I have to believe that there are good people. I cannot continue through this day and the next and the next believing every good deed is only a selfish act in disguise. I would... well, I would just rather not do that."

Andrew thought about her words and nodded. It was dangerous, he realized, but there was something to be said for a little bit of hope in the world.

"Now," she said. "Do you mind hanging my hammock for me, Andrew? I would myself, but... I..." she burped. "I do believe I am about to be sick!"

***

And sick she was. Quite a number of minutes later– when her near empty stomach was indeed *empty*– Andrew helped her into her hammock. Somehow, on the rocking cutter, the hammock managed to offer more stability than Lily expected.

With the moon rising high in the sky, the sea began to settle. Only marginally, but Lily would take what she could get.

She tried to sleep but could not. Perhaps it was the sea sickness. Perhaps it had to do with what she may dream. Perhaps it was the simple fear of the unknown. Lily had no clue where they were going or what awaited them when they arrived.

Beside her, her partner was not having the same trouble. Andrew snored softly as the waves lapped against the cutter's hull.

"You should be sleeping," a deep voice said, interrupting Lily's reverie.

She turned in her hammock to see the dark silhouette of Reyes emerge from the minuscule keep below.

"Mr. Reyes," she said. "Have you decided to grace us with your presence?"

In the pale light of the oil lamp, Lily could see that he was quite different from the slovenly shipmate she'd first seen on the dock at Gibraltar.

Reyes's hair was combed and his face cleanly shaven. His stained and rumpled clothing had been replaced by a clean pair of chinos, a white cotton shirt, and a black canvas vest.

"Mr. Reyes?"

The heavy-set man smiled. "Yes, it is me. I have dropped my disguise. I beg your pardon for the way I spoke with you at the Port. I have an image to upkeep."

"I'm sorry, an image?"

"I will explain," he continued in perfect English. "But first, are you all right?"

"I was rather sick," Lily said sheepishly. "But it is beginning to wain."

"Here." From his vest pocket he pulled a small object and passed it to her.

"What is this?"

"Ginger," Reyes said. "An old sailor's cure. Chew it and you will feel better."

Lily put a small piece in her mouth and immediately tasted the root's sharp tang. She grimaced.

"It is strong, but it will work," Reyes said. "Trust me."

"Trust you, eh?" Lily said. "A man who admits to

34

wearing disguises?"

"Perhaps 'disguise' is too strong a word," the big man shrugged. "It is more... an *affectation*."

"Oh?"

"What did Raúl tell you about me, Señora?"

"Only that you are an exporter of ham and that you would be taking us to Spain."

At the word 'exporter,' Señor Reyes stifled a laugh.

"And what do you know of *jamón ibérico*, Señora?" he continued.

Lily sighed. "I know that I tire of questions, Mr. Reyes. And I appreciate candor."

"I'm sorry," Reyes said. "You are right. Raúl was also right when he told you that I will get you to Spain. He was, however, wrong in calling me an exporter. In simple, candid terms, Señora, I am a smuggler."

"A... *smuggler*?"

"As requested, I am being candid."

"Yes, I'm sorry, I just–" Lily took a deep breath, tasting the burn of the ginger. "Mr. Reyes, it was not long ago that I was simply a professor of ancient history. I gave lectures and graded papers. Now I am sailing the Strait of Gibraltar with a ham smuggler off the coast of Spain. You will forgive my boorishness."

The large man nodded graciously. "Infinitely forgiven, Señora. But I should correct you. We are no longer in the Strait of Gibraltar, nor are we in the Mediterranean. This is the Atlantic."

Lily tried to looked steely, but there an undeniable fear she felt; realizing that they'd entered the great Atlantic on the small ship made her feel like a single snowflake in danger of being caught in a strong breeze and carried away, never to be seen again.

"It is all right," Reyes said, immediately recognizing her unease. "We are only miles off the coast and approaching the Gulf of Cádiz now. We should be in the Gulf water in a matter of hours."

"Where are we going exactly?"

"Well, Cádiz, of course," Reyes said. "It is a city on a sort of cape, and it lies north, up the coast from Gibraltar. It is not far, Señora. But with the current tide, it will take almost a full day to arrive there. This is why I suggested resting."

"I will," she said. "I believe you were explaining a little about yourself?"

Reyes smiled. "Yes, I was. I am a smuggler, although for the simple reason that I care not for taxes. Import and export taxes would make my business far too... expensive."

"Ah," Lily nodded with a smile. "I see. Simply keeping your overhead down, yes?"

"Of course."

"And this... *affectation*?"

"It may surprise you, Señora, to learn that I was educated at the University of Salamanca, receiving degrees in biology and economics. I also studied at *Le Cordon Bleu* in Paris."

"So being a ham smuggler makes complete sense," Lily said.

"Sarcasm, Señora, reflects only your ignorance," Reyes said.

"Why is that?" Lily said, feeling annoyed.

"Because *jamón ibérico* is a miracle of nature," Reyes said defensively. "And my years of study make me the perfect... *distributor* of it."

Lily bowed her head. "I'm sorry, Mr. Reyes. I did not mean to offend."

"With my education, I have learned how to raise my own pigs on my farm in Córdoba. I grown and care for the pigs and the oak trees that provide the precious *bellota* that makes *ibérico* so remarkable. Using my years of study, I have created a perfect life for myself. Did you know that *jamón ibérico* is banned in your country and can bring hundreds–upwards of even a thousand–dollars for a ham with the bone contained within?"

"*How much*?" Lily asked, her jaw dropping.

"Yes, exactly! I believe you are through mocking me now, yes?" he smiled, his goodwill having returned in spades.

"Is that why you were in Gibraltar?"

"What a better place to conduct business with travelers from around the world?"

"My lord," Lily said, shaking her head. "And this affectation of which you speak?"

Reyes smiled. "Do you know what would happen if *you* tried to sell *ibérico* to a crew of traders? You would be swindled. There are those who prefer to see what they expect to see, trusting only their limited expectations. And they believe a ham smuggler should look like a ham smuggler, no? Not an academic in a tie. The Reyes you met in Gibraltar is never swindled. He is seen as a dangerous, street-wise criminal."

"Perhaps you are right, Mr. Reyes." Lily looked at the man and did not want to admit just how right he was. What were her own expectations of him? Did she sell the man short based solely on his filthy clothes? She had a great deal to learn about the world, indeed. *And where is Hugo to teach me?* she thought dolefully.

"Are you all right, Señora?" Reyes asked.

"Yes, I'm fine. But I believe I owe you an apology," she began for the second time that day.

Reyes stopped her, just as Del Toro had. "Do not apologize, Señora. You are out of your depth, and unlike many in your current position, you are learning to carry yourself with grace. Continue doing that, and you will have nothing to apologize for."

He stood. "Now you must sleep. Tomorrow I will perhaps give you a taste of *ibérico*, only then will you understand."

"Thank you, Mr. Reyes," she said. With her sea sickness now fully abated, her eyelids were beginning to grow heavy.

"You are welcome," Reyes said. "And please call me Aurelio. I do loathe formalities, Señora."

"And you can call me Liliana."

The big man nodded. "Goodnight Liliana. Sleep now, you will need your rest. I will get you safely into Spain, I promise. From there, I will help you arrange transportation to wherever you wish to go. So please, fear not."

With that, the big-bellied man retreated, leaving Lily to drift off to sleep.

Before her eyes closed on that night, she realized that Mr. Reyes had managed to allay many of her fears with his simple logic and kindness. For that, she was grateful, because she knew all too well that a long road still lay ahead.

CHAPTER 5: The Inevitable Dangers Arrive (Come On, What Did You Expect?)

The sun rose on black sails approaching from the southeast, effectively ruining Aurelio's and Lily's hopes of a smooth end to their short expedition. Gone was Lily's safe entrance into Spain. Gone was Aurelio's hope of sharing his *ibérico* (in a purely culinary sense), and thus gaining Lily's professional respect.

Instead, our small gang of adventurers was left to battle for survival once again.

"How long until they reach us?" Lily asked.

Reyes shook his head. "Not long," he said. "The ships are large, much larger than mine. With the size and number of sails they have, they will travel faster." He looked at Lily ominously. "We cannot outrun them."

"So how long?" Lily asked, scooping up Brannigan's leather satchel and pulling it over her shoulder.

Reyes looked at her. "What are you going to do? Jump ship?"

Beside them, Andrew stopped snoring–finally. "What? Where?" he said.

"Get up, Andrew," Lily said. "We need to get off this boat immediately!"

"You can't do that, Liliana. We are over a mile from shore and perhaps fifteen from Cádiz. You will surely drown."

"What are me other options? If you can delay–"

"¡*Mira*!" Capo interrupted from the bow, pointing.

Lily and Reyes turned their attentions to the horizon. A pair of black sails approached from the northwest, probably sailing from Cádiz.

"My lord," Lily said softly.

"And you will swim into that?"

"We're trapped."

"What's going on?" Andrew asked groggily from his hammock.

"I said get up, Andrew!"

"Señora, please!"

"What would you have us do, Aurelio? As I said, we are trapped. I had hoped I was wrong in my doubts about sea travel, but apparently–"

"Liliana!" Reyes interrupted. "This is a smuggler's ship, do you not believe I can manage to hide contraband?"

"Uh, well," Lily began. "You... um. What did you have in mind exactly?"

The big man laughed. "Some smuggler you must think I am!"

"Mr. Reyes, please," Lily said formally. "This hardly seems the time to take offense. If you can just show us–"

"No, wait," he said, chewing a fingernail thoughtfully. "*El envío fue entregado antes de salir. Maldito! Hostia! Olvidado el envío. Leñe!*"

"Oh. That's a few bad words..." Andrew said as he rubbed sleep from his eyes.

Reyes turned to Lily, his face screwed up in consternation. "Señora," he said. "I, uh... I seemed to have forgotten that I had loaded multiple crates of *ibérico* onto the ship prior to our departure." He grimaced even as he said the words.

"I don't understand, Mr. Reyes. What are you saying?"

"The space I have partitioned for smuggling..."

"...is currently filled with *hams*?" Lily finished, her voice sharp. "And after you just scolded me for questioning your abilities as a smuggler! Mr. Reyes!"

"I apologize, Señora, I–"

"You made me feel guilty and everything!"

"Well, in my defense, the hams are safe–"

"No matter," she interrupted. "We'll just throw the hams overboard."

"What? No, wait, you can't!"

"Mr. Reyes, when it comes to our lives or *hams*, believe me, I choose our lives."

"Ugh. You're... You're right," Reyes said. "I would choose..." his voice trailed off.

"Mr. Reyes?"

"Ah, yes. Um, the ham–uh, I mean, your lives." He shook his head, perhaps trying to shake bad thoughts loose. "Do not worry, Señora. I will think of something." He looked back up at the horizon. "We have time. Not a lifetime, but time enough."

From the northeast, the sound of a diesel motor roared to life.

"What is that?" Lily asked.

"*¿Qué ves, Capo?*" Reyes asked his assistant who held a pair of binoculars.

"*Un pequeño barco. Un explorador, tal vez,*" Capo said after a moment. "*Cuenta con un motor fuera de borda.*"

"An... explorer?" Andrew asked, stretching.

"Get up, Andrew!"

"It translates to 'scout,' actually," Reyes said.

"I'm getting up!"

"And Capo says it has an outboard motor."

"How long, Mr. Reyes?" Lily asked.

The big man looked to the horizon. After a moment he turned back. "Not long now," he said.

Lily sighed. "Well," she said. "You know what that means, Mr. Reyes..."

The smuggler looked at her plaintively. "Not the hams..."

She nodded. "The hams."

***

Perhaps it was Aurelio Reyes' stubbornness, or you could chalk it up to Liliana's guilt at questioning the smuggler's life choices, but whatever it was, *something* persuaded Liliana to fold, allowing Reyes to keep his treasured *ibérico* onboard.

Which left our two contraband adventurers in quite a tight spot. Literally.

"Move a little to your left, Andrew. Yes, just a little..."

"Over here?"

"No, make that my left, Andrew, *my* left."

"Here?"

"Yes, better. Now your knee is not–"

"Oh, excuse me! Is that your..."

"Let's not talk about it. Please, I beg. I feel awkward enough as it is."

"Yes, good thinking. I certainly didn't mean to touch–"

"Andrew."

"Yes, right. Again, sorry Doctor. If we could, perhaps, not mention this to the Professor when we see him again?"

"I think that is a grand plan, Andrew. Grand. Uh, back to your left."

"My left?"

"No, no. *My left*. You were kneeing me again. Yes. Better."

Yes, a literal tight spot. As I said, one thing or another led to Lily and Andrew both squeezing into a smuggler's compartment *with* a dozen cuts of beautifully marbled *ibérico*–cuts ranging from bone-in back legs to cured loins to boneless shoulders (a rather grisly sight, really). Who knows what had convinced her, but at the moment she was busy lamenting her accommodating nature.

Lily shivered. They were mostly below the waterline, and the November tide was cold, lowering the temperature in the secret hold significantly.

"Are you cold, Doctor? I can–"

"Let's keep to business, Andrew. Shall we?" Good lord, she felt awkward enough!

She continued, "What do you see?"

As they were unfortunately positioned, Andrew was facing backwards, his head over her left shoulder, aimed at a tiny, foggy porthole just above the waterline.

"The ship!" he said. "The one with the engine, I think? It must have been that ship who signaled to lower our sails..."

"I can hear their diesel, yes," she nodded. "How close are they?"

"Well... right there." Here, Andrew maybe tried to point, setting off more grumbling and apologies.

"Can you see anything else?" Lily asked once this was finished.

"They've... come up alongside, I think." He shifted, craning his neck. "There's a big, *big* man about to board–"

Even as Andrew nearly completed the sentence, a double-tap *THUD* sounded through the boards above their heads.

"Yup. About to board!"

"Quiet, Andrew. Listen."

A deep, booming voice sounded, its timbre and volume carrying it down a ventilation duct just above them.

"Where are they?" the voice all but groaned.

"What are you doing on my ship?" Aurelio shouted. "You've no right to board–"

"I'm searching for escaped fugitives and I do have reason to believe they are aboard," the deep voice intoned woodenly.

"¡*Dios mío*! Did you stop every yacht on the Strait?"

"Yes."

Aurelio laughed. "Then I am not who you suspect, I am just the next unfortunate merchant who–"

The deep voice interrupted him. "I know ships," the

voice said. "And you are no merchant."

"What? Of course I'm a merchant, you think–"

"You have a gaff-rigged sail, but you have an extra sail above the main lug-sail. Also, your bowsprit is longer than average."

"*Si. ¿Cuál es tu punto?*"

"Your ship is made for speed," the deep voice continued.

"Many ships are made for speed. Just because–"

There was a *crack* and a muttering of curses. Lily only imagined it was a punch landing.

"Be quiet. I know a thief when I see one."

"Thief? I resent that..."

"What do you have below. What do you carry? Stolen goods? Guns?"

"Neither. What are you looking for again? You come onto *my* ship and–"

"Fugitives," the deep voice interrupted. "Murderers."

"Fortunately for you, I don't have any murders about, Señor... what's your name?"

"Konig," the deep voice rumbled.

"Señor Konig. And I didn't think Spain's coast was in your jurisdiction, amigo."

"I believe I asked what is in your hold, smuggler?" There was another *crack* of a punch.

"That's enough of that!" Reyes growled. "Stand down, Capo. It's all right."

"Take me down and show me what you are carrying. When I am good and satisfied, I will leave. Not a moment sooner. If you stand in my way, I'll–"

"You will *not* go down there," Reyes said, his voice

45

rising. "This is my ship and I'm the captain, and the day I defer to some Nazi giant–"

Another punch sounded, followed by the falling of a body. Our adventurers sure had heard enough of that in the past two days.

"I'm going up," Lily whispered. "I won't stand by and–"

The shouting of voices in German cut her off.

"What the..." Andrew began.

"What is it?" Lily asked.

"Some struggle. Over there! There's a second ship approaching, and there seems to be some kind of commotion on deck!"

"A commotion? What does that mean? What do you see, Andrew?"

"There's a–"

A rapid chatter of gunfire tore through the mid-day calm. Bullets *zipped* into the ocean and tore into the *Barco Jamón*'s hull, one round even cracking the grimy porthole from which Andrew gazed.

"Get down!" Lily squeaked.

Above them, Konig shouted something in German. His impressive footfalls pattered about before he jumped clear of the *Barco Jamón* and returned to his ship.

"Capo!" Reyes shouted. "¡*Al suelo y permanece abajo*!"

"Something's happening!" Andrew said.

"What? Did the Nazi–"

An explosion rocked the ship, tossing the small cutter in the sea like a toy in a bathtub. Lily screamed–she couldn't help it! Even Andrew let loose a rather effeminate *EEEP*!

The diesel motor returned to life with a roar, and Konig's ship outside turned sharply south, sending a spray of seawater across the porthole as flaming bits of wreckage fell from the sky.

"¡*Vamos,* Capo!" Reyes shouted. "¡*Leva las velas*!" A clambering of footfalls followed a moment later.

"They're... they're leaving?" Andrew said, his neck stretching dangerously to give him a better view out the porthole.

"What?" Lily asked. "Where are they–"

The secret panel holding our adventurers so tightly together popped open, sending them tumbling to the ground in a rather unfortunate pile.

"Excuse me, Doctor!" Andrew said, struggling to untangle himself from Lily.

"Andrew, are you always this clumsy–"

"Liliana," Reyes said, interrupting their griping. "They're going. Something's happened! I believe someone is attacking their fleet!"

"Did you open that door, Aurelio?" Lily asked angrily. "You could have given us some warning–"

"Wait, did you say they're going?" Andrew asked.

"Yes."

"What happened?"

The Spaniard shook his head. "I do not know. That beast Konig hit me. I had fallen when the ship exploded."

"Whose ship?" Lily asked. "Konig's ship?"

"No," Andrew said. "The other one."

"Yes, the other one!" Reyes said.

"Which one?" Lily asked.

"The ship that followed," Andrew said. "The second ship!"

"Whatever," Lily said. "Are we moving? Let's get out of here!"

"The sails are raised," Reyes said, turning and rushing through the small hold and up the steps to the main deck. Lily and Andrew followed at his heels.

At the top of the steps, he halted them. "Wait..." he said. "Stay hidden in case they watch!"

Burning pieces of wood were scattered across the deck. Slowly, Lily peeked over the edge of the stairwell, her eyes traveling across the ocean to the smoldering wreck that bobbed up and down on the white-capped and bubbly sea. In the distance, continuing *cracks* of gunfire sounded.

"Good lord!" Lily said. "What happened?"

"Some explosive, I would imagine," Reyes said as he twisted the wheel, leaving the smoking ruin behind them. "Quite a blow-up," Reyes laughed. Under his breath, he muttered, "Nazi bastards."

The jagged husk of burning ship turned in the tide and slipped below the waterline, leaving a trail of black and smoking wreckage floating in its wake. To the south, Konig's ship continued churning towards the collection of black sails. The distant exchange of gunfire continued.

"Some kind of gunfight," Reyes said.

"So someone is attacking the Nazis?" Andrew asked.

Reyes nodded. "It would seem."

"Are you all right, Aurelio?" Lily asked. A trickle of blood ran down the captain's cheek from a cut beneath his left eye.

The Spaniard nodded and wiped the blood away. "That Konig has quite a punch."

"Did you see that blue... thing?" Andrew asked. "Because I could have sworn I saw..."

"What, Andrew?" Lily said, turning to her young companion as a black ship sailed past, making its way slowly towards the melee to the south.

Young Caine shook his head. "It's nothing," he said. "Nothing."

CHAPTER 6: Oh Hey! It's What You've Been Waiting For: Brick and Nero! Ah Yes! Finally!

Swirls of mist and fog wrapped around the jagged peaks of the island, a wet cloak of gloom that crept down from the mountains and settled over remarkably lush green fields. The fields were expansive in their emptiness and desolation. But for the howl of wind, there was no sound.

If you were standing on the coast–white snowy cliffs facing you in the distance–it would seem a beautiful place. Point of fact, it *was* a beautiful place. But as with many exotic places, the island required the guiding hand of one who genuinely loved it and understood it in order to share the wonder with those unacquainted with its inherent charm.

Brick Brannigan and Archibald Nero were without such a guide.

Hands bound behind their backs, our two previously-missing adventurers were indeed alive, even if they were in a rather unfortunate position.

Still, alive is much better than dead, isn't it?

"I wish they'd give us some bloody water," Nero said.

"You've only been awake for a few minutes."

"Yes, but I'm thirsty."

Brick shook his head. "It was that worm," he muttered.

"You keep talking about a worm. Are you going to explain it further or–"

"Not now, no," Brick sighed.

"That's the fourth time you've said 'not now.' Am I ever to learn about this worm of which you speak?"

"I hope not," Brick said.

You see, the Professor had neither the patience nor focus to try and explain the nuances of the cursed Vøttur worm that had seized control of Mr. Nero in our previous adventure (you remember that, don't you? You read *Brick Brannigan is Knee-Deep in Peril!*, right?). Not that the Professor would have a problem explaining exactly how the Vøttur's complex physiology usurped control of the brain's basic functionality, essentially turning the victimized host into a walking zombie. In fact, the Professor had once lectured a group of PhDs on the Vøttur's dangerous capabilities. At the time, however, he'd had a full range of audio and visual aids– including 8mm film of a living victim in action and a few slides of a cross-sectioned Vøttur itself. At the time he'd also not been tied to a chair in a barn on a remote island.

Oh, yes, our adventurers were in a barn.

"I don't suppose you want to lend a hand, old boy?" Nero asked a nearby cow.

Unsurprisingly, the cow did not.

Brannigan struggled against his restraints as the feeling began returning to his hands. Until quite recently, you see, both our adventurers had been unconscious.

"Can you see out that window, Nero?"

The British pilot struggled in his rickety wooden seat. "A bit, yeah. Why?"

"What do you see?"

"A dark green cottage. Looks like there's grass on the roof."

"Do you see any people?"

"Just sheep. And rocks. And grass. Oh, there's the sea out there."

"Scotland, you think? The highlands, perhaps?"

The pilot shook his head. "Too rocky. And there's no sea near the highlands. More likely Ireland, although that house doesn't look very Irish to me. Plus, that sheep there doesn't have a black face. Memory serves that the Burren is known for blackface sheep, no?"

"I think?" Brick sighed, continuing to twist his wrists against his bindings. "My knowledge of regional sheep is perhaps not what it should be."

"Fair point. Not sure why I know so much about sheep..."

"Are you feeling all right?" Brannigan asked.

Nero shrugged. "A little sore, I guess, but otherwise all right."

Brannigan nodded, carefully observing Nero's every response as the Professor struggled to ferret out whether the Vøttur worm was yet living or dead. "And how's your leg?" Brannigan asked.

"My leg..." The Brit leaned as far forward as his bindings would allow. "Holy hell! There's a wound there! Is that a... Dear me, I think I've been shot!"

The Professor nodded. "Yes, you have."

"Great Scott! How did *that* happen? And who did it?"

"Who did it?" Brick asked.

"Yes, *who*? *Who* shot me, Brannigan?"

"Well." The Professor paused for a moment, feigning deep thought. (Of course, we as readers already know that Lily shot Nero while he was deep in the throes of the Vøttur's nigh supernatural mind control. But in her defense, she did it because Nero was seriously threatening our heroes' lives.) As we shared this aside, the Professor's "deep thoughts" did continue.

"Yes, Brannigan, *who shot me*?" Nero continued. "What the bloody hell are you doing? Thinking? Are you *thinking* about who shot me?"

"Uh, no." The Professor smiled. "Just clearing my head," he said. "I'm sorry to say this, but in all truth, I've absolutely no idea who shot you, my friend."

"No idea?"

"Nope! Although dollars to donuts, it was some Nazi scallawag."

"I imagine you're right about that, Brick. I just can't believe someone *shot* me! It's been a while since I've been shot. Although it looks like they put some rudimentary bandaging on it. You know, I haven't been shot since–"

"Uh wait, is someone coming?" Brannigan interrupted, hoping to stave off whatever anecdote came next.

"Well, no, not that I can see."

"Ah, yes, all right. And what about me? Am I all in one piece?"

Nero turned to Brick and gave him a once over. "Your face is a little knocked up. Two black eyes and there's a gauze wrap around your head–"

"Did you say *two* black eyes?"

"–all in all, you could be worse. You could be *shot*. And yes, two black eyes. But as I said, it could be worse. You could BE SHOT."

Brick nodded. "True enough, true enough."

The Brit sighed. "So we're in either Ireland or Scotland. In someone's barn. What for, do you think?" Nero asked.

Brick shook his head. "I've no idea." Now this, dear reader, was the truth.

The Professor had only awaken a few minutes prior to our arrival, his eyes opening even before Mr. Nero's. Sitting alone in the barn, he'd run through the last thing he could remember in rather frightening detail.

Brick had been struggling in the cargo hold of Nero's precious plane, the *Belladonna*, as she lost altitude over the Mediterranean. From the corner of his eye, he'd watched as Lily and Andrew had jumped from the falling plane and prayed the parachutes did their job. Once his friends had escaped, the Professor had subdued Zombie Nero in time to see the whitecaps of the Mediterranean waves.

He remembered a split-second of the crash, and that was it. He hoped he had been heroic; he hoped he had pulled Nero from the sinking wreck. Either way, they were both alive. And captive. But for what purpose, Brannigan could not fathom.

"Why didn't they just kill us?" he wondered aloud.

"What?" Nero asked. "Who kill us?"

Brannigan opened his mouth to answer. Unfortunately, that lingering doubt stopped him. What if Nero was still under the control of the Vøttur? His intense understanding of the worm assured him no Vøttur lasted more than a few days in its host, and even prior to the crash, Nero had been infected for at least 48 hours. But was there any way to guarantee old Nero was back?

Well, perhaps, yes.

"Nero," Brannigan said. "You remember that French bird you fancied in Tangier?"

"That French bird? You mean Miette?"

Brannigan nodded. "Yes, exactly. What did you think of her?" The Professor's memory reminded him that under the spell of the Vøttur, Nero's unparalleled interest in the fairer sex had been quashed absolutely.

"Miette?" Nero stared up into the mossy rafters of the barn's ceiling as his eyes lost their focus. "My goodness, Brannigan, what a specimen. There's a reason they call women the fairer sex, you know. I don't mind telling you, I'd do anything for a shag–"

"That's enough!" the Professor interrupted. "That's... plenty, Archibald, thank you very much."

"What? Well, you asked–"

"I just had to make sure you–"

"–wait, is this about Liliana?"

"What?"

"Liliana," Nero said. "Or 'Lily' as you so affably refer to her."

"What about Lily?"

"You did move in on *my* territory, Brannigan."

"Your territory? I'm sorry, I was under the impression that Dr. Halifax made her own decisions!"

"Well, you know what I mean, damn it."

"I like her, Arch," Brannigan said, earnestly. "I didn't

mean to..." The big man shrugged. "...move in on your territory, or whatever. I like her. And she likes me." He didn't really know what else to say.

Nero looked at him and smiled. "I'm sorry, my friend. You're right. I'm very glad you're happy."

Brannigan smiled as well. "Thank you, Archibald."

"Plus, it's been dreadfully long since any bird liked you, anyway."

"Hey!"

"Now where were we before we were sidetracked? Ah, yes! Who wants to kill us?"

"Oh, right, right, I forgot," Brannigan said. "The Cabal."

"The Cabal? Did they capture us?"

"Well our..." The Professor nearly explained how their plane crashed. He decided against it to spare Nero the heartbreak of losing his beloved *Belladonna*. "We were captured, yes!"

"Did you think they would kill us?"

Brannigan thought. "What they want, we do not have. When they discovered this, I would think they'd have killed us and gotten it over with."

"And what do they want that we don't have?"

Brannigan sighed. It was certainly annoying that Nero remembered almost *nothing* about their time in Tangier. Except Miette, apparently.

"If you don't remember, I don't think I should tell you," Brannigan said.

"Why is that?"

"Because I believe they mean to torture us, and it's harder to feign ignorance than simply be ignorant."

"Did you say... torture?" Nero's face paled.

Brannigan nodded.

"How do you know that?"

"Oh, just a feeling. If you've been in one situation like this, you've been in them all. Villains are so terribly predictable in their cruelty."

It was then that the voice from behind them chimed in, "You're not wrong, you know. I most certainly intend to torture you both."

Brannigan and Nero both turned, struggling to look over their shoulders at the voice behind them.

From the shadows stepped a lanky man with long black hair and a Fu Manchu. He wore a plain black suit and looked a bit more like an undertaker than Brannigan would have liked.

"My name is Mr. Shindo," he said, his voice soft. "And very soon you will both despise me. Now, shall we begin?"

CHAPTER 7: While We're At It, Let's Get Caught Up With Some Other People, Too (People with Friends in Low Places)

The locals had described the weather as "seasonal." Just about 40° with a tumultuous slate grey sky. It was dismal, dismal enough to make Fang miss the sun of the Sahara.

The Black-toothed villain was sitting at a wooden table in the green cottage's kitchen, drinking tea and watching the ocean. The monotony of waves seemed to impart a certain melancholy, he thought.

"Sir?"

Fang turned to see one of his loyal followers standing in the kitchen door. After the terrible massacre at the Temple of Aja, there were very few remaining survivors from his once mighty Legion of Madmen.

"Yes?"

"Mr. Shindo has made contact with the prisoners."

Fang stared at the young man, anger suddenly boiling in him. "Who sent Shindo in?" he asked.

"I did," a heavily accented voice said from the other side of the kitchen.

Fang turned to find Captain Heinrich Von Faust standing in front of the kitchen window, blocking the view of the sea.

Ah, Von Faust. That one-eyed, bald-headed, Nazi Captain and loyal member of the wicked Cabal. Once a mere pawn that Black Fang Delacroix moved about as he liked, the fascist loyalist was now a terrible thorn in Fang's side. A thorn that grew sharper by the day.

"I thought we agreed to let me speak to them first, Monsieur Captain."

"Why?" Von Faust said. "Mr. Shindo has performed his duties for the Cabal quite well, and there is no reason to believe this occasion will be any different."

"Yes, but Brannigan and I–"

"When it comes to Brick Brannigan," Von Faust said, "you do not think rationally, Herr Delacroix." The Nazi smiled, and his lips looked like two slugs.

Delacroix was going to say that–personal feelings notwithstanding–there was a chance Brannigan *would* speak to him. Mutual enmity aside, it didn't necessarily mean that the two men were diametrically opposed. To the contrary, in some regards they were quite similar. I said *some* regards. Only some.

Von Faust walked to the kitchen door and took the young Madman's arm, leading him out of the cottage and into the cold November air. The door slammed shut behind him.

Fang took a sip of his tea and watched the waves, trying to decide his next move.

Since departing from the ruins of *le Fugitif* in Tangier so many days previous, Fang had found himself in an infinitely more subservient position than he was accustomed to. This was not what troubled him, however. No, unlike what you may think, Fang was not a proud man. Instead, he was a man of principles–askew as they may have been, and when he found things not only out of his control but moving *away* from his desired outcome, he grew frustrated. Currently, he was quite frustrated.

If he had not had his men plant the Vøttur worms in the ice in Nigeria, Archibald Nero would not have been under his control and Brannigan most certainly would have escaped. Thanks to his ingenuity, however, Brannigan did not escape. Thanks to his ingenuity, Branngain was now tied up in a barn out back, awaiting questioning.

And yet, Von Faust would not let Fang perform the questioning, instead calling upon the barbaric Mr. Shindo to do his worst.

Fang sighed. It was terribly hard to fight the will of the Cabal, he realized anew, a lesson he'd actually learned when he was first forced to join their terrible ranks. There were just too many of them, and they were just too strong.

He finished his tea and stood, the thoughts in his brain finally aligning like the intricate workings of a clock.

"The other doctor," he said. "The woman."

Fang walked from the kitchen into a cozy sitting room where a fire burned in a great stone fireplace. In the far corner, sitting at a desk overlooking a narrow gravel road, a young Madman sat, one hand transcribing on a steno pad, his second holding a headphone tightly to his ear.

"Darius," Fang said. The young man did not look up. Fang cleared his voice loudly. "Darius," he repeated.

The young man looked up. "Yes, *Caïd*?"

Caïd, a title Fang's men called him out of respect.

The word made him smile, until he realized he'd been hearing it less and less in recent time.

"What have you heard, Monsieur Dufort?" Fang asked.

Over the past few days, the young man had been in charge of all radio transmissions, incoming and outgoing. At Fang's request, young Darius Dufort had assumed command of all radio traffic after his father Pierre Dufort's death in the Temple of Aja. The Legion of Madmen was a bit of a family tradition for some.

"Monsieur Konig has not found the other two, *Caïd*."

"He is checking ships, as requested?"

Darius nodded. "As you instructed, *Caïd*. But he has found nothing. On one of his last transmissions..." The young man broke off and flipped through his notes.

"What is it?"

"It was yesterday," Darius said. "Yesterday, Monsieur Konig reported an attack on two of the cutters off the coast of Cadiz."

"Was there any damage?"

The young man shifted uneasily in his chair. "One ship was lost, *Caïd*."

"Lost?"

"There was an explosion. *Le Chevalier Rouge* sank. The whole crew was lost."

Fang looked down at the woolen rug underfoot and closed his eyes. *How many more of my men are gone?* he thought. Perhaps the better question: How many were left? *Two*?

"What does he know of the explosion?"

Darius shook his head. "I have not been able to hail him on the radio since his report. He must be in pursuit of the *saboteur*. Or..."

"Or, Monsieur Dufort?"

"Or else his ship was lost, as well."

Little did Fang care for Monsieur Konig, just another one of the Cabal's murderers, but he would greatly lament the loss of his ship, *le Drapeau Noir*, the prize of Fang's small fleet.

"Keep trying," Fang said, patting Darius' shoulder. "Find Konig. Our resources have become... limited." It was hard for Fang to say it without thinking of the young man's dead father. "But we must locate the other two who escaped from Mr. Nero's plane, and only Konig can do it. We are very isolated here. This Dr. Halifax and Brannigan's assistant, Andrew Caine. We did not find the artifacts in the wreckage, nor on Brannigan's person. We have to believe Dr. Halifax carries them now."

"What can we do to find them, *Caïd*?"

Fang smiled his famous black-toothed grin. "Just because our resources are limited, Monsieur Dufort, does not mean all is lost. I still have a great many plans."

CHAPTER 8: ¡*Bienvenido a España!* *Y Me Disculpo por el Olor* (Lily & Andrew on the Rocks)

Lily sat on a bench overlooking the slow-moving Guadalquivir river, wrapped tightly in a long leather coat, hat resting in her lap. Despite the stench coming off her in waves, the late afternoon sun felt glorious on her face.

"I think I can feel my toes again," Andrew said from beside her. Like Lily, he was also wrapped in a newly acquired coat (his a navy blue peacoat, a shade too large for his lanky body).

Lily nodded. Her teeth had stopped chattering just a few minutes earlier. "I'm not quite there yet," she said. "But soon."

As promised, Aurelio Reyes had safely delivered Lily and Andrew to the city of Cádiz that day–just before lunch. As the *Barco Jamón* coasted past the *Castillo de Santa Catalina*, Reyes had pointed.

"Cádiz," he'd said. "One of our largest ports, and the oldest city in Spain."

"It doesn't even look Spanish," Andrew said. "It looks..."

"Moorish," Reyes said nodding. "Domes and towers, ornate tile work and geometric shapes. I told you this was an old city."

"How old, Aurelio?" Lily asked.

"It was founded by the Phoenicians. You tell me, Doctor."

"Good lord," she said. "It could have been founded as early as 1500 B.C."

Reyes laughed, twisting the ship's wheel, following the curve of the coastline. "Cádiz was founded in 1100 B.C. Not bad for an American."

Not bad, indeed. After docking amidst a flurry of Spanish Navy ships, Reyes had led Lily and Andrew down from the *Barco Jamón* and through the busy port towards the city, leaving Capo to tend to the ship.

"What now, Aurelio?" Lily asked. She had learned to trust the smuggler, especially after their encounter with the German Konig. Reyes had risked much in defending his cargo, and Lily would not soon forget.

"I'm sorry to say, Liliana, this is the end of the voyage for me. After this I must return to the *Jamón*. I have deliveries to make in Setubal *y* Lisboa. And I will have to hurry. I'll need to use the cover of darkness to enter Portuguese waters. The gentlemen of the navy are not too fond of my international forays," he said, glaring at a crew of midshipmen climbing a gangplank.

"Then... what is our next stop?" Lily asked, feeling suddenly nervous. "What awaits us in Cádiz?"

"Fear not," Reyes had said with a wink. "I promised to take care of you, and I will. You said, I believe, that you need to get to a major international city, no? The best I can do is Sevilla, it is not perfect, but it will have to do. It's not far, and from there you should be able to charter a plane. I would put you on a train now, but you may have heard about the riots that have arisen. Well, there have also been demonstrations and railroads have been affected. But, all is not lost. I have a man I trust who is always happy to move my contraband, for a taste." From inside his black vest, Reyes pulled a wax paper-wrapped bundle tied with a string.

"*Jamón*?" Lily asked.

Reyes nodded. "*Si, Jamón.*"

"And your friend?"

"For once, you need not worry. His name is Juan and he is as boring as you can imagine. For once, I imagine you are happy to hear this–especially after our recent excitement. He is... how would an American put it? He is... not a character. Well, not like me, at least." The big man laughed.

"I'll be sorry to see you go, my friend," Lily said. "Thank you for your help."

The big man had paused, only momentarily, a kind and genuine smile on his face. "Before Raúl departed Gibraltar, leaving you in my care, he revealed to me that you are a friend of Hugo Brannigan."

Lily blushed slightly and nodded. "I am."

Reyes nodded in return. "Then you have nothing to thank me for, Liliana. People need to help other people. And besides, I owe Hugo Brannigan my life."

"You, too?" she asked incredulously.

Reyes laughed. "Yes, me too. When you find Brick, tell him he is welcome at my homestead whenever he likes. It has been far too long."

"I will tell him, Aurelio."

Our trio of adventurers continued towards the outer fences of the port, walking along a stone esplanade that looked out over the Gulf of Cádiz.

"Is he well?" Reyes asked.

Lily did not respond. She searched for words, coming up empty-handed.

Reyes paused. "What is it?"

"The Professor is missing," Andrew said.

"Missing?"

Lily nodded. "We believe him kidnapped."

Reyes stared out at the blue ocean. "*Dios mio*," he said to himself. "*Dáselos el infierno, mi amigo*." He turned to Lily. "And you two are his rescue party?"

"Something like that," she said.

"*Que lástima*," he muttered. "I wish I could go with you, my friends. But I fear I would be more trouble to you than help. You see, on the mainland, I attract the attentions of *la policía* far too quickly. The one drawback of my chosen occupation." He shook his head.

Lily felt that wellspring of courage bubble deep down in her heart. "We will be all right, Aurelio. Hugo will be all right. Trust me." She smiled.

There was something in her eye that made Reyes believe her, unquestionably. "You are remarkable, Liliana," he said. "I have much faith in you. That being said, I will do everything I can to help."

From his pocket, he pulled a thick wad of banded currency. "Take this," he said. "It is all I have, perhaps a few hundred or few thousand *pesetas*, but it is better than nothing."

"Aurelio, we can't take–"

"Don't be ridiculous, Liliana, take it."

"Aurelio–"

"Andrew," the Spaniard said, turning to young Caine. "Take this money."

"Yes, sir."

"Use it as you see fit."

"Yes, sir."

"But Aurelio, you needn't–"

"Liliana, please do not take me for too kind a man yet," the smuggler said. "You've not yet seen your new accommodations."

"What do you mean?"

"Well, you will still need to be smuggled out of the port. Which is doable, but not easy."

"All right..."

"Options are limited and, oh, I forgot to say welcome to Spain! You are now on Spanish soil–"

"Aurelio, you're making me nervous."

"It's not so bad," the Spaniard said. "Not really."

***

It turns out boring Juan Lima was a Portuguese truck driver. At first, Lily had taken this as good news. Riding in a diesel truck was infinitely preferable to sailing on a ham smuggler's ship. When she got a look at Juan's truck, however, her opinion on the matter... changed.

"He delivers... fish," she said (a revelation based solely on the smell alone).

"*Un poco* fish, Señora," Juan said, climbing down from the truck's cab. "*Pero pulpo*, as well. *Mucho, mucho pulpo*."

"Lots and lots of what?" Lily asked.

Andrew and Reyes spoke at once. "Octopus," they said.

Reyes found this amusing. Andrew, on the other hand, looked a little sick.

"Octo... oh dear."

"Liliana, wait, it's all right," Reyes said.

"No, I'm... I'm fine," Liliana said, trying to overcome the initial surprise. "I just need to get used to the idea of spending time beside crates of octopus, that's all. I'm not such a fan of seafood."

"Crates, Señora?" Juan asked.

"Juan..."

"*Yo no uso las cajas. Los pulpos están vivos. Las células se congelan, pero vivos.*"

"What did he say?" Lily asked. "I definitely heard the word 'no'..."

"He spoke very quickly," Andrew said, scratching his head. "But I heard the word 'vivos,' which means 'alive.'"

Lily gulped. "Alive?"

Reyes sighed. "Yes, Liliana, I admit the octopus are alive. But they are frozen, so they aren't moving or anything. They are frozen alive to maintain freshness for the trip."

Lily blanched. "Frozen alive? Strangely enough, I am quite familiar with that process, Aurelio."

"Oh? Well, they aren't in boxes because–"

"Wait," Lily interrupted.

"–anyway the fish, the fish *are* dead."

"Just stop, Aurelio. Please. I don't think I want to know any more. That's okay. I understand that this is the next leg of our journey, and that is all I need. This truck will get me that much closer to Hugo."

Reyes nodded. "It will."

"Andrew," Lily said. "Climb aboard. It's time to go."

She turned and shook Reyes' hand. "Thank you, Aurelio," she said. "You have done much for us."

"I only wish I could do more, Liliana," he said. "Take care. Use my money. And take care of Brick. He is a good man, deserving of a good woman."

"Aurelio, how–"

He smiled. "I am Spanish," he said. "I am wise in the ways of love."

She blushed. "Yes, well... I'd better get going. Before I lose my nerve."

"Good luck."

"Thank you."

She turned and climbed into the covered bed of Juan's truck, casting one glance over her shoulder as Aurelio waved his goodbye.

***

If we can fast-forward a few hours in just a few a sentence or two: The trip from Cádiz to Sevilla is mostly desert. Rocky, sandy, desert. Lily and Andrew indeed made the trip in the back of Juan's fish truck.

Exciting, huh?

Yes, you would think so. Thankfully for our travelers, the journey from Cádiz to Sevilla was reasonably short. Unfortunately for our travelers, the roads were rocky, and they were still riding in an ice truck filled with living octopus and dead fish. Rather unlucky, really.

On the other hand, neither Lily nor Andrew understood how lucky they really were. In truth, it's hard to feel lucky when you are sharing an oversized ice bucket with dead fish, but what can you do? As our adventurers chilled with the *pulpo*, Juan Lima got them through the port authority security and a few spots of trouble between Cádiz and Sevilla. It turns out that even soldiers do not like the smell of fish that much.

When Juan pulled open the rear gate of his truck and lifted the tarp covering his bevy of aquatic creatures and smuggled fugitives, Lily's lips were blue.

"Are... w-w-w-w-we... th-th-th-there?" she said through chattering teeth.

"*Si*, Señora. *Bienvenido a Sevilla*." He took her hand and helped her from the wet bed of chipped ice. When she leapt to the ground, chips and flecks fell off her soaked body and clattered to the pavement like poker chips. She could not help but shiver.

She stood on the loading dock of a busy market. A dozen trucks identical to Juan's were backed up to the dock, burly workers in aprons hauled wooden crates onto hand trucks, laughing and speaking quickly in Spanish.

A moment later Andrew spilled onto the loading dock beside her. Ice clung to his hair and eyebrows. His lips were blue, as well.

"Are... w-w-we... at... Se-Se-Se..." He shivered. "Se-Se-Se–"

"I th-th-think," Lily said.

Behind them on the stone wall of the old building was a sign made from colorful tiles that read "*Mercado de Triana.*"

Lily read the sign and looked at Juan. "S-S-S-Sevilla?" she asked.

Juan nodded. "*Sí.*" After a long moment, he took a step back and waved a hand in front of his face. "*¿Qué es ese olor?*"

"He's not r-r-r-really asking w-w-what I th-think he's asking, is h-h-he?" Lily said to Andrew.

"Yes," Andrew said. "Apparently we s-s-smell."

"It's your truck, Juan. You c-c-carry the stuff all day!" She shivered again.

"*Sí*, Señora. But I no sit in it." He smiled.

"Yes," Lily sighed. "That is true."

Juan turned to Andrew. "*Hay puestos de control,*" he said, his voice low. "*Hay gente que buscan para ustedes. ¿Entiendes?*"

"Uh... *¿H-h-hay gente... en busca de... n-n-nosotros?*" Andrew cast a worried glance at Lily. "*¿Nosotros?*"

Juan nodded. "*Sí, exactamente.*"

"Oh. That's bad."

"What, Andrew?"

"Juan says there are people looking for us. He s-s-says there were..." he turned to their driver. "*¿Puestos de control?*"

Juan nodded.

"Checkpoints," he said, turning back to Lily.

"Checkpoints," she said softly. "And they're looking for... Americans?" Lily asked Juan.

"*Sí, estadounidenses. Dos personas.*"

"And we will... stick out," Lily said.

"Especially like this," Andrew added.

Our adventurers took in their wet and disheveled appearance.

"Andrew," Lily said, pulling clumps of ice from her hair. "Give me Aurelio's money."

Straightening her filthy clothes, Lily took a deep breath and walked up to the nearest truck driver, a tall, thin man in a long leather coat smoking a cigarillo.

"Señor," she said. "How much for your coat?"

"*¿Qué?*" he asked.

Lily reached out and pulled gently on the lapel of his coat. "Your coat," she said. From behind her, Andrew whispered a word. "*Abrigo*," she said. She raised her hand with the money.

The man smiled. Lily pulled a few bills of cash free and handed them to him in exchange for the leather coat.

"*Gracias*," she said, turning away. After a moment, she paused. Turning back, she said, "That too," she pointed at a matching flat-topped cordobés hat.

"*Usted conduce un negocio duro*, Señora," the man said with a grin. "*Pero usted es muy guapa. ¿Cómo podía decir que no?*"

She took the hat and gave her best smile. It was a knockout.

She's certainly getting more comfortable with this whole adventure bit, isn't she? Andrew couldn't help but think with a smile.

***

Our two adventurers had parted ways with Juan, thanking him and wishing he and his *pulpo* the best of luck before slipping into the busy *Mercado*. With what little money they had left after purchasing Andrew's peacoat from a young sailor on leave, our intrepid duo had purchased a pair of ham sandwiches from a bearded vendor—it was not *ibérico*, rather cheap cuts of *serrano* instead; Lily was quite shocked to see the price of *ibérico* per pound—and made their way back outside, collapsing onto a bench overlooking a broad river that seemed to bisect the town.

Before partaking in the sandwiches, Lily and Andrew shared the *ibérico* Reyes had given them. Absolutely dumbstruck that such divine flavor could come from a pig, they shared a moment of culinary reverential silence. And now here they sat.

"I don't know why I got the sailor's coat," Andrew muttered.

"Because the sailor was the first man who agreed to sell his coat. You're warmer now, aren't you?"

"I am, you're right." He took a bite of his sandwich. "What now, Doctor?"

Lily finished her sandwich, throwing a small piece of bread to a nearby pigeon. "I have been wondering that for a while, Andrew."

"And?"

"And... I realize that we need more information."

"What do you mean?"

From Brannigan's satchel that still hung across her shoulder (you remember that, right?) she pulled the metal skull that Brick had once removed from a Clockwork Man in the basement of a Nigerian temple (and you remember *that*, right?).

Jewels set into the metal glinted in the bright sunshine. While not the Eye of Aja—the stone safely contained inside–the smaller precious stones on the outside were still worth a pretty penny.

"With these jewels, we can get anywhere," she said. "I remembered I had them somewhere between Cádiz and that marketplace. With these, we can charter any car or boat or plane. We can literally get anywhere in the world."

"But?"

"But where do we go?"

"Where would the Professor be?"

"Yes, that is indeed the question, isn't it?"

Andrew was silent.

"If you were a criminal, Andrew, where would you take Hugo?"

Andrew stared off at the slow moving river.

"I have no idea," he said.

Lily watched the pigeon pick at her discarded bread. Then she turned and watched the river flow beneath a long bridge connecting one side of the city to the other. *What would Hugo do?* she wondered. She thought of the time spent with him in Tangier. Liliana Halifax, while not accustomed to the globetrekking lifestyle, was a terribly quick learner. And remember, she still did have that adventuress blood flowing through her veins.

"Me neither." She smiled. "So you know what we need to do? We need to ask a criminal."

CHAPTER 9: Monsieur Delacroix Gets To Thinking While Mr. Shindo Gets To Explaining

Fang was watching.

Von Faust was standing on the gravel driveway beside a black military jeep speaking in hushed and hurried tones to the young Madman he'd led from the cottage.

From Fang's position in the open doorway, he could not hear what was being said. Regardless, he found it disturbing.

Fang and his Legion of Madmen had an interesting relationship with the Cabal. At times strained, at times mutually beneficial, it always proved... complicated. When two headstrong organizations were merged, there inevitably tended to be some amount of power struggle. In the case of the Fang's Legion of Madmen and the Cabal, however, that was not really an issue. It had been made abundantly clear to Fang that he was *beneath* the Cabal. They required his might and resources and intelligence, but only in the same capacity a rifle needs a bullet. Unfortunately for Fang, he was just as disposable.

But his Madmen, he realized, were different. They helped him maintain his minimal dignity. They were loyal. They had fought and died beside him and would continue to do so.

Right?

This, yes *this*, is why Fang was so troubled. And why Fang watched.

The young Madman standing beside Captain Von Faust was nodding as the Nazi soldier continued speaking. Nodding perhaps a bit too eagerly.

"Captain," Fang said, rousing Von Faust's attention. "Are you departing?"

Von Faust turned towards Fang, a look of annoyance evident on his face. "What?"

Fang pointed at the jeep. "Are you going into town?"

Von Faust looked at the jeep. "Town?" he asked. "No. Not town."

Fang stared at him, begging the question *Then where?*

"We're going to the airfield," Von Faust said. "We're meeting a plane."

"Someone is arriving?"

Von Faust offered only a forced smiled. "Someone," he said finally. Finished with Fang, Von Faust turned to the young Madman and muttered a few words. The Madman smiled.

"What's your name, soldier?" Fang asked his loyal follower.

"Lessard," the soldier said. "Alain Lessard."

Fang searched his memory, but the name meant nothing to him—a fact that in itself prompted some guilt, seeing as there were only two Madmen on the island with Fang (Darius Dufort and this fellow, apparently named Lessard).

"Lessard," Fang said. "What are you doing?"

Lessard opened his mouth when Von Faust spoke for him. "He is assisting me, Herr Delacroix. He is to drive me to the airfield. Do you find that agreeable?"

In fact, he didn't. But he nodded anyway. "Certainly," he said.

"Fine, fine. I'll let you get back to work," Von Faust smiled. "*Auf Wiedersehen.*" The Nazi waved dismissively and climbed into the jeep.

Work? Fang thought. *What work is there for me to do here?*

***

Speaking of work:

"Ah, no, that's all right, you don't need to get to work yet!" Nero said.

The Professor turned his attention to Mr. Shindo. "Torture, eh? Don't you want to question us first? What if we are amenable to talking?"

Mr. Shindo pyramided his fingers. "Are you amenable to talking?"

"No," both Nero and Brannigan said in unison.

"Although," Nero added. "If you could perhaps give me an idea of what kind of torture we're talking about—"

"Archibald!" Brick scolded.

"What? I'm just curious."

"Be strong, my friend. He's not yet begun!"

"It's true," Shindo said. "But I doubt you will last long." The funereal gent crossed the space of the barn, his shoes *crunching* on hay, and took a seat on a barrel

77

across from our adventurers.

"I have been asked to meet with you on behalf of my employer, the Master of the Cabal. We believe that you gentlemen are in possession of certain relics we require."

"Relics?" Nero said. "What on Earth are you on about? We've a chance yet, Brick," he said, turning to his bound partner. "He's looking for some kind of relics, it's a good thing we–"

He stopped when he looked into the Professor's face. If a face could read *SHUT UP*, the Professor's most certainly did.

"Oh," Nero said. "That bit about ignorance, eh?" The Brit strained against his bonds as he took a deep breath. "Yes, well." He turned back to Shindo. "I'm sorry, do carry on."

"Professor Brannigan," Shindo said, "what do you know of the Cabal?"

Brannigan looked into Shindo's pale eyes. "Enough not to help when given the opportunity."

Shindo smiled. "You've spent far too much time with Quincy Max. I see the old man has filled your brain with his rhetoric."

"Dr. Max has done no such thing," Brannigan said through gritted teeth. "He's merely given me the facts and let me draw my own conclusions."

Shindo smiled. "The facts? Professor, you as an academic should appreciate the danger of facts taken out of context."

Brannigan did not respond. Instead, he began the slow and tiring process of breaking his bonds. With remarkable force, he began to pull the rope apart, even as he rubbed it up and down against the rough wood of the chair, his strength quickly returning.

"I'll give you an example," Shindo said, taking a long, thin cigarette from his pocket and slipping it between his lips. "Dr. Max explained to you that the Cabal originated in Nigeria, correct? Dr. Max believes our organization originated as the Axé of Ogoun on what is now known as the Niger Peninsula. How am I doing so far?" As Brannigan contemplated Shindo's words, Shindo lit his cigarette with a match and took a deep drag, slowly expelling smoke up into the air.

"Keep going," Brannigan said, struggling to squeeze as much curiosity into his tone as possible (while he continued working on his bonds).

Shindo nodded. "According to your Dr. Max, the Axé of Ogoun gave way to the Cabal of Angelus Mortis, a secret society bent on... destroying the world?" Shindo laughed. "Is that even what he says? At this point, I have a hard time getting Dr. Max's 'facts' correct, as they are so preposterous."

"You're doing a fair job," Brannigan said. "Please, continue."

"I am sorry to report, but your good Doctor is wrong about a great deal, Professor Brannigan."

"Like what?" Brick said, feeling the rope begin to fray against his wrist.

"Like... this Cabal of Angelus Mortis. What a ridiculous name. I've never in my life heard it other than in the theories of Quincy Max," Shindo shook his head, puffing on his cigarette. "We're a Hermetic society, entrenched in arcane teachings of the esoteric. This theory of Dr. Max's is nothing short of offensive."

"Which particular theory is that, Mr. Shindo?" Brannigan said, feeling his bindings fray further.

"His theory of our plot to destroy the world!"

Now, up until this moment, Mr. Nero was sitting quietly, listening to Mr. Shindo and Professor Brannigan carry on. But at the mention of world destruction, Mr. Nero decided it was time to add to the provocative discourse. "What the bloody hell are you on about? Destroy the world?!"

"Calm down, Arch," Brannigan said. "It's all right–"

"You see, Professor Brannigan? This is the stigma your good Doctor has attached to our organization. We are now seen as a secret society of villains! The truth could not be farther from Dr. Max's assertions."

"It's hard to make that distinction when you ally yourself with Nazis," Brannigan said.

Shindo shook his head and tapped ashes into his free hand. "Our German brothers are a young, burgeoning nation starting fresh after the insults of Versailles. What have they done to gain such hatred?"

"They violated the treaty in rearming," Brannigan said, clenching his muscles tightly and straining against the ropes. "Have you forgotten the Great War?"

"I've not forgotten, Professor, but is rearmament such a crime? They are an independent nation like any other, struggling to find their way in this mad, mad world. 1935 is far more complicated than 1914, Professor. And the Germany of 1935 is far different from the Germany of 1914."

Brannigan felt the ropes give, if only slightly. "There are those–myself included–who fear what is happening in Germany."

Shindo shrugged. "Fear all you want, Professor, but you have no grounds. The Cabal relies on the might of this newborn army to assist us in gathering our relics from the farthest reaches of the Earth. We have libraries upon libraries of texts–many of which were falsely believed to have been lost forever to time–that will require much scrutiny if we hope to locate and liberate all the relics."

"If you do not mean to destroy the world, Shindo, why gather these relics?"

Shindo took a self-satisfied drag from his cigarette and smiled wanly. "You are a scholar, Professor, what do you know of translation?"

Brannigan sighed. "I know it is an art as much as it is a science. There are nuances of language far beyond simple conjugation."

Shindo nodded. "Now, I said we were Hermetic. Where Dr. Max calls us the Cabal of the Angelus Mortis, in truth we are the Hermetic Brotherhood of Pandora. The term 'Cabal' originated with our founder, Edgard Tóth." Shindo smiled. "I know what you are thinking: Why the Cabal? Well, honestly, he liked the sound of it."

Brannigan sighed, even feigning curiosity was becoming difficult. "Why Pandora, Mr. Shindo? And what does this have to do with translation?"

"What does the word 'Pandora' mean to you, Professor Brannigan?"

"Pandora refers to the Greek myth of the first mortal woman who was given a box and told to protect it, but never to open it. Curiosity got the better of her, but when she opened it, she learned it contained all the world's evils, which were then released because of her foolhardiness. It is a fundamental tale of Greek mythology, Mr. Shindo. Most children know it." Brannigan frowned. "I have to say, given the chance to reflect on it, I am *more* disturbed by your choice of the name Pandora."

"The tale is a bastardization based on patriarchal bullheadedness and mistranslation, Professor Brannigan. The original Greek tells of an all-giving goddess, not an all-gifted mortal. At the turn of the century, a scholar named Jane Ellen Harrison discovered that not only did Pandora never have a box at all, but no evils were released. She *gave* life, she did not unleash evils, Professor Brannigan. Hesiod's original myth tells us this. Mistranslations by Erasmus of Rotterdam have created an entire world of confusion around dear Pandora."

Brannigan sighed. "And what, you take this myth as inspiration? You believe these relics were scattered gifts from Pandora's box?"

"Your understanding of our creeds is shallow and incomplete, but in some measure you are correct."

"It's a myth, Shindo," Brannigan said angrily. "Even if Erasmus mistranslated it, that doesn't give you *carte blanche* to unite relics to destroy the world. Also, the Cabal has been around for centuries. Have your goals only become 'noble' in the past thirty-five years?"

"They won't destroy the world, Professor!" Shindo said, raising his hands triumphantly. "Brought together, these relics will unite all the blessings of the world, bringing us to a new beginning! Abandon your maddening quest and turn away from the ravings of Quincy Max. With your help, we will no doubt be able to bring this world into its next dawn of enlightenment. In the future, they will look back on us as we look back on the House of Medici, the Khans, the Merovingians, the Habsburgs, or even the Julio-Claudian Dynasty. Do you not wish to be a part of the New History, even as it is written? Now join us in our quest and help us fulfill this ancient promise!"

"Excuse me," Nero said, clearing his throat politely. "How does this not sound like the end of the world?"

Shindo ignored Nero. Instead, he focused on Brannigan. "What say you, Professor?"

Brannigan smiled. "Mr. Shindo, you name conquerers, tyrants, and killers as role models and figures of inspiration. In doing so, I believe you have... well, tipped your hand." He shook his head. "I'm sorry, but no."

Shindo–who had apparently grown quite excited in telling of the Cabal's true history–lowered his hands and sighed dejectedly. "It is as I had feared. You are both beyond my influence. It is regrettable, for you at least. *Der Klinge* will be disappointed to know that I failed in my first endeavor. But all is not lost," he said. "I have further... *options* at my disposal."

Nero shuddered. "Is it time for the torture bit?"

"It is, indeed, Mr. Nero. You see now why I wish you had been persuaded by my logic, instead. This line of questioning can become so terribly... messy."

"You're forgetting one thing, Shindo," Brannigan said.

"And what is that, Professor?"

"In both versions of the Pandora myth, one item is ever-present, regardless of whether it was contained in a box or otherwise."

Shindo frowned. "And that is?"

Brannigan snapped free from his bonds faster than a flash of lightning. "*Hope!*" he shouted.

Before Mr. Shindo could move from his position on

the barrel, Brannigan lashed out, one enormous fist *cracking* across their interrogator's arrogant face. Shindo toppled backwards with a gasp, crashing to the floor.

"Great Scott, Brick!" Nero shouted as the Professor untied his ankles from the legs of the chair.

"Let's go, Nero!"

"What? Free me, you dolt!"

"What do you mean? Haven't you been working all along on breaking your bonds and freeing yourself this whole time?"

Nero blushed. "Well, no, not really. I was... well, I was listening to his story. That chap was rather compelling!"

"Damn it all, man!"

Rushing behind Nero, Brannigan used his brute strength to tear the ropes asunder (believe it, dear reader, it's much easier when your hands are not bound!).

"Now get up, Nero, before those Nazi buffoons return!"

With Nero free, our two adventurers were up in a flash, and faster than a buttered bullet, they were out the door and into the cold November air, never looking back.

CHAPTER 10: Von Faust Continues Planting Seeds, Der Klinge Makes His Arrival, and Disaster Comes One Step Closer...

Brannigan kicked down the rear door of the barn, Nero nipping at his heels.

"Where the hell are we going, Brick?"

"Away, Nero! Keep up!"

"Keep up? *Keep up*?! I've been shot, remember?"

"How could I forget?" Brick muttered, returning to help his friend.

As I said, the green cottage and barn sat by the coast. Unfortunately for our adventurers, behind the barn, the lush green terrain became rockier and steeper, the field of sheep quickly giving way to a sharp incline leading up towards a low mountain peak.

"Wait, stop, please!" Nero urged, taking cover behind a small copse of pine trees.

"What's wrong?" Brannigan said, slowing beside his partner.

"We need a plan, Brick," Nero said as he collapsed onto a rock, breathing heavily.

"Yes, I suppose we do," the Professor said, scratching his bandaged head. "Seeing as we're still not certain *where* we are."

"I think I've got a better idea on that front, ol' chap." Nero pointed.

Upon the peak of the barn they'd just evacuated waved a flag on a short pole. It was a white flag with a horizontal red and blue cross on it.

"Ah, brilliant!" Brick said. "That's..."

Nero nodded excitedly. "Yes, it's..."

"...uh..."

"How about..."

"Finland?" Brick said.

"I thought that cross was blue?"

"Ah, yes, of course."

"It's not Norway, is it?" Nero asked.

"No, that one's red with a blue cross."

"Oh fine, fine."

"At least mine was the right background color."

"Mine had a cross," Nero grumbled.

"All the Scandinavian ones have crosses."

"Not Greenland."

"By the curse of Perry's Black Ships, that's correct, isn't it?" Brick shrugged, resigned. "*Touché*."

"I have it," Nero said.

"Wait, look."

"At what?"

"Oh, nothing." Brick muttered swears. "I was trying to buy time."

Nero smiled. "Couldn't think of it, eh?" he laughed.

Brick shook his head. "Alas, no."

"The Faroe Islands!"

"Ah, the Faroe Islands!" Brick shook his head. "Well-played, Arch."

"Thank you very much."

Yes, dear reader, our adventurers have finally caught up with the rest of us. If only they'd had the benefit of the book's give-away title like we did...

"But now what?" Nero continued.

Brick scratched the stubble that was growing on his face. "My knowledge of the islands is minimal, honestly–"

"–as is mine."

"–but depending on which island we're currently located, we could be quite isolated. If my memory serves me right, we'll need to get to Tórshavn in order to get on a plane. That is, unless there is a private strip about."

"What about a boat?" Nero asked.

"It's the Faroe Islands," Brick said. "There are boats everywhere."

"Then let's go back down to the water, I'm sure–"

"The cottage is down there, Arch. I don't know how many Nazis are here, let alone Fang's Madmen. Our best bet is to get up and over this hill."

"Then what are we waiting for?"

Hey, good point, Archibald. Before the Professor and Nero could conceive of a smart or even nigh appropriate response, our two adventurers took off, dashing up the incline towards the steep emerald hills that lay beyond.

**

There was a radio tower broadcasting a homing beacon and a path of electric lights installed in the long packed-dirt runway. Other than that, the plateau was vacant.

No, strike that. Other than the homing beacon, the lights, *and* the army jeep bearing Von Faust and Lessard, the plateau was vacant.

Silently, they waited.

Occasionally, Von Faust would check the watch on his wrist as he stood leaning against the jeep. Behind him in the vehicle's driver seat, Lessard yawned, his mind wandering.

The sky was darkening, and a light rain had begun to fall.

"Did you mean what you said, sir?" Lessard asked after a few minutes in the rain.

Von Faust, turned away from young Lessard, smiled. Since joining the Cabal, he'd made his share of mistakes, but he'd also learned the power of *suggestion*.

"What do you mean, soldier?" he asked, turning to face Lessard.

"What you said back at the cottage." Lessard shifted in his seat, feeling suddenly uncomfortable under Von Faust's stare.

Still smiling, Von Faust asked, "What did I say that interested you?"

"This... Cabal," Lessard said. "You hope to... change the world?"

Von Faust nodded. "One relic at a time."

Lessard wiped drops of rain from his brow and studied his fingernails. In truth, he felt as directionless as Black Fang Delacroix. Unfortunately, he lacked Fang's focus to keep him on the villain's "straight and narrow," and he found himself tempted by the even darker threats.

"What have you been thinking, Herr Lessard?" Von Faust asked, a self-satisfied feeling filling him like a warm glow.

"Just about your offer," Lessard said. He went back to studying his nails.

Von Faust opened his mouth to speak, ready to finish the deal, when the distant *GRRRRR* of airplane props interrupted him.

"Ah," Von Faust said, turning his back on Lessard. "Here they come."

***

"Do you hear that?" Nero said, looking up from his bandaged leg.

"Better than that," the Professor smiled. "I see it." He pointed. "And there's our private airstrip."

Nero looked up and caught sight of the silver-hulled plane quickly, even in the darkening sky. "That's a Douglas DC-2," he said. "Twin-engine cargo plane."

"American?"

Nero looked away, tightening his bandage. "American built, yes. But it's used by a number of countries."

"Germany?"

Nero looked up and nodded. "Unfortunately."

The roar of engines changed as the pilot throttled back, decreasing speed.

"What do you think, Brick?" Nero asked. "Can we make a move on 'em?"

"You know more than I do, Arch," the Professor said. "How many men could fit on that thing? And can you fly it? More importantly, can you fly it with a bum leg?"

Nero smiled. "You doubt me, Brick. I could pilot anything with a stick or wheel, my friend, shot or otherwise."

"All right then. How many men could be on there? At most?"

"It's a fourteen seater," Nero said, adjusting himself on grass and leaning forward to peer over the thick hedge. "Plus the possibility of a pilot and copilot. So... sixteen, max?"

Brannigan pointed. "Plus those two is eighteen," he said.

The Professor had just spotted Von Faust and young Lessard, the duo parked at the far end of the landing strip. Von Faust stared up into the sky with his one eye, a look of unquestionable pleasure on his face.

"Bloody hell," Nero said.

"We'll have to wait, I'd say. We'd have the element of surprise on the plane, but there's no way we could sneak up on Von Faust and that young soldier. Not from this distance!"

"What is Von Faust doing?"

"Meeting the new arrivals, I'd imagine. Let's see who's come to visit."

***

Nero and the Professor ducked beneath the shrubbery for cover in the wake of the plane as it sailed overhead before touching down. The DC-2 rumbled down the dirt runway, tires sinking into the soil as it slowly turned to mud. The ship coasted slowly to the end of the runway before killing its engines. A moment later the hatch opened, and Nero and the Professor watched as a pair of men exited. The first was an old man; the second a giant. *Der Klinge* and Konig.

"*Guten tag*, Herr *Klinge*," Von Faust said. The Nazi Captain stood just below the lowered stairway, raising one arm in salute. "*Heil* Hitler!"

Der Klinge nodded solemnly and raised a half-hearted salute. "*Ja*," he said impassively. "*Heil* Hitler."

"How was your trip, Herr *Klinge*?"

"Long," the old man said as the giant Konig helped him into Von Faust's jeep. "You have captured this man?" he asked. "You have this Brannigan in your possession?"

"I do, sir. But–"

"More importantly, the Cipher, Heinrich. Do you have the Cipher?"

Von Faust opened his mouth, searching for words. "Uh, ah... not yet, Herr *Klinge*," he admitted. "It was not in their possession when we apprehended–"

"The Cipher is not here?" the old man asked, his brow furrowing. "Where is it, Heinrich?"

"We are ascertaining that information now, Herr *Klinge*. Mr. Shindo is–"

"That damnable American has a worst track record than you do."

"Sir, I believe Mr. Shindo can–"

"What about Delacroix?"

"Sir?"

"Where is Delacroix?"

"He waits back at the cottage."

"Has he spoken to this Brannigan?"

"No, sir. I believed it unwise to–"

"That's enough," the old man said, looking up at his huge assistant. The two shared something in a brief and silent exchange. The old man turned back to Von Faust. "We will speak further at your headquarters. My assistant will mind the plane," he said. "Let's go."

"But, Herr *Klinge*. I assure you, the plane will be–"

"Herr Konig prefers to mind the plane, Heinrich," *Der Klinge* scowled. "Show me what you have accomplished. Take me to this Brannigan. Now."

***

"They're leaving!" Brannigan said, pointing.

"Hugo, I believe I'm having a small problem–"

"We can make a run for the plane before Von Faust returns to the cottage!"

"Hugo–"

"–and if we are lucky, we can be in the air before Black Fang even knows that we have esca–"

"Brick!"

"What? What is it, Nero?"

"I believe I'm having a problem," he said.

The Professor directed his attention to Nero's leg. The pilot was seated and focusing on his wounded, bandaged leg. The gauze and makeshift dressings on his wound were stained red with blood.

"I don't know if I popped stitches or–"

The Professor knelt. "Does it hurt, Arch?" he asked.

Nero swallowed. "A bit," he admitted.

Brannigan shook his head. "I'm sorry, my friend. I paid no heed to your troubles. I was stupid."

Nero laughed. "It's all right, we needed to escape, Brick. I just wish those bastards hadn't shot me!"

Brannigan blanched and forced a smile. "Uh, yes, *those bastards*. Right. Those bastards!"

"But your plan," Nero said. "I believe it's sound."

"My plan?"

"Make for the plane, old boy."

"Ah, yes, right." Brannigan glanced over his shoulder. "Do you think you can fly it?"

"Were you even listening to me, Brick?"

"Of course, silly me. But look!" The Professor smiled and pointed as Von Faust's jeep puttered past, *Der Klinge* seated in the passenger's seat, Von Faust relegated to the back. "Our visitor departs."

"Wasn't there another man?" Nero asked.

Brannigan nodded slowly. "I believe there was, although the body of the plane blocked my view. What did you see? You've the eyes of a hawk, after all."

Nero shook his head slowly. "I admit, I'm not certain." He turned to the Professor. "What do you think?"

Brannigan took a deep breath. "Well, to quote G. Legh's Accidence of Armoury, 'no time better than even now'!"

"What?"

"There's no time like the present, my friend!"

With that, the Professor leapt over the small shrub and began his mad dash across the field.

Meanwhile, on the south face of the hill, Von Faust & Co. continued their winding trek back to the cottage on the coast, soon to find only disappointment awaiting them.

***

The plane seemed... empty.

Brannigan had crossed the runway in a flash, his Herculean stride carrying him from his hideout with Nero to the belly of the DC-2 in a matter of moments.

No one waited on the tarmac, no one lurked in the passenger's compartment.

Alone, the Professor checked the cockpit and the cargo hold, finding the cockpit empty but the hold filled with a collection of mysterious crates bearing a rogue's gallery of customs stamps from a dozen countries.

"What in the name of Hannibal's elephants...?" Brannigan said, kneeling beside a crate and running his hand over the impressed stamps. "If Quincy was here, his head would be a-spinning!"

"*Es tut mir leid zu unterbrechen*," a booming voice behind him sounded. "*Bitte kommen Sie mit mir*, Herr Brannigan."

The Professor whipped around, eyes wide. "Damn it man, where did you come from?" Standing in the doorway to the cargo hold was a giant of a man, his hands seeming to approximate the size of cantaloupes.

"*Ich habe auf dich gewartet*," the giant said. "*Sie sind sehr schnell für einen Mann mit einem Schnurrbart!*"

"I've almost no idea what you're saying, my friend," the Professor said, backpedaling. "My grasp on German is elementary at best. I heard a few words... uh, 'for me,'

94

'quick,' and... really, did you say 'mustache'?"

The giant took a step towards Brannigan (quite a mistake) and was met with one of the Professor's world renown haymakers. A shot like that would flatten the very Black Hills of Dakota.

Unfortunately, the giant Konig was not the Black Hills of Dakota. The punch impacted the German's solar plexus and rebounded as ineffectually as that of a housefly.

The Professor reeled backwards, cradling his fist. "Sword of Damocles!" he shouted. "I believe you must work out regularly!"

He swung again, this time aiming for the giant's jaw. The huge man caught the Professor's fist mid-air, squeezing Brannigan's fist mercilessly and twisting his arm away.

"*Mich nicht kämpfen, Schnurrbart Mann. Sie werden nicht gewinnen.*"

"It's... not... a... *mustache!*" Brannigan said, fighting to speak every word. He swung his left hand–far from his forte–and caught the giant unawares, sending the huge German stumbling backwards as he released Brick's right paw.

"Bloody hell," the Professor said, looking down at his numb right fist. "You nearly crushed my hand! And it's *a la souvarov*, not a damnable mustache, for pity's sake!"

He looked up in time to see the melon-sized fist of the Nazi giant coming at him like a cannonball.

Unfortunately, lightning quick reflexes or not, even the Professor could not avoid that.

It was, as they say, *curtains*.

CHAPTER 11: In Which Our Spanish Adventurers Find a Friendly-ish Face Where They Least Expected

They'd bickered for a few minutes before finally deciding to go with Dr. Halifax's suggestion: the American Consulate.

"I still think we should have gone to the police," Andrew said. "I'd feel... safer."

"We're not here to practice safety, Andrew," Lily said. "Lest we forget, safety and caution are not the same things."

"Oh?"

Lily smiled, her adventuress blood bubbling once more. "Of course not. One is so much more... boring."

"Oh dear," Andrew said.

"Plus, I remember going to the Consulate in Tangier with Hugo. I... well, I have a good feeling about this."

Andrew nodded. "All right," he said. "Let's see if you're right."

After backtracking to the *Mercado* and receiving some directions from a florist, Andrew and Lily set off, crossing the Guadalquivir River, leaving Triana, its narrow streets and Moorish architecture behind them. Our duo of adventurers were forced to ask only three random pedestrians for directions before they found themselves on the edge of the *Plaza Nueva*, an elevated statue of Fernando III staring down at them.

The square was broad, filled with a good number of people enjoying the afternoon sunshine. Palm trees sprouted up over the square, and our lost adventurers began crossing the crowded plaza slowly, taking in the sights.

"That's City Hall there," Andrew pointed. "I think." He smiled awkwardly as they passed a street musician. His doleful guitar strummings nearly lost in the din of an angry crowd congregating before City Hall.

"Didn't Aurelio mention protests?" Lily asked, taking a step closer to Andrew and lowering her voice. "I admit, I know little of Spain's current political clime."

"I don't know anything myself," Andrew said, raising his voice slightly. "But I think I've found our destination!" He pointed to the far end of the Plaza where an American flag hung over a double-doored entranceway.

The Consulate was a rather small affair, manned by a minimum number of people. Lily and Andrew, however, had not the time to wait in line before something terribly strange happened.

They saw Quincy Max, or rather, they *heard* Quincy Max.

"Students!" the old man shouted. "In my day students were never this *rowdy*! They learned, they didn't protest!"

"Dr. Max?" Lily found herself asking.

"They–" The old man paused momentarily. "Excuse me, did someone say my name?"

Dr. Halifax and Andrew stepped from behind the short line of people leading up to the front desk and found the bent shape of Quincy Max approaching.

Lily could not help but smile, her less adventuresome half feeling admittedly relieved.

"Oh Quincy, I'm so *happy* to see you!" she blurted. "I–oh I just feel so lost!"

"Quincy?" the old man shouted. "*Quincy*?!" Quickly, he turned, his head shaking vigorously as he began his long walk back to the private offices.

"What, why...?" Lily paused, cursing her poor memory. "Oh blast," she said, remembering Hugo's words about the Max family being "quite large." Apparently, she'd just found another. "Dr. Max," she called. "A moment, please!"

The Max brother paused, back still turned to our adventurers. Shaking his head, he turned. He gazed at Lily sharply before he began to make his way back towards the lobby. When he reached the main reception desk, he waved, "Come."

Lily and Andrew scooted around the waiting line and made their way past the desk. "Excuse me, Mr. Max, I'm dreadfully sorry I–"

"Young lady," Interrupted the mysterious Max. "I may not be Quincy, but I am indeed a doctor. Please do try not to insult me further."

Lily blushed. "Apologies, *Dr.* Max. My name is Liliana Halifax and I am a professor at your brother's Institute."

"Lovely," the old man said, his voice unmistakably snide. "Is there something you want?"

"A moment to talk," Lily explained, religiously patient. "If you would be so kind as to take us some-where private, I believe I have some information you would like to hear."

The Max brother looked at her, and for a moment Liliana believed he was about to send her and Andrew back out into the street. He did not, however, as a charitable air must have come over him.

"Oh, all right," he sighed. "But let's hurry up."

The grumpiest Max brother (so far) led our adventurers back into his office, a dark mahogany number eerily reminiscent of Mortimer Max's office in the American Legation in Tangier. Okay, *more* than eerily reminiscent. It did, in fact, look like the exact same office.

"Sit, sit, sit, I don't have all day."

Lily and Andrew took residence in a pair of chairs that faced Dr. Max's desk. As expected, he sat behind the desk and took a drink of dark coffee. The name placard on his desk read *REGINALD MAX*.

For a long moment, nothing happened. They stared at him, and he stared at them.

"Well, what do you want?"

Lily cast one glance at Andrew, her face betraying all of her fears. The same fears that had all but evaporated when she'd first laid eyes on Reginald Max had resurfaced in spades upon discovering his... unpleasant disposition.

"As I said, my name is Liliana Halifax, and I am here from your brother's institute back in the States. I–"

She stopped, remembering words of wisdom a few gentlemen had imparted on her. Señor Reyes, Señor Del Toro, and even Hugo. She needed to trust people, and she needed to conduct herself with grace. Also, she could not overlook the–

"Madame, can you speak? If you are troubled, I would be grateful to offer my assistance by throwing you out onto the sidewalk."

She smiled congenially and decided to finish her train of thought. Where were we? Ah, yes. She could not overlook the power of:

"Brick Brannigan," she said.

The stingy old man, mouth open and ready to rebuke, froze.

Was it not Señor Del Toro who had said, "All you needed to say was 'Brannigan,'"?

"Brannigan," Reginald Max said, his voice soft. Beneath his long white beard, his mouth was an inscrutable line.

"Yes," Lily said. "*Brick Brannigan*."

Slowly, ever so slowly, the old man smiled, his icy mask seeming to melt instantly.

"Welcome, friends," he said.

Together, Lily and Andrew breathed a deep sigh of relief.

***

"You wouldn't believe it," Reginald was saying, laughter lines that had been hidden now appearing at the corners of his eyes, "That devil Brannigan got me drunk on Sherry at a bullfight. I was so *angry*, but I swear, my child, I'd never had so much fun before in my life!"

Reginald was laughing, Lily was laughing, even Andrew was laughing. Our adventurers had found a safe place, and for the first time, they could truly exhale in peace (without fear of pirates, freezing to death, or sea sickness). It was a remarkable feeling, let me tell you.

"But *why* on Earth are you looking for criminals?" Reginald asked.

"I told her we should go to the police," Andrew interjected.

"Ah, well, I wouldn't go that far, young sir," the Max brother said with a sigh. "You are foreign. And while the Spanish *policía* are both kind and capable, they... well, they have their hands rather full at the moment."

"Speaking of, what is going on outside City Hall?" Lily asked.

"Political upheaval, I'm sorry to say."

"Upheaval? But I thought that since the war, things in Europe had stabilized!"

Reginald laughed. "Goodness, my dear, you are certainly out of touch, aren't you? Things on the continent are the worst they've been in some time, and there are many who believe that they will only get worse! Some say a civil war is brewing here in Spain. And don't get me started on Germany!"

"Oh." Lily shuffled her feet and cleared her throat. "I am a little more entrenched in... old things," she admitted sheepishly.

"And that's fine, at times like this, there is an unmistakable comfort to be found in *old things*, indeed! But, again, why do you want to find criminals?"

"Hugo," Lily said, her voice growing suddenly solemn. "Hugo is missing."

Lily recounted the tale as she saw fit–an abridged version, at least. It was long enough–albeit only just–to make up a full novel, after all (you read it, right? *Brick Brannigan is Knee-Deep in Peril!*). When she was finished, she leaned back and sighed.

"So you see, Reginald, we are... well, at a bit of a loss at the moment."

"Indeed you are, my child, indeed you are." Pensively, the old fellow lit a pipe and sat back in his chair. "Perhaps you could... No, wait! I've the most splendid idea, of course!"

"What? You do? What is it?"

Rising to his feet as quickly as the old timer could, Reginald Max pointed the stem of his pipe at Lily and said, "When was the last time you went to church?"

***

The church in question, dear reader, was the *Catedral de Santa María de la Sede*, also known as the Seville Cathedral–or simply *Sevilla Catedral*, for you Spanish speakers. I'd go in depth describing it, but even the combined literate mastery of Shakespeare, Milton, Melville, and Dickens would fall short (so you can imagine how I might fare). Flawless marble, lavish stonework, endless gilding, a breathtaking altar, and more flying buttresses than even *Notre Dame* could shake a stick at–and we haven't even gotten to the bell tower constructed from a repurposed mosque minaret. The *Sevilla Catedral* is as beautiful as it is unique.

"I wasn't expecting this..." Andrew said as he followed Lily and Reginald Max across *Avenida de la Constitución* towards the great looming structure.

"Neither was I," Lily said, her mouth hanging open. "But my goodness."

"Truly one of a kind, isn't it? I think it rivals the

Rouen Cathedral, perhaps even the Duomo in Florence. Although, I quite like what they're doing to that *Sagrada Família* in Barcelona."

"It certainly is beautiful, Dr. Max. But... I'm sorry, sir," Lily said, her thoughts turning to Hugo and his frightful predicament. "What are we doing here exactly?"

Reginald Max turned and winked at Lily over his shoulder. "Patience, my dear. Patience."

Dr. Max led our adventurers through the doors on the West facade and crossed the grand, empty space quickly, his footsteps *clicking* across the marble floor. Lily gasped as her eyes adjusted to the darkness and came to rest on the huge golden altarpiece that rose from the polished floor to the massively high ceiling, showing vivid scenes from the old testament. Even Andrew could not help but stare in awe at the marvel of the cathedral as he passed an old woman kneeling, lighting a candle in prayer.

"Come now," Dr. Max said softly, urging his slowing companions on.

He led them halfway down the long nave before turning to his left towards a grand doorway that was closed. With a sigh, he pushed, forcing the door open with a *creak* and bathing our adventurers in golden sunlight. The rustle of leaves in the wind, the chirping of birds, and the bubbling of fountain soon followed. Dr. Max closed the door behind them.

"I see you like our Cathedral," he said with a proud grin. "But a mass will be starting soon, so I don't want to stay for long. But this is the Orange Tree Courtyard, and I believe we will find just who we are looking for here..." He turned, squinting into the sunlight.

The courtyard was a large rectangle with a small fountain in its center. Rising in even intervals from the stone patio were six or seven long rows of orange trees, green and rife with brightly colored fruit. Above them, the mosque minaret–the *Giralda*–rose against the perfect blue sky.

"Have you come for a rematch, *Viejo*?" a voice called from across the space.

"*No me pongas a prueba, niño!*" Dr. Max said. "*Te has ganado, pero fue sólo suerte.*"

Lily looked at Andrew. "What is happening?" she asked. "And who is speaking?"

"A priest," Dr. Max answered. "*Padre* Francisco. We have gotten to know each other quite well," he smiled. "Through our games of chess."

From the deep shadows beneath a small tree, a short, slim man emerged. He had a well-trimmed beard and laugh lines around his eyes. Ah, but his eyes were deep and dark, and while there was an unmistakable kindness there, Lily could see something unknowable in them, as well. From the tangled branches over his head, he snatched an orange and began to peel it. "*No fue suerte, Viejo,*" Francisco said. "You have taught me well."

Reginald Max smiled and embraced the much younger man. "*¿Cómo estás*, Francisco? *¿Y cómo está su madre?*"

"She is nearly as old as you, *mi amigo*," Francisco said. "But she is well, nonetheless. Who are your friends?"

Reginald explained as cursorily as he could manage– it still took a few minutes–before the young priest took a deep breath and shook his head.

"A terribly unfortunate situation," he said, his voice growing serious for the first time. "I see now why you have come to me."

There was a moment of silence as the young priest took a bite from the freshly plucked orange.

"I don't mean to speak out of turn," Lily said, "but I believe I am a bit confused, myself," she admitted. "I do not know why we have come to see you, *Padre*."

"*Padre* Francisco is... well," Reginald stroked his beard, thinking. "How would you say it, Francisco? You are... modern?"

The young priest smiled mysteriously as he wiped a streak of juice from his lip. "I welcome all to the services of *La Catedral de Santa María de la Sede*, whereas there are those who have been stationed here for far too long, men who are content to exclude those deemed less than savory."

Lily weighed the young priest's words and remembered what Reginald had said. "Less than savory," she repeated. "You mean... criminals?"

Francisco nodded. "*Confesión*," he said. "Chosen profession aside, there are men with bloody hands that desire the rites of *penitencia* as much as those with clean hands. It is very important to some."

"And they cannot receive it from other priests?" Andrew asked.

Francisco shook his head ruefully. "The older priests forbid it. I do it in secret because I believe it to be right. I speak with the men and I urge them to turn themselves in, to correct their paths before they are truly lost. In some cases it works." He looked at the cobble ground beneath his feet. "In some it does not," he admitted.

"So you see now why I have brought you to here," Reginald said.

"But I do regret your coming, *Viejo*," Francisco said, his voice low. "*El secreto de la confesión es sagrado*. It is sacred, Reginald. You would have me break it?"

"No, Francisco, you know I do not want to put you in such a position–"

"But you have, *amigo*."

"My friend's life is at stake, Francisco," Reginald said softly. "Just point us in the right direction."

Lily spoke up, unable to reconcile the turmoil on the young man's face. "Do what you believe to be right, Señor. If that means turning us away, so be it. But I would not have you break your vows. Not even for Hugo."

Francisco looked at Lily, perhaps taken aback a bit. She did not have the forthright pushiness that Reginald Max did. In truth, even Andrew was surprised at her admission.

"This man," Francisco said, "you are here because you love him, no?"

Lily took a breath. "I have known Hugo for... well, a very short time. But yes, Father, I do believe I love this man. I am willing to cross the four oceans and seven seas to find him."

Padre Francisco looked into her eyes and took a breath. After a long moment, he said, "Please excuse me, my friends. Take a moment of peace in the garden, and I will return." Slowly, he stood and walked from the courtyard, his shoulders bowed slightly as if beneath a heavy weight.

"I hope he can help us," Andrew said.

"No, Andrew," Lily said. "He needs to do what is right. We were, perhaps, wrong to come here." She turned to Reginald Max. The older man squirmed under her gaze.

"I'm sorry, Dr. Halifax," he said softly. "I care for Brick Brannigan a great deal, and like you I would do almost anything to save him. I do not regret this, even if it puts *Padre* Francisco in an unfortunate position."

And that was that. No one spoke for the next few minutes. Our three adventurers waited in the small courtyard as the sun began to slip lower in the sky. The birds chirped, the fountain bubbled, and the wind slipped through the trees ever so gently.

When *Padre* Francisco returned, the weight that seemed to burden him was gone.

"Well?" Reginald asked.

"I can tell you."

"You prayed on it?" Andrew asked.

The young priest shook his head and smiled. "I called the man on the phone and asked if I could tell you." He shrugged. "He said that he cared not one bit!"

"That was easy," Lily said with a grin. "Thank you, Father. *Gracias*."

"Do not thank me," Francisco said. "I am glad I could help. And I am grateful for your understanding, *Señora*."

"Many people have helped us," Lily said. "I am endlessly surprised and grateful for the kindness that has been shared with us."

Padre Francisco smiled. "The world has more good people than bad," he said. "It is good to be reminded of this from time to time. And as this evening will prove,

Señora, even some of the bad people are better than we can believe."

"Which bad person have you got for us, Francisco?" Reginald asked.

"A man who has done terrible things who I believe I can save."

"A... murderer?" Andrew asked with an audible *gulp*.

"Perhaps. His exact crimes are not known to me, but he is most wanted by the police. Because of this, I know not where to find him."

"But he left you his phone number?" Lily asked skeptically.

"I know it because he calls for me often. His conscience weighs heavily on him."

"Oh no, surely you can't..." Reginald began, a bright flicker of recognition crossing his face. "Not–"

Francisco nodded. "Si, *Viejo*. *La Tempestad*."

"The what?" Lily asked.

"Oh my word!" Reginald said. "Not him!"

"It means 'The Storm,'" Andrew said.

Francisco grimaced. "His true name is unknown to us all. He is the scourge of the underworld, a criminal mastermind. And I believe he is the only man who can help you."

The conversation fell into silence as a strong and baleful wind ripped through the courtyard, forcing Lily to hold her flat-topped *cordobés* hat on her head. Above them, the deep bell of *la Giralda* rang ominously.

Francisco handed Reginald a folded piece of paper to Lily. Inside was scribbled the name of a restaurant and a time. "He will only meet you alone, *Señora*. He is safe, but use caution regardless."

"You are certain I am safe?" Lily asked.

Dr. Max spoke up. "No! Not with *La Temp–*"

"No, *Viejo*," Francisco interrupted. "If you've ever trusted me, trust me now. *Señora* Halifax will come to no harm on this night. You have my word. And the word of *La Tempestad*."

The wind continued blowing, and beneath the long leather coat, Lily shivered. "I will go," she said. "I trust you, Father."

She looked at the time written on the paper. "We should go," she said. "Thank you again."

The priest shook his head. "Do not thank me. I hope only that I have not let you down. I will pray for you and for your lover, *Señora*."

Lily smiled at the use of that word (lover). "Thank you, Father." She stood, a fresh determined energy present in her step. "Let's go, gentlemen."

She led Reginald and Andrew from the courtyard after brief goodbyes, Reginald one step behind her and Andrew at the back. The young man was delayed because he could have *sworn* he saw a subdued flash of color appear momentarily on the parapet above them before disappearing just as quickly. Was it, perhaps, blue?

"What was that?" he said to himself. After a moment, he shrugged and continued on, not thinking twice before returning with his party to the busy streets of Sevilla, not realizing it was the second time he'd seen that strange flash of color in the past few days.

It almost seemed to be following them.

CHAPTER 12: All Right, Let's Get This Story Moving (In Earnest), and Nothing Does That Better Than A Dead Body!

Brannigan opened his eyes to the sound of muted arguing. He was back in that damnable barn, affixed to a new chair–this time with chains.

"Of *course* I made that point, *Der Klinge*," Shindo said, sighing. He stood in the corner with his back turned to Brannigan. "I understand our mythology and legacy as well as anyone, seeing as I learned it from you. I can make a compelling case in a short amount of time, I assure you."

"It would seem you cannot, Edmond. I appreciate your efforts, my son, but I have to say, this is appearing to be little more than a resounding failure."

"*Monsieur Klinge*," Fang said, entering the barn at a slow walk. "If you would allow me–"

"Stop, *Herr* Fang," *Der Klinge* interrupted, scowling. "You have done little but disappoint me. Why in the name of *die heilige Mutter* should I let you speak with the prisoner?"

"Without my help, he would not *be* here, *Monsieur*," Fang said defensively. "If you have forgotten, it was *I* who had the worm planted in the ice, it was *I* who controlled *Monsieur* Nero and prevented the escape from Tangiers, and it was *I* who successfully moved the prisoners from the depths of the Mediterranean to the safety of this farm without detection. Your *Monsieur* Von Faust has done nothing but–"

"Stop, *Herr* Fang," *Der Klinge* repeated angrily. "I do not broker argument. It was under your watch that *Herr* Brannigan and *Herr* Nero escaped, was it not?"

"It was under the eye of *Monsieur* Shindo–"

"Silence!" the old fascist shouted. "Please leave, *Herr* Fang. You have annoyed me enough for one afternoon. Brew us some coffee and stay out of our way."

Brannigan watched Fang's face as the evil French-man held his tongue. It was a silent film, and a tumul-tuous one at that. His eyes sharpened in anger and then turned down to the floor. *Is that shame I see?* wondered Brannigan. *Or embarrassment, perhaps? Sadness? Or just deep and impenetrable fury?*

After a quite pregnant pause, Fang turned and left the barn. In his wake, Von Faust and the giant Konig en-tered, making the room a bit crowded with fascists.

"I say, this room is getting a bit crowded with fascists!" Brannigan said with a chuckle.

Shindo turned around quickly, his eyes narrow with anger. On seeing his face for the first time, Brannigan's chuckle bloomed into a full-throated laugh. The interro-gator had a black eye and a broken nose (judging from the white athletic tape stripped across it and cotton balls plugged in each nostril).

"Hah! I seemed to land a solid one there, eh Shindo?"

Der Klinge took a step forward. "*Herr* Brannigan, welcome back to us. I feared you would not be waking before nightfall."

"Oh? How long was I out, old timer?"

Der Klinge was unperturbed by Brannigan's jab. "Over an hour. My name is *Der Klinge* and it seems you were no match for Konig's strength," he said, gesturing towards the giant.

"How could I be, Mr. *Klinge*?" Brannigan smiled. "I'm just a man. I imagine your Konig friend could knock over the damned Empire State Building!"

Der Klinge smiled. "He will try soon enough, *Herr* Brannigan. It won't be long before we march into your New York City."

Brannigan smiled coldly. "Try it. What did Abraham Lincoln say? 'All the armies of Europe and Asia could not by force take a drink from the Ohio River.' We wouldn't let you bastards cross State Street north of Battery Park. No army will we ever allow to step foot on Broadway or Bowery, Lexington or Canal. Over my dead body. And I don't even *like* New York!"

"Enough of this!" *Der Klinge* shouted again, perhaps finally getting a little rattled. (I mean, what villain would not be rattled by such a rousing Abraham Lincoln quote?) "Enough stalling! Nothing has happened! Nothing at all. Just talking and traveling and more talking. It's ridiculous! Konig, what chapter are we in?"

The old man leaned in as the giant whispered in his ear.

"*Twelve*?!" *Der Klinge* shouted. "But nothing has happened!"

"Plenty has happened," Brannigan said defensively. "Never underestimate the unforeseen consequences in part two of a trilogy!"

"Consequences!" *Der Klinge* spat. "You speak of

consequences when chained at my mercy?"

"There are always consequences," Brannigan said, the words ominous. "If you do not understand this simple fact, then you cannot win, old man."

Der Klinge smiled. "You are captured, *Herr* Brannigan, and even now await your own torture–which I assure you will be a long and terrible ordeal–while your friends are either gone or scattered to the wind. You are alone and you cannot hope to be saved. There is no chance of it. Haven't you wondered where your dear Nero is? In your escape you were captured, *Herr* Brannigan, and he was killed."

Brannigan took a deep breath, fighting off the wellspring of sadness that had opened in his chest. "I have hope eternal," he said. "Even in the face of death. I can mourn my dear friend later, and I will, but for now I must have hope. In the darkest of times it is easy to feel hope when you have something worth living for."

"And what is that?"

Brannigan smiled and thought of Lily, wondering where she was and what she was doing. As he said, while he was afraid, he had not lost hope. Lily was coming, of that he was certain.

"That is for me to know, and you to fret over," Brannigan said.

Der Klinge scowled. "The Eye of Aja," the old man said, his voice like a sheet of granite. "Where is it?"

Brannigan arched his back against the chains, the bones in his spine *cracking*. He ran his tongue over his back right lower molar unconsciously, a habit he had acquired when in times of great strain. "At the bottom of the damned Mediterranean, *Klinge*," he said. "When you crashed my plane you kissed it goodbye."

"And the Cipher of Dumuzid?"

"Laying beside the Eye in the wreckage. It seems Fang is not the only person liable to make mistakes, is he?"

Konig took a step forward and hunched over to whisper once again into *Der Klinge*'s ear.

When the old man turned back to Brannigan, there was something like victory in his eye. "Konig informs me that he has debriefed *Herr* Fang. You see, as my French associate was saying, it was *he* who was in control of your friend Nero as the plane was going down. *Herr* Fang was watching through Nero's eyes and controlling your friend's every move. He saw the woman escape with it."

"What woman?" Brannigan said lamely.

Der Klinge's smile grew larger. "Yes, as I suspected." He turned to Konig. "Do not give up on finding the woman. As we thought, she has what we want."

Konig turned to leave, trudging heavily. *Der Klinge* turned back to Brannigan, his eyes squinting in thought.

"No, wait!"

Konig stopped in the door.

"Do not find the woman yourself. Instead, take control of the radio from *Herr* Fang. Call out to our agents throughout Europe. Make contact with those who would help move people across borders illegally. No doubt she is coming to rescue her lover. Little does she know that she is also bringing us exactly what we most desire. Let her come, and tighten the net with each passing day."

Brannigan's mouth fell open and he cursed his stupidity. And he'd had the temerity to scold *Der Klinge* for having no foresight in regards to consequences!

When the old man turned back to Brannigan, he looked quite satisfied, indeed. "Like all Americans," he said, "you talk too much. Hope, *Herr* Brannigan, can be such a dangerous thing. You see, it clouds your vision. And when your vision is clouded, you cannot see what is right in front of your face."

The Professor swallowed and looked at the ground. *Der Klinge* was right in this case, it had clouded his vision. He could think of nothing but Lily, never pausing on the fact that she was bringing the Cabal exactly what they wanted.

"Now, before another pesky chapter break interrupts us further," *Der Klinge* said, not without a hint of exasperation, "Why don't you tell me where the map is?"

"What?"

"The map, *Herr* Brannigan. The most important relic of all. I know you liberated half of it from the peaks of the Andes and the remainder from the foothills of Tibet. Its halves have been reunited, and now with the Cipher of Dumuzid, it is all we need."

"How do you know that?" the Professor asked, dumbfounded, a terrible pit opening at the bottom of his stomach.

Der Klinge kept up his sinister grin. "That is unimportant," he said. "Why don't you cease your stall-ing and get to it?"

Brannigan closed his eyes. He could not remember a time when defeat seemed so imminent, wrapping its cold arms around him like the sea. In his mouth, his tongue touched the very back right lower molar once more, and he remembered Quincy Max's words as clear as day. *We must protect the map and its secrets at all cost, Brick. The lives of the innocents populating this beautiful planet far outweigh our own. Never must we forget this simple truth.*

"I can't tell you, *Der Klinge*, because it would be... well, just a really bad idea."

"Then you will be tortured. There is little you can do to stave off the end, despite your hope. Truth is such a simple thing to extract. We will learn this truth, one way or another."

"No," Brannigan said simply. "You won't."

With that, he used his tongue to push off the fake crown acting as his lower right back molar, exposing the caplet of poison within.

Der Klinge understood what was happening before anyone else. His eyes grew wide in shock. "No! Konig, grab him! Quickly!"

Even as Brannigan bit down on the caplet, releasing the poison, a smile tugged at the corner of his mouth. He closed his eyes and thought of Lily as the caplet burst and the poison was released.

When Konig reached the Professor it was already too late.

Brick Brannigan was dead.

CHAPTER 13: Madness Visits *El Corazón de la Bula* (As Does Our Adventuress Lily)

Lily stood in a dark alley, long coat flapping in the wind that tore through the lonesome backstreet, one hand holding her *cordobés* hat despite the chin strap she had tightened. A swarm of butterflies was running amok in her stomach, and her courage was beginning to falter. *I am alone in a back alley in Sevilla, preparing to meet with a criminal mastermind in hopes of striking a bargain to save the life of my new love. Why would I* not *be nervous?*

Perhaps a hundred yards away, warm golden light poured from an open doorway, carrying with it the tempestuous rhythms of flamenco music. Lily listened to the clatter of castanets and thunder of the handclaps overwhelming a fleet of nylon-stringed guitars and tried to calm herself. She was early. *La Giralda* would ring when it was time for their meeting to begin.

Lily had spoken privately with Dr. Max prior to leaving for the meeting, knowing full well that his warnings would do nothing to deter her.

"Francisco is..." he shook his head. "I fear he is being quite foolish. *La Tempestad* is a menace, Dr. Halifax. He has been the scourge of Sevilla for a very long time. Robbery, blackmail, graft, murder. I know Francisco is a man with a good heart, but I fear that he is blinded by his compassion, blinded perhaps by his hope that the criminals whom he has counseled can be saved. Unfortunately, most are beyond salvation."

"You would have me not go, Doctor?" she'd asked him.

He took a very long time to answer. "In all honesty? I just don't know."

Anxiety notwithstanding, she had gone, and now here she stood, awaiting the toll of *la Giralda* and watching as men and women walked laughing into the loud restaurant called *El Corazón de la Bula*.

Perhaps this is a mistake, she thought. *Am I safe here? Am I to be murdered in a dark alley by a man called* La Tempestad? *Will I ever see Hugo again?*

As if in answer, the bells of *la Giralda* tolled eight, and she knew it was time.

***

El Corazón de la Bula was deceptively large inside, but its grand size was all but cancelled due to the oppressive number of patrons that filled the space. The room was dim, but still awash in colors. Dark reds and blues and purples, giving the room an eerie, dreamlike quality, exacerbated by the pounding of handclaps, footstomps, and amplified guitar. Men and women crowded the huge room, moving in a storm across the broad dance floor. Above, a mezzanine ran a ring around the room, and from her vantage Lily could see that it too was filled with bodies. A huge rectangular bar filled the wall to her left, with men and women surrounding it jubilantly. Round tables circled the bar, most filled with numerous small tapas plates being picked at by sweaty dancers as they exited the madness of the dance floor. Opposite the bar, over the ocean of the dance floor, was a stage filled with musicians, most clapping, accompanying the three acoustic guitarists.

"¡*Fuera del camino*, *Vaquera*!" a man grunted as he pushed past Lily, the scent of wine heavy on his breath. She stepped aside as he stumbled past her to the bar.

Lily reached deep into the pocket of her long leather coat and returned with the note *Padre* Francisco had given her. She read the words carefully:

There is a table in the back right corner of *El Corazón de la Bula*. *La Tempestad* will wait for you there when the bell of *la Giralda* signals eight o'clock. Use discretion.

Here it was, eight o'clock. And so *La Tempestad* would indeed be waiting. Lily closed her eyes, took a deep breath, and stepped forward into the maelstrom. She knew exactly what she was doing, and never did she forget for whom she was doing it.

As Lily struggled around the outer ring of the dance floor, a woman approached a microphone, receiving a smattering of applause from the crowd. She began to sing, a full-throated wordless melody that brought the dance floor into a frenzy. Lily, kept the brim of her hat low and slipped through the crowd, pushing her way towards the back of the room.

In back, beneath the overhanging mezzanine, the thrum of music was lower and the space less crowded with dancers. A few tables were squeezed into a small alcove in the very corner, most of them empty. To the left of the alcove was a second, smaller bar, not nearly as full as the first but far from empty. Lily walked past it and into the heavily shadowed alcove.

A group of young men had pulled two tables together and were arguing vehemently in Spanish. Lily ignored them. She had found what she was looking for.

In the absolute corner, his back to the wall, sat a chiseled, scar-faced man with pitch black hair highlighted by flashes of silver at his temples. He wore a sharp suit and partook generously from a long-necked glass liquor bottle and plate of indistinguishable food before him.

Lily approached the table slowly. As she did, she saw that the man's right eye was milky with blindness and drooped lazily to the right. His skin was pitted and a scraggly mustache stained his upper lip. *Quite an unattractive fellow*, Lily thought as she arrived at his table.

"*Toma el asiento, Vaquera,*" he said, his voice low and gravelly. "*Antes de dibujas la atención innecesariamente a nosotros.*"

"I don't speak Spanish," she said, slipping into the seat across from him.

He smiled and Lily hated it. His teeth were a fine tobacco brown and at least three were missing. "You speak no Spanish, but you understand."

She did not respond, instead she loosened her chinstrap and pushed the *cordobés* hat back on her head, revealing more of her face.

"Where did you get that?" the ugly man across from her asked. "I do not believe you have been to *Córdoba*. Take it off, unless you think yourself some woman *ranchero*. You look ridiculous."

Lily's cheeks burned as she slipped the hat off her

head and laid it on the seat beside her. She felt the flush of embarrassment rising in her face.

"I ask for discretion from an American," he muttered, shaking his head. "¡*Qué cosa más tonta que hacer*! You stick out like *una vaca en una iglesia. Ridículo*."

Lily self-consciously rubbed her cheeks and pulled long strands of hair off her forehead. *Ridículo*. She did not need a degree in Spanish to understand that word.

The man took a forkful of some kind of meat from his plate, slopped it around in a watery tomato-based broth. "Are you hungry, *Vaquera*?" he asked.

In truth, Lily was getting quite hungry. She began to shake her head and thought better of it. "What are you eating?"

"*Criadillas*," he said. "A... local delicacy." He pushed the plate towards her.

From the empty place setting before her, Lily unrolled a napkin and silverware tumbled free. She lifted a fork and stabbed a piece of the pale meat.

"*Criadillas*," she repeated, putting the piece into her mouth and beginning to chew.

The Spaniard nodded. "Bull testicles," he said.

Lily stopped, the piece of meat sitting on her tongue. *Oh lord,* she thought. *Oh, oh no. What do I do? Spit it out? Finish eating it?* She looked at the man across from her and scowled.

"*La Plaza del Toros* is just around the corner," he said. "And while it is not season for the fights, it is still a delicacy. In the season of the bullfights, there are those who would pay a great price for the prizes of bulls vanquished. *Criadillas* give those who eat them bravery and strength. It would seem that you need both, no?"

Her two good eyes fixed on his one good one, Lily finished chewing and swallowed, absolutely unwilling to let the man across from her make her doubt herself again.

"Not bad, *señora*," he said, smirking, "for an American."

"If you are finished..." she began, taking a hit from his long-necked bottle and tasting the sweet burn of brandy. She made a face as she swallowed the last of the liquor and cleared her mouth. "...perhaps we can begin, *La Temp–*"

As if he had not barbed her enough, the ugly man (or *hombre feo*, if you'd like to insult him in his own tongue) continued. "Don't say that! *Mujer estúpida, yo no sé por qué–*"

"I've had quite enough of this, I think," Lily interrupted. "Obviously you agreed to meet me for some reason. So if you have information to share, get on with it. Otherwise, I'm leaving. Believe it or not, I have better things to do then sit here and be insulted by a man whose face looks like it was just squeezed through the large intestine of a barnyard animal."

The ugly man (*hombre feo*) did not respond. Instead, he sat with his mouth hanging open, bravely parading his tobacco brown teeth once again.

"Well?" Lily asked, already beginning to feel the sting of guilt that inevitably followed any insult she was lucky enough to marshal.

When *Hombre Feo* did not respond, she took her hat from the empty seat and stood.

"Wait, *señora*." He licked his lips and looked down at the plate and bottle before him. Slowly, he pushed both away. "*Mil disculpas*," he said. "I... I apologize. *Padre*

Francisco would be quite ashamed of my behavior. Please, sit."

Slowly, Lily returned to her seat.

"In truth, I wanted you to remove *su cordobés* so I could see your lovely face."

"Uh huh," Lily said. "Butter me up after you're back on level ground, buster."

Her newly companionable companion nodded. "As you Americans say, fair enough. For the purpose of this conversation, please only call me Felix." He reached across the table to shake her hand.

Lily extended her hand out to him only to have him raise it to his lips and kiss it, instead. She suppressed a shudder.

"The drink makes me impertinent," he said, gesturing to the bottle. "And tonight there are extenuating circumstances that..." he sighed. "That do not help matters."

Lily wasn't certain what to say. Should she feel bad for the man? Should she respond with rudeness in kind? It took not even half a moment to realize that acting in such a way was simply not her style.

"Think nothing of it, Felix. You are here helping me. I would be remiss not to act with grace," she said, thinking of Del Toro.

The man now known as Felix smiled again. "And you are my guest, *señora*. I must act with the same grace, or what kind of host would I be?"

Lily smiled and bowed her head slightly, waiting the Spaniard's next move.

His eyes moved across the area cautiously, from the bar to the dance floor to the double table of rowdy young men over Lily's left shoulder. Finally he said, "Your friend is missing, yes?"

She nodded. "Yes."

"And you believed him to have been smuggled from Spain?"

"He was involved in a plane crash off the coast of Gibraltar. He was rescued by ship and I believe he was moved."

"Moved?"

"Yes. Those who took him would want to move back to the security of their lair."

"Lair? You deal with some kind of villains, no?"

"I do, indeed, Felix."

The Spaniard leaned back, pushing his chair up onto two legs and reclining against the wall. "What makes you believe his is not in Spain even now?"

"He could be," Lily said. "But if he was, would that not also be your area of expertise? Smuggling a man *into* the country?"

Felix smiled. "Smuggling someone into Spain is much easier than you think, *señora*."

"This I've already learned."

Felix smiled again. "You say he was involved in a plane crash. Are you certain that he still lives?"

Lily met his sharp one-eyed gaze head on. "Yes," she said. "I know it."

"All right, what else can you tell me?"

Lily started at the beginning and gave every detail she could remember to Felix. Every name, every locale, every extraneous adjective. When she was done, the Spaniard nodded solemnly.

"I have good news, *señora*, and bad news. Which would you prefer first?"

"The bad news."

"The bad news is that what you are searching for is far beyond my abilities. In my personal opinion, you will not find this man. If he was taken by the calibre of villain of which you describe, he is probably dead already. You hold back information about *what* they want of him and *why*, but I have killed enough people to know when a life is about to be extinguished. I believe your friend is not long for this world. I am sorry."

Lily looked at her hands on the table and took a deep breath, ice-cold dread filling her stomach. *Is Hugo really dead?*

She looked up, burying the darkness deep inside. "You said you had good news?"

Felix *La Tempestad* nodded. "You are strong, *señora*. I like that. If you did not already have a man, I would ask you to be my woman."

Lily smiled a cock-eyed smile despite herself, despite everything. "And the good news, *La Tempestad*," she said.

Felix frowned briefly and began speaking much more quickly. "I wish you had not said that, *señ–*"

"*La Tempestad*?" an angry voice said from behind her. Lily glanced over her should to see a square-jawed young man rise from the double table behind her. She immediately realized her mistake. What had Felix said? *For the purpose of this conversation, please only call me Felix.* Lily had revealed too much.

"Get down, *señora*," he said, rising quickly and pulling a long-barreled pistol from inside his coat.

Lily slipped out of her chair and ducked as the remaining men from the table behind her all stood as one angry body.

"*¿Está usted La Tempestad?*" the square-jawed young man said. "*Usted puta rata, está arruinando esta ciudad, arruinando este país. Una revolución está llegando, hijo de puta, y está usted con nosotros o contra nosotros.*"

Felix *La Tempestad* raised his pistol and pointed it at the young man. "*Jode la revolución, hijo. ¡Vete a la mierda!*"

He pulled the trigger and the pistol cracked through the flamenco music. Lily screamed as the young man collapsed beside her, blood pouring from a nickel-sized hole in his forehead. Behind her, the dead man's companions rushed forward.

Felix's pistol fired again and again, bodies dropping around him. The cavalcade of young men pulled their own pistols and began firing, the small alcove quickly filling with smoke and madness as the gunfight grew. Lily scrambled backwards as tables flipped, scattering glassware and bottles to the ground with crash after crash. From the dance floor, men and women screamed. Gunfire continued as bodies all around her dropped. She continued scuttling away, moving as far from the gunfight as she could. Behind her, the dance floor was emptying in a stampede. She had nearly escaped the alcove when her breath caught in her throat as a strong hand caught her hair and lifted her. Helplessly (an adverb she despised being applied to her), she grappled with her attacker to no avail.

Looking up, she saw a tall scowling man with blood running down his face. "*Mujer maldita y amigo de un cerdo. Vaya con dios ahora.*" He aimed a small revolver at her temple.

From the hollow of his neck, the long point of a dagger burst with a spray of blood. Lily–at this point quite traumatized–screamed again as the now dying man released her hair and she fell to the floor. She wiped blood from her eyes and looked up to see a dark-eyed man pull the dagger from the dying Spaniard and push him to the floor as bullets *whizzed* harmlessly over his head. A royal blue scarf was tied over the his head and pulled low enough to cover his eyes, which were revealed through two meticulously-cut eye holes. Below his right eye was a small white *fleur de lis*. Over his broad shoulders, he wore a long blue cape. He smiled a debonair smile and ran a finger over each half of a pencil-thin mustache.

"What... the... hell?" Lily muttered, eyes wide.

"*Ne parlez à personne de cette, mademoiselle. Vous ne m'avez pas vu. Je n'existe pas.*"

With that, the tall stranger turned in a flourish of cape and cowl and disappeared into a growing melee, knocking bodies aside as he passed.

Lily blinked her eyes, now certain that she must have taken a not insubstantial blow to the head, and turned back to *La Tempestad*. He lay in the corner, unmoving.

She crawled over bodies and under tables until she was at Felix *La Tempestad*'s side. His eyes were both open, but now his good eye seemed to be as vacant as his milky eye.

"Felix," she said. "Felix!"

The villain turned his head towards her. "*Lo siento, señora.* This has gone to hell, and me soon along with it." He coughed and a long snake of blood ran from the corner of his mouth. Lily's eyes moved down from his grizzled face and found four gunshot wounds to his chest. He was certain to die, she realized.

"Felix," she said. "I will stay with you. I'm sorry this has happened. I–"

"Do not lament a bastard such as I, and an ugly one, at that. I must tell you..." he coughed again, struggling to take a breath.

"It's all right," she said.

"No," he whispered, his voice failing, "I must tell you..."

"It's all right," she repeated, knowing he stood at death's door and wishing Father Francisco was there. She held his hand. "You will be all right, Felix."

His lips moved, but very little sound escaped. Lily leaned her head close, her ear almost pressed to his mouth, and listened to his dying words.

CHAPTER 14: The Alhambra, The Curse of Ximénes de Cisneros, and The First Man With No Name

The sun was rising slowly over the eastern horizon.

Dr. Liliana Halifax stood alone beneath the stilted arches of the Arabesque-adorned hall leading into the Court of the Lions, and waited. She straightened her *cordobés* hat self-consciously. After a moment, her hand came to rest on the pistol she now wore in a holster on her right hip. She waited for a man with no name, pondering her fate, and thought that the events that had taken place at *El Corazón de la Bula* felt like they had happened such a very long time ago.

It may have felt like a long time ago, dear reader, but it was less than ten hours previous that Felix *La Tempestad* had given her a set of instructions she hoped would lead her in the correct direction.

After *La Tempestad* finished whispering in her ear, his eyes closed and he began the great voyage. Through the smoke and gunfire, Lily slipped away from the flamenco club, disappearing into the dark streets of Sevilla, the *policía* arriving at the scene only moments later.

She ran through the streets, watching for landmarks that she could remember in the darkness, the words of

La Tempestad ringing in her head.

"Be at the center of the Triana Bridge when la Giralda *strikes nine. Wave your hat over your head as a signal, and the date will be set. A man with no name will meet you at the Court of the Lions at dawn tomorrow."*

As he expired, he'd pushed his now holstered pistol into her hand, urging her to take it. *"Be careful,"* he whispered, *"and forgive my rudeness."*

At first, she'd run. When sure the police would not apprehend her, Lily had slowed down and surveyed her surroundings, knowing she was not far from the Triana Bridge. "I crossed it with Andrew," she said. "I can find it again. I know I can."

Unfortunately, in the darkness things were not quite so easy.

Now the toll of nine approached, and she felt no nearer to the Triana Bridge than she was when she started. Faster and faster she went, tearing through the darkened streets like a mad woman.

Finally, she turned a corner and found the beauty of the broad Guadalquivir before her. She ran towards it, coming to a stop on an esplanade that ran alongside the great river. To her left was a bridge in the distance. She looked at her watch. She wouldn't make it in time. To her right was a second bridge, this one much nearer. The lights that ran along it were familiar, as were the circles built into the bridge's architecture.

"That's the one," Lily said, smiling.

And so she ran, crossing the distance in a blur. As she reached the bridge, her legs seemed to turn to lead, willing to carry her no further. She pushed further, finally skidding to a stop in the center just as the bells of *la Giralda* rang behind her. Recalling Felix's last words, she snatched the *cordobés* hat from her head and waved it in the air madly, hoping to God that someone some-where was watching, hopefully this Man With No Name. She waved and waved and waved. Anyone watching would see in each pass of the hat an undisputed desperation.

When the bells ceased, there was no signal in response, no acknowledgement. The city returned to its sleepy quiet. Lily stood in the center of the bridge, catching her breath, and listened to the Guadalquivir gurgle under her feet.

After a few minutes in silence, she walked slowly back to Dr. Reginald Max's office at the Consulate where she found Andrew and Brick's bag (still containing the Eye of Aja and the Cipher of Dumuzid), and began preparing for the next leg of their journey.

And now here she stood, a scant nine and a half hours later, in the Court of the Lions of the great Alhambra Palace and Fortress, over 150 miles from Sevilla. Under any other circumstances, Lily would only marvel at the magnificence of the six-hundred year old Moorish structure that had seen its share of kings and sultans. Today, however, she had other things on her mind.

Like where was this Man With No Name? The sun had climbed above the horizon, and her instructions had said 'dawn.' It was surely dawn, was it not?

Even as this thought flitted across her mind, a shape emerged from the shadows at the far end of the Court of the Lions. Over the bubbling fountain, Lily identified the figure as a man, middle aged, with pale white skin and patchy brown hair. He wore a long coat, not unlike hers, and walked slowly, his hands deep in his pockets.

He stopped before the fountain and ran a hand

through the water, lifting it so drops fell from between his long fingers. "Here I am," he said, his voice very high pitched and soft. "Why not show yourself?"

Lily emerged from her own shadows and stepped into the open air of the courtyard. She felt very much like a *vaquera* indeed when she tipped her hat at the stranger.

"Good morning," the stranger said.

"Hello."

The stranger looked her over, from her weatherbeaten boots to her crips *cordobés* hat, eyes lingering for a moment on the leather bag slung across her chest which contained the Eye and the Cipher. She tightened the strap and turned it away from him.

"What is your name, fair lady?"

"*Dr.* Halifax," she said.

The stranger did not reply. Instead he began to take a few steps towards her, casually, his eyes moving from the arches of the surrounding passages to the tops of the Spanish fir trees that grew beyond the court.

"Dr. Halifax," he said. "Welcome to the Alhambra. Have you been here before? Have you been to Granada before?"

"Neither."

"Ah, then you must be especially excited," he said. "This is quite a wondrous place, is it not? It has much history wrapped up in its lovely walls. Much blood, too."

"It is lovely, yes. Mister... uh, well, sir. I believe we have some business to–"

"Not so fast, Doctor, I believe someone of your academic standing would like to hear something about such a place before we get to *business*, as you put it."

Lily cocked her head, becoming more unsure of this

fellow by the minute. Her hand found the butt of the pistol once again. Despite the recommendation coming from a man who had died protecting her, Lily suddenly felt quite unsafe.

"All right," she said. "If you feel so inclined."

The stranger nodded. "I do, yes." He smiled and Lily could not help but feel disturbed at the snake-like quality of his face. "Because, you see, I have much history wrapped up in these walls myself."

Lily took a subconscious step backwards. "Please," she said, urging him on.

"I don't know how good your history is, Doctor, but in 711 Moors invaded Spain from Africa, eventually conquering most of the Iberian Peninsula. What followed was a nearly eight-hundred year period the Spanish have come to call–"

"The *Reconquista*," Lily said. "Yes, I know."

The stranger smiled. "But in that time, the Moors certainly left their mark on this country, and perhaps one of the most beautiful relics is this one, the Alhambra."

Lily nodded. "Yes, I am well-versed in European history, sir," she said. "What of it?"

"Well, in 1527 Charles V, the Holy Roman Emperor, built a palace inside the Alhambra," he pointed vaguely. "...over there."

"Yes, I am familiar with Charles V."

"Ah, all right, then tell me this, Doctor, where is Charles V buried?"

"He is buried in the Pantheon of Kings in *El Escorial* in San Lorenzo de El Escorial."

"You are, well, *half*-right, Doctor," he smiled.

"Half right? I don't believe I am, sir," Lily said.

"Charles V is buried alongside–"

"I said half-right because indeed *most* of Charles V is buried in *El Escorial*. Note that I said 'most.'"

Lily frowned. "What are you talking about?"

"Are you familiar with the Regent of Spain Ximénes de Cisneros? Proponent of the Crusades and one-time Grand Inquisitor?"

Lily nodded. "Yes."

"Do you know anything of his relationship with Charles V?"

Lily shook her head.

"It was strained, to say the least. Ximénes de Cisneros was strong-armed by a number of people into recognizing Charles V as co-ruler of Aragon, Catalonia, Valencia, Naples, Sicily–"

"What is your point, sir?" Lily said impatiently.

"My point is that not long after this recognition, Ximénes de Cisneros died under what can be called 'mysterious circumstances.' Now, he had acted as regent for some time, and he had many loyal followers, followers who went on to wait over *forty years* for Charles V to die before finally taking their revenge."

"What are you talking about?" Lily asked. "I know nothing of this."

The stranger smiled. "Shortly before his interment in 1558, Charles' coffin was opened and his skull was stolen."

"That is not true, it can't–"

"It is, trust me," the stranger said, his voice rising sharply. "His skull was stolen by priests loyal to Regent Ximénes and it was returned... *here*."

"Here?" Lily asked, skeptically. "Why?"

"Because it was cursed, you see. Ximénes de Cisneros was the Grand Inquisitor, and in his time there were those he spared in order to maintain their services privately. Men and women of great power."

"If you're talking about witches or–"

"'Witches' is such a blunt and filthy word," the stranger said. "I'm speaking of men and women with... unknowable and equally unnatural power. As Grand Inquisitor, Ximénes de Cisneros had the power to save them, and indeed save them he did by granting them clemency in exchange for this power. It was this that created in them such a great loyalty. After his death his followers waited until Charles succumbed to Malaria and died. It was then that they took the skull of the emperor, and using their remarkable powers they put a curse upon it. When that was done, they buried it in secret catacombs beneath the Palace of Charles... here in the Alhambra."

"Lies," Lily said, slowly shaking her head. "All lies."

"I assure you, señora, it is all true."

"How do you know? And why should I trust you? I don't even know your name."

"I know, Doctor, because it was *I* who stole the skull from the catacombs."

"You did... what?"

"I stole the skull from deep beneath the lowest levels of the Palace, and the curse–perhaps meant for the heirs of Charles–was lain upon me instead." He smiled dolefully. "If a curse is the price I must pay for loyalty," he shrugged. "So be it."

"Loyalty?" Lily asked, baffled once again. "I'm here for no skull. What are you talking about?"

"The skull of Charles V, you see, was the first relic I was able to secure... *for the Cabal*..." He smiled, his snake-like visage becoming something wholly sinister.

"The Cabal!" Lily gasped.

"And the relics you carry with you now will be my second... and my third. I will be looked upon as a hero."

Lily turned and began running, one hand digging for the pistol on her hip. She risked one glance over her shoulder, and it was long enough to see that the stranger was chasing her at a mad and barely human gallop.

She screamed as the stranger began to change... to *transform*. His hair grew longer and wilder, his skin paler. His bones groaned and creaked as they stretched.

He isn't human, Lily realized. *He isn't human, at all. At least not anymore.*

CHAPTER 15: The Body of Brick Brannigan and the Potential Fates That Await

Der Klinge was cursing, his face a twisted mask of fury. Around him, Konig, Shindo, and Von Faust looked on.

Professor Brick Brannigan–newly liberated from his chair and chains, to say nothing of mortal coil–was laid out on wooden table in the corner. Soft light from a window beyond glowed on his now lifeless body.

"You said you searched him, Von Faust!"

"I did–"

"Apparently, your searching abilities are as lacking as your skills in acquisition. *Where is the eye*?! *Where is the Cipher*?!"

"I thought they were with–"

"If they are with this woman, *where is she*?! Agents have scoured the continent since the crash, and they are empty-handed. At every turn they come up empty handed, or are faced with impossible coincidences. Konig himself was victim of an engine fault on a ship off the coast of Spain that nearly resulted in his death. What madness is this? It is beyond coincidence. She seems to have become a ghost, and a cursed ghost at that!"

"But you said–"

"What I said to Brannigan was said to force his hand. I am not so confident we will find her, you fool!" the old man shouted at Von Faust. "If she comes to us, it may very well be the only way in which we will find her. Why can we not find this woman?"

"One may suggest fate, *Monsieur Klinge*," Fang said, stepping from the shadows.

"What? You are mad, Fang! And didn't I tell you to leave and make us coffee? Have you coffee?"

"Brannigan is blessed with an unnatural luck, *Monsieur*," Fang continued, ignoring the old fascist. "Perhaps now you understand why defeat is so easily met upon his introduction."

"Shut up, you frog. Be gone with you! Fetch my coffee."

Turning surprisingly sad eyes upon his felled adversary, Fang slipped back into shadow as *Der Klinge* continued his tirade, his wrinkled face reddening. Fang had suspected the presence of a poison capsule, even suggested it to Von Faust–or at least tried. The fascist officer had shouted him down and continued blindly. If anyone could begin to fathom Brannigan's hidden arsenal, it was Fang.

Mid-tirade, Fang could not help but ask, "And what of *Monsieur* Nero?"

Der Klinge stopped. He turned to Von Faust, as though struck by a wholly original idea. "What of Nero, Von Faust?"

"As I said, sir, Herr Nero escaped. He is not dead, as you assured Brannigan, only missing."

"Then he is next." The old man turned to the giant standing mute in the corner. "Konig, *find Nero*! He is somewhere on this island, lurking! Find this man, and bring him to me alive! He has much to answer for."

***

Poor, unfortunate Archibald Nero was having a hell of a time–and he'd yet to learn of his dear friend's passing.

Nero limped around the cab of the DC-2 parked on the runway, blood soaking through the bandage on his leg (where Lily had shot him; you do you still remember that, don't you?), trying to bring the big plane to life. He'd labored for nearly an hour with little to show for it besides aggravation. The instrument panels, overhead lights, and radio were dark. He flipped a half-dozen switches on a panel before returning to the pilot's chair.

"Why are we getting no power?" he growled. "I need this bloody radio to work!"

After Brannigan had been apprehended by Konig, Nero watched uselessly from the shrubs as the Professor was hauled off by the giant, leaving the plane unguarded. Since the departure, he cursed his injuries and helplessness, wanting nothing more than to bring the radio to life and call for help. Even in this regard he was unsuccessful.

Less than a minute after entering the plane, Nero realized it was no normal DC-2. Strange pieces of machinery had been added to the plane, Nero assumed to help outfit it for long-range flight. The foreign additions, however, were also added to the cockpit controls– including a mysterious keypad. Nero's attempts to bring life to the plane had been an abject failure, and he was beginning to believe that was no mistake.

"They've done something to protect this bird from unauthorized use," he muttered. "Damn their German ingenuity!"

As if in response, Nero raised his eyes and found himself staring–through the rain-speckled windshield of the modified DC-2–into the face of Konig the giant as he approached the powerless aircraft, his dark eyes roving across the runway.

"And things seemed bad enough," he muttered.

Konig caught Nero's eye through the windshield and smiled.

"Damn it," Nero spat. "Damn it all!" He retreated into the cargo portion of the plane and began to toggle levers, bringing a pair of hydraulic pumps to life. With a mechanical *whurrr*, the pumps rose the ladder into the plane and sealed the door with a *thump* and *hiss*.

A moment later, a solid blow sounded against the DC-2's riveted aluminum skin. A second and finally a third followed. Then it was silent.

Nero could all but hear Konig's rumble of anger.

Turning his back on the door, Nero limped past the small port side windows–ignoring Konig's seething glare–and returned to the cockpit, his teeth gritting in frustration.

"You're a smart man, Nero," the Brit said to himself. "Positively brilliant, old chap, now why not sack up and get this bloody bird in the air, eh?"

A few more jabs at the instrument panel yielded similar results (that is to say: none).

Nero took a deep breath as the whole plane seemed to shake beneath his feet, nearly toppling him to the cockpit floor. Somewhere outside, Konig was up to something, the great giant apparently not easily dissuaded.

From a heavy metal box at his feet, Nero lifted a sub-stantial iron wrench and brandished it at the instrument panel he believed responsible for his accumulating defeats.

"This is your last chance, you cursed Babbage Engine," Nero sputtered. "If you do not acquiesce to my courteous requests..." he dialed a few more buttons. Nothing. "...then you will acquiesce to my brute *force*!"

He swung the wrench, bringing it down on the instrument box with a smash, resulting in a few kicked sparks and a brief blinking of light as the panel momen-tarily glowed to life.

Nero pushed a few more buttons before flipping a smattering of switches.

"Still no power, eh? I'll show you, you bastard, you electronic sentinel, you stubborn box of–"

The plane shook beneath the fists of the giant, finally tossing Nero to the ground and sending blood running freely from his wounded leg. He cast a wary glance at the rear of the plane as the sound of rending metal crept towards the cockpit.

Little did Nero know that Herr Konig was making an entrance where no entrance previously existed.

"Enough talk," Nero said softly. He rose to his feet and brought the iron wrench down on the keypad with a two-handed swing.

The panel smashed, raining numeric keys across the floor.

Nero turned from the ruined gatekeeper device and flipped a switch. The instrument panel flooded to life.

"No failsafe? Hah! Did you learn nothing from the

Maginot Line, you fascist goons?" Nero laughed. "Some contraption! Impervious to all... except a great big wrench!" He dropped the wrench on the floor and began pre-flight prep (albeit slightly abbreviated).

Konig had a 9 inch panel half-peeled free from the DC-2 when the pair of props began turning. With a double back-fire, the two engines roared to life, and Nero could not help but laugh.

The wheels began to turn as Konig tore at the plane's skin, veins bulging from his arms and huge head. When his boots left the ground, he began to shout in German.

Over the sound of the engines and across the length of the plane, Nero could hear the giant's roars.

"*Sie werden nicht entfliehen*! *Sie werden nie entgeht mir*! *Ich werde dich finden*! *Ich werde dich finden und ich werde dich töten*!"

"I don't bloody speak German," Nero laughed as he gave the yoke a slight twist and the altimeter jumped.

He didn't need to see it to know that the giant had been shaken loose. He had escaped.

***

Attentions in the seaside cottage had been aroused by the DC-2's double back-fire. Everyone was standing outside when the DC-2 cleared the trees and hills and rose into the sky.

Everyone, including *Der Klinge*.

He turned to Von Faust, his face shaking with fury, and asked, "Von Faust, can you please tell me where my plane is going?"

Von Faust, face even paler than the average aryan,

opened his mouth, but could locate no words.

In the rear of the group, *Monsieur* Fang simply shook his head, the faintest hint of a smile perhaps–*perhaps*, I said–playing across his lips.

CHAPTER 16: In Which a Grand Escape Plan Meets a Premature Yet Nevertheless Moderately Successful Conclusion (Also Known As: WELCOME TO SCOTLAND, ARCHIBALD!)

Something was wrong.

(Yes, try and wrap your mind around that revelation given the ominous chapter title you've just taken in.)

Archibald had been forced to utilize his Swiss Army Knife of cockpit repair–in this case, a heavy iron wrench–twice more since taking off from the remote Nazi airstrip on the Faroe Islands. Once he employed it judiciously against the radio; once he employed it against what he took to be the autopilot device.

In both cases, his heavy-handed tinkering was unsuccessful.

He'd been airborne for almost an hour before he destroyed the radio, spending the better part of those fifty-some minutes desperately attempting to call for help. He'd been forced to abandon Brick, but Archibald would be damned if that meant he would leave the good Professor behind. He'd attempted a dozen or so mayday calls before dropping the wrench on the nigh paper-thin radio casing, ending the radio's life.

The autopilot was a bit more complicated. You see,

Nero had taken off under the impression that the plane operated under his own deft instruction. As it turns out, the Douglas DC-2 switched to autopilot once the runway was cleared and the altimeter passed 5,000 feet.

The ascent continued automatically, the yoke turning to adjust course despite Nero's yanking in an opposite direction. After abandoning the yoke to the autopilot and a brief consultation of the charts and maps (to say nothing of a glance or two at the magnetic compass and heading indicator), Nero was able to chart the plane's direction as pointing ominously towards Berlin.

Upon this realization, the Brit searched for a parachute, came up empty-handed, and finally made a few off-color exclamations that I, your narrator, will not share, seeing as we are in mixed company.

When his steadfast and usually unflappable British countenance had returned, he made the decision to swing the ol' wrench once more.

However, despite Archibald Nero's determination, the autopilot could not be... well, dissuaded.

It seems as though the modified DC-2 had its heart set on Berlin, and so to Berlin it would go.

Abandoning the cramped and frustrating cockpit, Archibald traveled to the rear of the plane, feeling the whipping cold air rushing through the torn skin of the plane where the giant had attempted to gain entry. Past the cargo hold and emergency exit he slid, eyes sharp for tools along the way.

Near the tail, he found two things he needed desperately:

1. A flight control system repair kit, containing a collection of pushrods, tension cables, chains, and weights, proving that the Germans were indeed as conscientious as Archibald had hoped (and feared).

2. A wound ripped in the side of the DC-2, large enough for a grown man to slip one full arm through.

You see, if Nero could not steer the plane thanks to the damnable autopilot, he would do what he could to sabotage it. Archibald Nero would *not* be ending his madcap journey in Berlin. No sir, no how.

From the repair kit, Nero attached a length of chain to a rusted turnbuckle, ensuring that the eye bolt connected with the chain and the hook faced outward. Onto the body of the turnbuckle's metal frame, Nero attached a weight for posterity, fully realizing that the airspeed would be offering enough of a challenge without the damn hook being too light.

Satisfied that his jury-rigged device was sufficient, Nero left it on the floor of the craft and returned to the cockpit to do all that was left to do: wait.

And wait he did. Mr. Nero sat in the leather pilot's chair, the most pertinent navigational chart spread across the yoke, one eye on the tachometer and one on the compass. In his hand was a broken nib of a pencil, and patiently, ever so patiently, Nero charted his supposed progress across the expanse of the North Atlantic as he approached the frigid North Sea.

Archibald Nero was plotting a plane crash, his own plane crash. And this was to be his second plane crash in a remarkably short period of time. I believe this is what the collective they refer to as "pressing your luck."

Nero stared out the DC-2's windscreen and tried to remain calm. The wisps of altocumulus clouds passed by, painting a cotton-like haze across the great tide of the sea. In the distance, Nero imagined the approaching Shetland Islands to his left and north shores of Scotland to his right.

Unfortunately for him, the DC-2 was plotted to bisect these two landmasses by no small margin, carrying him straight over the heart of the North Sea to Germany, ergo the need for his "jury-rigged instrument." All he needed now was some divine timing.

And so he waited, plotting on the chart, consulting the tachometer, magnetic compass, and wristwatch.

The sun began to sink as the miles ticked away.

"Well, old chap, I believe this is as good a time as any," he said to himself. "Don't muck it up. Brick's life is on the line." He sighed. "Yours too, of course. But that goes without saying."

He shrugged and left the cockpit for the last time, closing the door behind him.

In the narrow, coffin-like tail section of the plane, Nero took up his instrument and laid the pencil on the DC-2's metal floor, pointing towards the cockpit. Over the bumps and shudders of the plane, the pencil wobbled back and forth moderately, but maintained a roughly stable place. Nero hoped it could act as a makeshift gimble once he started fussing with the rudders the old-fashioned way.

"All right, you barmy old bastard," he said, sidling up to the DC-2's starboard side. "It's time."

Holding the length of chain tightly, he slipped his hand through the ripped skin, immediately feeling the intense burning cold of the wind at 10,000 feet.

"Good lord!" the Brit shouted against the roar of the rushing air. "That's bloody *freezing*!"

With the chain dangling, he began to swing it, the weighted turnbuckle immediately making the weary muscles in his bicep ache. Through the shredded plane's skin, he locked his eyes onto the cable controlling the main rudder system.

You see what he's doing, don't you dear reader? No? Well, Archibald means to manually pull the cable that will turn the plane's rudder, taking him off course from Germany and pointing him towards mainland UK. I don't know about you, but I'd rather go to the UK than Germany circa 1935, eh?

His first throw nearly carried the chain away in the wind, a last second catch on a chain link saved Archibald's instrument.

His second throw was only marginally better.

His third, well, let's just skip right to it, shall we?

It was his seventh throw, just when the salty Brit was certain he could take the cold no longer, that finally latched onto the onto the DC-2's rudder cable with a *clang*.

"Good show!" he shouted to no one. "That's a good start, Arch."

Pulling a blue and numb hand back within the plane, Archibald squatted and braced his feet against the inside of the craft, squaring his body to the starboard side and closing both hands around the chain now affixed to the rudder cable.

He looked down at the pencil and pulled with all his might, fighting the plane's autopilot.

Slowly, ever so slowly, the pencil rolled across the floor towards the port side of the plane.

"We're turning," Nero said through gritted teeth. "We're turning! Scotland here we come!"

Once he had the rudder shifted, all he had to do was

maintain his grip and wait, as each mile flown at that angle would aim the craft away from Berlin and towards the United Kingdom.

When he switched the hook from the rudder cable to the elevator cable, it honestly took so many throws that neither I nor Nero managed to keep count. When he finally snagged the elevator cable, he was so damned tired he couldn't even celebrate.

"All right, you filthy muggins, down we go."

Angling the chain in his grasp upwards, Nero pulled with all his might.

He might, perhaps, have pulled a *little* too hard.

The plane plummeted, angling the dual props at a 60° angle to the ocean, sending Nero rising off the ground in a remarkable display of anti-gravity.

Unfortunately–or fortunately, it could go either way, really–the engines stalled. Now, I say this could be fortunate because dear Nero had no bloody way of stopping the plane (his thought process was literally "one thing at a time").

The plane fell from the sky.

Through the jagged hole in the DC-2's skin, Nero saw the white-capped North Atlantic rushing towards him and prayed to any god who was listening that he could survive this impending catastrophe. Brick Brannigan had saved him, and Nero *could not* die in debt to that arrogant bastard.

It would just be... embarrassing.

The DC-2 impacted a wave mid-swell, and Nero saw only darkness.

An Intermission of Sorts: Briefly Visiting a Pair of Friends, Old and New

In an office in the rural midwest of the United States, approximately 4300 miles from Dr. Liliana Halifax, approximately 3600 miles from the last known location of Archibald Nero, and approximately 3400 miles from the final resting place of Hugo "Brick" Brannigan, a bearded elderly gent drank a cup of tea and looked out at the leaves as they made their slow change from green to yellow to orange to brown. Soon, the trees would be bare, the leaves replaced by boughs resplendent with snow.

Were things different, the good Dr. Quincy Max may be humming or smiling, perhaps even whistling. However, with things as they were, he was not. Instead, the old man's brow was furrowed; lines of worry creased his already wizened face.

On his desk was a creased and crinkled telegram. Beneath the Western Union seal, it read:

My Dear Brother,

Over the past few days, I have come to know well your Dr. Halifax and her young assistant, as they have found me here in Sevilla, and in the short time since my previous telegram, much has happened. They asked my help, and I have obliged as you would expect. It is in this matter that I must beg your forgiveness. I have been the instrument of introduction between your Dr. Halifax and a man who operates illicitly under the moniker of La Tempestad. He is of questionable moral standing, but I have, under good authority, come to trust him in some measure. The trouble is that your Dr. Halifax has not been out of contact for 24 hours and I know now where she has gone. I fear the worst. I have contacted another gentleman I trust in hopes of locating your dear colleague, but my efforts have proven unsuccessful.

I will continue in this endeavor, but with each passing hour, my hopes dwindle.

Please contact me ASAP if you come into possession of additional information.

Cordially yours,

Reginald

Quincy had immediately dispatched a telegram to his brother, outlining what Hugo and Lily's mission was, and adding as many pertinent details as he could fit. Now, he was forced to wait. After receiving the first telegram from Reginald, explaining that Hugo was missing, Quincy did not believe things could get worse.

Now Lily was missing.

The fate of the very world was at stake (you remember that, don't you, dear reader?), and to make matters worse, two of Quincy Max's closest confidants were now missing, perhaps even... *dead*. The old man felt a cold hand clutch at his octogenarian heart, the same cold hand that had clutched at his heart since receiving Reginald's first telegram.

Yes, the fate of the world was indeed at stake, but

dear Quincy Max could not get the faces of his two friends from his mind, and there was nothing else he could do.

And so, he waited.

***

Approximately 4200 miles away from the Quincy Max Institute and the lonely cup of tea, a dark-haired French pistol climbed into her charter plane, heading north, bringing with her a host of firepower large enough to force the chartered pilot to recalculate his ballast. This *mademoiselle* sat in the co-pilot's chair, determined, spinning the cylinder in her literal revolver as she prepared herself for the battles yet to come, hoping that the intel she'd received was correct.

The engines started, and the chartered craft taxied towards the runway as the Tangier sun slipped below the western horizon.

CHAPTER 17: The Alhambra, The Ongoing (and Troublesome) Curse of Ximénes de Cisneros, and That *Second* Man With No Name

Lily knelt behind an ivory wall, intricately carved with arabesques so beautiful as to be considered art. Unfortunately, it was also porous, offering achingly little shelter from the prying eyes of her pursuer.

But when you're running for your life, you will take shelter where you find it.

"Come out, *señora*," a guttural and raspy voice slithered. "You cannot escape me, not here in my home. No one knows the passages of the Alhambra Palace like I do. I have lived here for so long. So very, very long."

The voice was so different than the voice she'd heard originally. Gone was the high, nasally whine of the Man With No Name. It was replaced by a sound she could only charitably consider human.

As I'm sure you remember, dear reader, Liliana is currently running for her life from a ~~Man~~ Beast With No Name in the grand corridors of Spain's Alhambra. She is doing her damndest to meet up with a smuggler's associate to get her hands on information that would possibly lead her to info on her beloved Hugo "Brick" Brannigan...

But you remember that, don't you?

She held her breath and closed her eyes, reliving the transformation that her pursuer had undergone when he'd taken up his pursuit. His limbs had stretched and grown, his arms extending long enough that his loping run soon transformed from two limbs to four; his pale white eyes had soured and widened, becoming a feline yellow; and his teeth and nails had grown, leaving the realm of human and quickly entering the realm of predator.

No, he was not human, certainly not human at all.

In her hand, Lily held her pistol, hammer cocked and finger wrapped tightly around the trigger, ready to put a round into the beast if necessary.

Easy as it was to imagine doing this, she knew it would be infinitely more difficult to *actually* shoot the beast.

A faint *click click* accompanied each step the beast took as it moved towards her, its long claws tapping against the palace's stone floor. Lucky for our adventuress, it also acted as a lovely tracking sound.

As the *click*ing approached, she began to creep backwards, slinking towards an entryway into a long a twisting corridor. In her breast pocket was a fairly rough sketch of the palace's layout, given to her by Reginald when she'd parted ways with him, the most he could offer to get her to the Court of the Lions. She would consult the map again if she could, but dared not with the creature so close by. The crinkle of paper would herald her death, of that she was certain.

And so she crept blindly, moving out of the unnamed chamber and into a corridor leading into the depths of the palace, all the while holding her breath and tracking

154

the beast's movements thanks to the *click* of its claws.

Around a corner she slipped, finding herself back outside. She knelt in a large courtyard, a long, placid pond sat in the center of the courtyard, flanked by two long well-trimmed and sculpted shrubs. Porticos lined the walls at either end of the courtyard. A gentle wind crept through the air, its whisper interrupting the gurgle of distant fountains.

With a light-footed leap, Lily hopped the shrub and landed behind it with barely a sound. Through the knotted branches and greenery, she saw a large, dark shape emerge from the doorway opposite her location.

"*Señoraaaa.....*" the voice called. "*¿Dónde estás?*"

Through the bush, Lily leveled her pistol. She could not see much, but she could see enough to know she felt more comfortable with a pistol pointed towards that inhuman beast.

This is what we're dealing with? she couldn't help but wonder. *Relics with a power to do... that?* She felt the weight of the Eye of Aja in her shoulder bag along with the Cipher, and had to hope a similar fate did not lay in store for her. Never had she been involved–or even *heard*–of anything like this happening. *I'm an archaeologist and adventuress!* she thought, *Not a pulp heroine!*

One eye closed as Lily fixed her aim, her finger tightening on the trigger as The ~~Man~~ Beast With No Name approached.

Scant feet away, the creature stopped as a patter of feet cut through the relative quiet of the courtyard. With a snort, its head snapped to the right, glaring at the north portico nestled at the far end of the courtyard. Jaws opened and a roar escaped pale lips as the creature opened up and galloped towards the door.

Lily backpedalled, moving towards the south portico, leading her as far from the beast as she could get. From her pocket, she whipped out the map as the dark shape of the creature rounded the corner and disappeared into the palace, its roar echoing throughout the ancient building.

Holding the creased paper up to catch the early morning sun, Lily scrambled to read.

Unfortunately (are you getting as tired of seeing this word as Lily is?), the damnable creature was forcing her to move *deeper* into the palace's compound. Given the layout of the palace, she was moving towards an exit, but she would need to cross the expanse of the structure to get there.

"I cannot get a break, can I?" she muttered, stuffing the map back into her pocket as she turned and ran towards the south portico, leading her out of the moorish architecture and into the renaissance architecture of the Palace of Charles V, a huge square structure shoe-horned into the heart of the Alhambra.

Lily passed through an arched entryway and found herself in a wide colonnade, a circular shape set inside of the square structure of the building. She pulled the map from her pocket once again, shaking her head in the dark space, when she heard a snort from behind her.

The beast stood over her, its head cocked at her, golden eyes wide, fanged mouth grinning.

"I have found you, *señora*," the beast hissed. "*Su carne me saciará, estoy seguro de esto. No he sentido el toque de una mujer en un largo tiempo. No me vas a tocar, pero todavía va a tocar.*"

Liliana did not even hear the beast; her eyes were fixated on its twisted and unnatural body. Long limbs sprouted from a hairy torso. The small head hovered at the end of a long, bent neck. The hands and feet each bore only three long, hairless fingers.

As the creature finished speaking, a long, thick tongue slipped from between the fangs and extended towards her face.

Such a gesture may seem like creepy *subtext* to us, dear reader, but in Lily's position, it was far from *subtext*. It was basically just, well, *text*.

For Lily, there was one way and one way only for her to answer such a bold and forward gesture.

The revolver in her hand exploded, sending the .32 calibre bullet charging through the beast's chest. Black blood exploded from the creature's back, spattering across a column in a spray.

Lily did not stay to watch the results. She turned and ran into the palace.

Columns passed her in a blur as Lily searched for a hall or doorway, anything to put distance between herself and the beast. She was now mapless, having dropped her only guide back at the feet of the creature. Skidding to a halt and turning left, Lily found herself in the center of an open, circular patio, a ring of columns bracing the palace's second floor, nothing but blue sky overhead.

She was a real *vaquera* now, she realized, feeling every bit a bullfighter as the beast emerged from a portico at her back and faced her.

Lily lifted her pistol once more and aimed, firing four more shots into the beast, each drawing blood.

The ~~Man~~ Beast With No Name howled a laugh, even as pools of black blood gathered beneath its body.

"You cannot stop me, *puta*," the beast roared. "*Su*

muerte es segura."

The pistol clicked empty, and slowly, Lily lowered her hand, slipping the pistol back into her holster. She looked behind her. *Can I run?* she thought desperately. Was this the end? *Am I really going to die in Spain? Without ever seeing Hugo again? Seriously?*

"*Pas ne courent, mademoiselle,*" a smooth voice whispered from the darkness of the colonnade. "*Vous ferez la créature en colère. Avez-vous n'apprenez rien en Espagne?*"

"I'm getting a little language overloaded," Lily said breathlessly. "I usually do all right, but... good lord!"

"I said 'do not run, you will make it angry,'" the suave voice translated. "'Have you learned nothing in Spain?'"

"I'm not running," Lily said, casting a glance over her shoulder. "But now what?"

From behind a thick, stone pillar, the mysterious masked stranger from *El Corazón de la Bula* emerged, winking at Lily as he did so. Wrapped in a royal blue cape, he opened it slowly to reveal two long daggers that hung sheathed on his belt. His clothing was otherwise black, except for a blue scarf tied around his head that obscured the top portion of his visage. Two blue eyes stared at her, the white *fleur de lis* ever present on the fabric beneath his right eye.

"I am here to save you, *mon cher*. And then, once this task is completed, I will take you on the town, show you the beauty of *Espagne*, share with you a bottle or *deus* of Champagne, and then take you to bed as only *Le Duc* could. My skill as a lover is known the world over, *mon petit amant*, and I will–"

"I–you–why I should–" Lily sputtered, digging for

some response. "You arrogant–"

"*Mademoiselle*, do not thank me just yet, *s'il vous plaît*," *Le Duc* said with debonair grin as he slipped the two daggers from his belt. "Wait until I have saved your life. Then you can thank me with your lips and your–"

"Why you conceited little–"

The ~~Man~~ Beast With No Name roared (again), interrupting Lily's tempestuous rant and bringing her back down to Earth.

She turned in time to see it charge.

CHAPTER 18: Unceremonious Last Rites, Performed by a Bastard for a Hero

Fang stood at the mouth of the graveyard, listening to muted voices speaking in German and staring at the canvas body bag at his feet. His mind was a storm of thoughts, both good and bad.

Brannigan, his oldest and fiercest adversary: dead.

The sound of jackboots on damp ground came from behind him, interrupting his scheming. He turned to see a pair of soldiers–*his* soldiers–emerge from a cloud of cold mist, each bearing a long-handled shovel. Perfect for digging a grave.

"*Monsieur* Dufort," Fang said with a nod, "*Monsieur* Lessard. Good day."

Over the German whispers, soggy footsteps, and the lapping of waves on the rocky shore, Fang could make out three words shared between his loyal madmen before his presence silenced them.

"*Est-ce vrai?*" one voice had asked another. *Is that so?*

Three words, yes, but it was enough. Even if Fang had been unable to detect who had spoken the words– which he, in fact, had–he already would have known. Those three words heralded the birth of doubt, a characteristic unwelcome in any army.

Lessard spreading Von Faust's lies, Fang thought. His loyal madman Darius Dufort was succumbing to diminishing loyalty to Black Fang Delacroix. Such was the risk of exposing your loyal followers to a band of wild fanatics. Fang had anticipated such trouble, but not so quickly. And admittedly, the untimely demise of so many of his dear men had not helped prevent this.

He sighed.

"*Monsieur* Lessard," Fang said, his voice low and sharp with as much menace as he could inject. "*Vous êtes aussi courageux que votre bouche*?" he asked.

"*Moi, Herr* Delacroix?" Lessard replied, his face innocent, but his smirk belying much.

The hair on Fang's neck stood on end. "*Herr* Delacroix?" he asked, incensed. "*Un mot gentil est suffisant pour abandonner votre maître et votre pays? Vous êtes pathétique*?"

Lessard took the insult with a stone face. Beside him, Darius turned his gaze to the muddy ground.

"*Herr* Von Faust *et Der Klinge* have given me far more than a kind word," Lessard replied in a neutral tongue. "This world is changing, *Herr* Delacroix. There are only two sides. Life is perhaps more black and white than you believe."

"Perhaps," Fang replied. He closed his hand around the almost forgotten albeit ever-present scimitar hanging at his waist. With a slight *hiss*, the blade slid free from its sheath.

"Fang!" a voice shouted from behind him. "Stop delaying the men. They have much work to do."

Slowly, Fang returned the blade to its sheath. Lessard stepped past him with a cavalier stride. Dufort followed him.

"*Et vous*, Darius?"

"I miss my Father, *Caïd*," Darius said, his voice low. "His death brings me much sadness. And where there is much sadness, there is the potential for much foolishness. Forgive me. *Je suis trop vous abandonné.*"

With that Darius strode past Fang, the shadow over his face promising Black Fang Delacroix that he would never again hear one of his men call him "*Caïd.*"

***

The shovels bit into the cold, wet earth, and Black Fang Delacroix watched from a distance as his two fallen soldiers bent to the command of Captain Heinrich Von Faust.

"Unmarked, *Herr* Von Faust?" *Der Klinge* asked with an evil grin. "You are bad."

"This Yankee scum deserves worse than an unmarked grave," Von Faust said. "He has caused us much trouble."

"That he has. But there are some who would demand honor in any burial," *Der Klinge* continued, testing his subordinate.

"We've no time for ceremony," Von Faust said. "What we do, we do only to dispose of the body. If it proved more convenient to burn it, we would burn it. If we could sink it in the ocean, we would sink it. Dirt just so happens to be the easiest solution for us. Honor is not for our enemies."

Der Klinge smiled broadly. "That is right, Von Faust. Quite right."

And so, in the ten or so feet of once-green grass between the aged and unadorned tombstones of Gabriel Sigrunarson and Kaspar Mikkelsen, *Monsieurs* Lessard and Dufort dug six feet down into the mud, preparing the unmarked grave.

"I believe once we find what we came to these cursed islands for, we'll be able to acquire transportation in Klaksvík," Von Faust said. I know I have apologized already, but I cannot begin to apologize–"

"That is enough, Von Faust," *Der Klinge* said. "I was angry when we lost our plane, and I am still angry, but dwelling on your failings does not help my heart. And I need my heart strong for what lies ahead, no?"

The old man turned to Von Faust and cast a pair of eyes on the younger man that looked like two black holes.

"I... well, I–"

"Do better, Heinrich," *Der Klinge* said. "That is the last time I will offer such advice. It is also the last time I will allow for such advice. Do you follow?"

Von Faust took a deep breath and nodded, believing that he had dodged yet another bullet–and perhaps he had.

Lessard and Dufort had slowed, the quick progress becoming quite a struggle as the wet earth had been transformed into a substance not markedly dissimilar from permafrost. The deeper they dug, the colder the ground became. The colder the ground became, the more likely a little bit of water would be a little bit of ice.

"That's enough," Von Faust shouted, waving his fascist hand proudly. "*Herr* Lessard, *Herr* Dufort, climb out."

Tossing their shovels free of the hole, the men climbed free, one at a time, their uniforms and faces filthy, their lips blue.

"I believe that is more than adequate, men," Von Faust said, looking into the pit with a look on his face that could only be described as glee. "Why don't we–"

"Whaa you *gêant stupide*–" came a strange muted shout, cutting Von Faust off.

Der Klinge, Von Faust, Lessard, and Dufort turned to see *Monsieur* Delacroix hanging by his neck from Konig's great fist, the Frenchman's feet kicking ineffectually.

"Konig, where did you come from? And what are you doing?" Von Faust asked, taking a step forward. "Put *Herr*–"

"No," *Der Klinge* interrupted. "Konig, what did he do? Why have you done this?"

Fang's hands closed over the huge fingers of the giant, struggling unsuccessfully to pull free so as to take a breath. His face becoming a fiery red, his mouth hanging open, his eyes bulging.

Konig opened his mouth and spoke, his voice so low as to almost be lost in the wind. "*Er war mit dem körper.*"

Der Klinge turned his gaze to Fang. "What were you doing to the body, *Herr* Fang?"

Fang, mouth still opened, struggled to respond. But where he'd hoped to form words, a soft "*Ehhhhhhh*" was all that escaped his mouth.

Der Klinge waved a hand. "Konig."

The giant opened his hand and Fang fell to the ground, panting as his face returned to a normal color.

"Speak, frog," Von Faust said with a goading kick. "Speak!"

"Honor," Fang whispered, his throat raw. "I do not share your sentiments regarding honor. Honor is due to all, even our enemies."

Der Klinge took a step forward and looked down at the Frenchman in unveiled contempt. "And this, *Herr* Fang, is why you will never be a true member of The Cabal." He shook his head, disgusted, before turning away.

"Yes, Fang, you are nothing!" Von Faust rebuked him like a child. With a giggle, he turned to Konig and pointed at the body. "Well, Konig–"

"Wait," *Der Klinge* said, turning back to face Fang as the Frenchman raised himself onto one knee, his breathing still labored.

"If you believe in this... this *honor*, *Herr* Fang, then I charge you with finishing these 'rites' as you would call them."

"It is only about respect, it is no 'rite.' Do you want me to–?"

"Konig was going to drop Brannigan into the pit and be done with it, but if you feel so strongly, so... weak, then do it yourself. You won't cease fussing with the body, anyway."

Slowly, Fang rose to his feet, mud now splashed across his once impeccable clothing. Dufort took a step towards him, but Fang waved him off with a muffled curse. He cleaned a streak of mud from his cheek and arranged himself before returning to the grave, taking a knee, and slipping his arms beneath the canvas-wrapped body of Brannigan. With a grunt, he lifted the body, revealing his remarkable strength. He turned to the hole.

One slow, difficult step. A second. A third. With teeth grit, he made his way to the open pit. At its edge, he grunted as he lowered to the ground once more, his arms shaking as sweat formed on his face. Gently, Fang lay the body on the ground at the grave's edge. He rose and leapt down into the fresh pit, his boots impacting loudly against the frozen bottom.

Above him, the Cabalists stood looking down at him. Von Faust laid a boot across the body and began pushing it towards the edge.

"Stop," Fang said. "Leave him."

Von Faust withdrew as Fang pulled Brannigan's body over the lip and lowered it to the bottom, laying it down peacefully against the ice. He lay one muddy hand across where he imagined Brannigan's face to be and bowed his head. When he was finished, he stood.

He saw five unforgiving faces staring down at him.

"How does that feel, *Herr* Fang?" *Derr Klinge* asked.

"How does what feel?"

"The bottom of an unmarked grave. I want you to understand that is what awaits if you cross me. Any patience I had is now gone. We are too close to victory to supplicate ourselves to the whims of fools."

Fang stared at *Der Klinge* for what seemed like a very long time before he said, "If you wish to bury me, bury me. If not, shut your mouth and give me a hand." He raised his arm, extending an open hand to whomever cared to help.

A moment passed in silence.

"Well?"

Finally, *Der Klinge* nodded and Konig grasped the Frenchman's hand, pulling him roughly from the grave.

Der Klinge turned to the cemetery's entrance and walked away silently, Konig at his side.

Von Faust nodded in the direction of the hole. "Lessard, Dufort," he said before turning and scuttling off after his master.

As Lessard and Dufort got to work, Black Fang Delacroix gave the grave and its surrounding tombstones one last glance before turning and disappearing into the mist. Strangely, no one ever noticed his ever-present scimitar was missing.

When the two French soldiers were finished, Brick Brannigan was six feet under, and all but lost to our heroine.

CHAPTER 19: Archie's Alive; Aye, Tis Scotland, Indeed!! (aka Try to Read This Fool Scribe's Take on a Scottish Accent)

Nero opened his eyes, rather surprised to see a hospital room rather than puffy clouds and St. Peter tending to a large gate.

"I'm alive? Bloody hell."

"Oh!" a voice *eek*ed from the far side of the room.

A shape rushed into view.

"Ye're aweeke?" a beautiful red-haired woman in a nurse's bonnet asked in a heavy Scottish brogue.

"I'm awake," Nero said. "Am I alive? I'd assumed yes until I saw your face. Now I'm assuming I must be in heaven, my lass." He lay a hand on her hip. "Because you're an angel."

The nurse pulled back. "Whot?" she asked, swatting his hand. "Best watch yer damn hands, ye *Sassenach*."

"Pardon me, miss," Nero said, sitting up in bed. "I certainly didn't mean to–"

He stopped, mouth hanging open.

"Whot es et? Ye all roit, ye Tommy?"

Ah, the inevitable has finally happened: Nero's memory has been restored–or at the very least, given a bloody good shake. For better or for worse, everything he'd forgotten was *back*.

"He shot me!" Nero shouted, his voice rife with consternation. "That bugger, that brazen bloomin' Yank shot me. Well, *he* didn't, Lily did, but she did so at his insistence. I can't very well blame her, can I? But... what the... how the..." Nero gave his head a good shake as though something had come loose and he was trying to make it right. "Brannigan!"

Still, things did not seem... fixed.

"I said ye all roit, Tommy?"

Nero turned to the nurse. "My name is *not* Tommy, madame," he spat. "If you'll please tell me where in the name of Oliver Cromwell's boots I am, I would be grateful!"

"I know yer name inn't Tommy," the nurse said. "It is an *exprression*. Ye're in Balfour Hospital here in Kirkwall, Scotland, ye radge bosstard."

"Radge?" Nero groaned. "It's been far too long since I've been to Scotland. What does radge mean again?"

"It means ye're dead mad, ye tube."

"Tube? What is...? Ugh, never mind." Nero whipped back the sheet that covered him, revealing a blue hospital gown that ended above the knee, his wounded leg properly dressed and bandaged for a change.

"Shot, I don't bloody believe I'm–"

"Down wit ye!" the nurse said, grabbing the sheet and pulling it back over Nero. "Ye're shot! Ye need *rrr*est."

"No, madam, what I need is to help my friend, even if he is responsible for this gunshot. Well, not that he didn't apparently have good reason. Have you ever heard anything about mind control? I have to tell you, it's– well, maybe I won't go into that just now. But worms?

Hell!" Once more, he pulled the sheet back.

"Git in yer bed, damnit!" the nurse pulled the sheet back over him.

Nero clamped his mouth shut and took a deep breath through his nose. It whistled, undermining his apparent minimal authority.

"Miss... uh, what's your name, dear?"

"Yoo call me 'lass' or 'dear' agin an I'll give ye somethin' ta regret, ye hear?"

Nero sighed. "I apologize, madam, what is your name? Where are my manners? Let me introduce myself. My name is Archibald Nero." He extended his hand to her.

"My name's Emma Louise Duffy, Mr. Nero, an it would please me greatly if ye'd lay yer head doun an let me git Dr. Campbell, aright?"

"Now, one moment Ms. Duffy, I apologize for my rush, but I cannot stay here, you see I've got a friend who–"

"Stop, Mr. Nerro. Ye survived a bloody plane wreck in the ooshen. Until the Doctor–"

"A plane wreck indeed. What is that, my second in a week? Third? I should *not* be flying with that damnable record!"

"Are ye listenin Mr. Nerro?"

"What? Oh, well, to be honest I was not, no."

"Ye bloody bampot, I shud–"

"Ms. Duffy, do you mind my asking why you seem so terribly bothered? I love the Scottish spirit, but you seem downright furious."

Nurse Duffy took a breath and began "I–" but that was as far as she got.

She took a breath, realizing that she had been taking out quite an amount of anger and frustration on this Mr. Nero, certainly not his fault.

"I apologize ta ye, sur," she said, exhaling. "Imma jes finishing oot a double, an the blinkin' nurse who's to take oover is late. If she wann't late–"

"You wouldn't have to deal with me, is that right?" Nero asked with a sly and empathetic smile.

"Ay, it tis," Nurse Duffy responded. "For tha, I apologize, sur."

"Don't be ridiculous, Ms. Duffy," he said with his most dashing smile. Despite herself, she smiled in response, but when Nero went to pull of the sheet once more, that delicate smile waned.

"I see ye wan ta get up, is tha roit? Well, 'til the Doctor gives the a-okie, ye'll not be movin anywhere, ye hear tha Mr. Nerro?"

"I do hear it indeed, Ms. Duffy. But let me tell you something."

"Oh?" she raised an eyebrow dubiously. "An wha's tha?"

"Well, I have a dear friend whose life is in great danger due to something that is sort of my fault, but not really. Regardless of blame–and I have a bit of blame I'm ready to put on him, let me tell you–I can't leave him to die. At the very least, and I do say 'very least,' please let me speak to this Dr. Campbell so I can try and get released as soon as possible. I must honor my friend and do everything in my power to save him."

"Tha I unnerstan, Mr. Nerro," Nurse Duffy said, "but the prollem is that Dr. Campbell inn't here jes now."

"Where is he?"

"*Thas* the prollem, you see we're a smoll 'ospital, an he's oot tending ta patients."

"The on-duty doctor in a hospital makes house calls!? What do you mean? Is this backwards place really still the United Kingdom??"

"Not hoose calls, sur. Naw really. Really there was'n emergency at the base an he got the call to help oot, ye see? There was a crosh."

"A... crosh?"

"Ay, a plane crosh like yers."

"Ah, a *crash*," Nero nodded.

"Ay, thas wot I said–"

Nero smiled. "Then you know what that means," he said. "If the mountain won't come to Muhammad..."

"No, sir. Abslootely no. Imma the oonly nurse on dooty roit now. If the other nurse were here, it'd be different, but as it tis–"

Nero interrupted with a point over Nurse Duffy's shoulder.

She whipped around to see Nurse Hannah Douglass in the doorway.

"Sorry I'm late, Emma. The bloomin' traffic ta git here wuss a nightmare."

Nurse Emma Duffy stared at her angrily.

"What? Wha's tha look yer givin me? Oh, tha pilot's awake, is 'e?"

***

Nero, donning a pair of borrowed pants, a shirt two sizes too large, and his own boots (still wet), slipped into the passenger side of Nurse Duffy's black Peugeot.

She slammed the door beside him and glared at him.

"I canna believe I let you tolk me inna this," she growled. "This is a bod idea."

"Bad idea or not, I believe it is what must be done, Ms. Duffy," Nero said, "And I can't begin to tell you how grateful I am for your assistance." He leaned towards her, amping up his Nero charm.

"Yeah, thas enuff," she said. "Don git fresh, ye hear? You kin thank me later. An in the meantime, call me Emma. I think we're pass the formalities, okie?"

She turned the key and the engine coughed to life.

"Emma?" Nero smiled his Nero smile. "It is genuinely a pleasure. Please, call me Archibald."

Despite the anger and annoyance, the slightest–and I do mean *slightest*–hint of a smile tugged at the corner of Emma's mouth. Let me tell you, dear reader, there really is just *something* about Archibald Nero...

"What base is this exactly, Emma? I'm not familiar with Kirkwall. I've been to Edinburgh, but that's it."

"We're on an island colled Orkney at the tip top of the UK. Edinburgh's is sooth of 'ere, jes about 500 kilometers by rood."

"Than my calculations were perfect! Bloody brilliant!"

"Yer wha?"

"Eh, nevermind. It's quite a long story. So... the military base?"

"Ay, iss an RAF station colled Hotson."

"Hotson? You mean Hatson? RNAS Hatson?"

"Ay, Hotson."

"I think I've heard of that, I have." Nero thought. Had he been there before? Long ago? He racked his brain unsuccessfully. He'd traveled the globe, and he knew he was getting old when his memory started getting foggy. "I can't bloody remember," he shrugged.

They passed through the checkpoint at the gate with Emma explaining they were there to see the doctor. In the distance, a long pillar of smoke was rising off the tarmac; in the air, the smell of burning gasoline was heavy. In light of recent developments, Nero could only hope for the safety of the pilots involved.

"The hospital facilities shud be oover thatta way," Emma said as they rumbled to a stop at an intersection, gesturing to the left.

"No, that way," Nero said pointing to the right.

"Whot? Thas na right. I've ben here. Doctor Campbell willa be over thare." She pointed again to the left.

Nero smiled and pulled the wheel to the right. "Accelerate, Emma," he grinned. "And trust me just once more. I have a different idea."

"A different–?"

The Peugeot trundled to a stop outside a nondescript building with armed guards outside. In the distance, a pair of planes took off, their engines roaring up into the air, making Nero a little jealous.

Inside, Emma followed closely behind Nero, her face worried.

"Do ye know whot yer doin?" she asked. "If yer lyin, the MPs'll have oor nicks!"

"What happened to your Scotch will?" Nero asked with a grin.

"Thas different!" Emma said, scowling. "I've no idea how ye convinced me o' this, but it was a mistake, it twas."

"You can't leave now, Nurse Duffy," he smiled. "I'm under your care and supervision!"

Nero walked down a hall, and following either his nose or foggy memories, he turned left and stopped outside of a door. He knocked twice before entering.

Emma looked at the name placard and gasped as she followed him inside.

The door read *COLONEL ANGUS McBERNN*

"I'm here to see the Colonel," Nero said to a petite woman behind a desk. "My name is Archibald Nero and I come bearing information that involves the very fate of the entire Kingdom."

"Do ye have an appointment, sir?" the woman asked, her accent lighter than Emma's.

"Uh, I'm sorry?"

"An appointment. The Colonel is very busy. And there's just been an accident, as ye see," she gestured over her shoulder at the window. Through it, Nero could see a fire brigade working to extinguish the remains of the crash.

"I see, madam, and I'm sorry but I do not have an appointment. I need to see the Colonel immediately."

As he spoke, a door to the left of the young woman's desk opened and a red faced man stepped out in full uniform, a hat under arm.

"Amelia, I need to be gooin to the hospital noow," he roared in a gravely voice. "I canna see McMannus flyin the next trainin mission afta tha roit mess, but who kin tell rully." He looked up at Nero and frowned.

"An who might yoo be?" he asked.

Nero bowed slightly and extended his hand. "My name is Archibald Nero, sir, and I need to speak with you about dangers that threaten all of Her Majesty's Kingdom."

The Colonel looked at Amelia.

"Does this mahn have an appointment?"

"No, sir, Colonel."

"I didna think he ded," McBernn spat before stomping past Nero.

"Wait, sir, did you hear what I–"

"I've gut a mahn boornd badly an in hospital. I canna be talkin to ye, mate. I've no time for theories when a man is dyin."

"I have a friend who is dying, sir," Nero pleaded. "He's just a few hundred miles north in the Faroe Islands. His life is–"

McBernn, at the door, turned and scowled at Nero again. "If yer man is in the Faroes, yer buggered. Ye 'spect me ta invade bloody Dinmark? Tis not even on oor soil. I canna doo it. You wanna git to the Faroes, I canna help yoo, brother. I 'pologize fer tha, but it tis the trooth."

He nodded briefly before donning his hat and pulling the door shut behind him.

"Damn it all," Nero said.

"Less go find Dr. Campbell," Emma suggested, relief–albeit wholly *sypathetic* relief–obvious on her face, realizing that could have gone much, *much* worse. "Perhopps the Doctor kin make a suggestion thot'll help ye go ferward, all right Archibold? Maybe we can coll fer 'elp? Or perhopps we shud go back to the hospital?"

Nero raised a finger excitedly. "No! That's a brillaint idea, Emma!"

"Goin back to th'ospital?" she asked.

"No, of course not." Nero smiled devilishly. "Your other suggestion, of course. In order for it to work, I'll need to... well, borrow a uniform."

"Oh bugger me," Emma muttered. "Whot ever did ay say yes fer?"

CHAPTER 20: Trifle Not With An Angry Adventuress

From a crouch, *Le Duc* launched himself up over the head of the creature and landed on its curved back with a shout of French.

"*Préparez-vous à votre mort, bête!*" he shouted victoriously (a fine choice of adverbs, if not a bit premature).

The beast roared, throwing back its monstrous head, slamming the flat of its skull against *Le Duc*'s temple. Eyes blinking, *Le Duc* shook his head as one dagger dropped from his hand and clattered to the stone floor of the colonnade.

"Hold on!" Lily shouted, sprinting towards to melee, her long vaquero's coat flapping against her flanks as her *cordobés* hat flew off her head and fell to the ground.

Even as she watched, the creature seemed to change, its unnatural body shifting to accommodate for the addition of a rider. The spine realigned, bending downward to bring *Le Duc* within claw-range even as its long, distended forearms stretched painfully, skin growing taut as the bones grew.

"Be careful," she called, pulling a six round speedloader from a pocket. With one hand, she struggled to open her revolver as she ran, her hands clumsy in their ignorance. "The creature, it's... it's *changing*!"

Le Duc's vision finally cleared of stars in time to see a skillet sized claw slice past his face.

"*Mon dieu!*" he squeaked. "I did not think I was within–"

"It's changing, I told you!" Lily hollered as she slapped her cylinder closed, skidded to a halt, and raised her pistol.

"Best put your head down, *Monsieur* Duke," she said. "I'm a beginner..."

"*Est-ce une blague?*" he asked, eyebrows high.

Lily smiled. "This is no joke," she said, feeling a strange, unfamiliar adventuress' calm begin to take over. She was meant for this, remember?

The gun fired, sending a hot piece of lead 2,500 feet per second straight into the ~~Man~~ Beast With No Name's head.

Lucky shot? Perhaps.

But where you'd expect a ghoulish spatter of brains or at least minimal splash of blood, there was only a dull *THUNK* accompanied by a red droplet or two. A moment later, the beast's thrashing ceased as it all but forgot the addition of *Monsieur Le Duc* and turned two golden eyes towards Lily.

"Oh my," she whispered. "I'd hoped that would... you know."

"*Exécuter, mademoiselle, cette créature signifie pour vous détruire!*" *Le Duc* shouted as the beast opened up a four-legged gallop across the expanse of the yard straight for Lily.

She took a deep breath and sighted once more, feeling that calmness steady her hand. "If your head is too thick," she began, "perhaps my luck will fare better..."

The gun roared in her hands, its recoil fighting back against her grip. She emptied the remaining cylinders into the creature's chest, each round biting free a piece of flesh and exposing sour yellow bones within.

Still, the beast could not be dissuaded.

Really, it was some kind of curse.

Holstering her revolver once more, Lily began to backpedal. "Anytime, *Monsieur* Duke!" she called over her shoulder as she turned and made for the closest column. "I'm not one for that damsel in distress bit, but I could reconsider!"

She leapt behind a pillar just as the charging monster ripped past, newly-born horns tearing through the old stone like paper, causing the great stone beam to wither slightly and bow beneath the weight of the structure above. Lily gasped as the pillar cracked and groaned under the strain.

On the beast's back, *Le Duc* had decided to try to get involved, and currently he was busy hacking and slashing at the creature in vain. Shreds of its leather-like hide began falling to the ground, withering and curling even as they touched the stone.

Lily watched in consternation, doing everything in her power to keep at least one pillar of cut stone between her and the monster as she struggled to regroup.

"It's as if it's invincible," she whispered to herself. "The bullets are useless, as is the Duke's blade. It must have a weakness..."

The monster charged again, this time impacting a column head-on and splitting it like a tree trunk. As a wedge of stone fell, its head pushed through the opening, revealing a heavily plated skull, completely unlike the skull that she'd seen only moments earlier.

"It's evolving," she gasped. Somehow, the creature was changing, its body shifting and growing to better suit it to the current situation. *If we were in water*, Lily thought–torn between amazement and terror, *it would probably grow fins!*

As another pillar toppled, a portion of the second floor colonnade broke free and collapsed, the huge rectangular piece of stone crushing one of the beast's legs and tossing *Le Duc* from its back.

"*Cette créature est une terreur*!" he exclaimed. "I have seen nothing like it! *Pas une chose maudite!*"

"Nor have I, *Monsieur* Duke," Lily said, rising to her feet and helping *Le Duc* away from the creature. "Lucky for us, it has been trapped by its own foolishness."

"*Oui*, indeed it–"

He stopped, eyes wide.

Despite the stone weighing a few tons–and remaining immovable, even to the abomination–the body would not be foiled.

Lily and *Le Duc* watched as the ten foot tall creature became fifteen, became twenty, its body growing so quickly as to force pieces of its hide to split and tear, unable to accommodate the horrid and unnatural expansion. Even as it did, a fifth leg sprouted from the creature's side, bones emerging from nothing and growing outward, joints appearing and twisting the bent hoof downward to touch the stone flooring even as the crushed leg turned black and fell away.

Slowly, the creature rose to its full, newly formidable height.

"*Dieu ait pitié de nous*," *Le Duc* said, making the sign of the cross.

"Your God has abandoned you," the beast rasped through a fang-filled mouth.

Lily stared, speechless, and could have sworn the creature was smiling.

Before either adventurer could react to the beast, it swung, slashing across *Le Duc*'s chest and throwing him into the center of the stone patio as blood rushed down his black tunic.

"*Tuez le putain de chose*," *Le Duc* shouted, "or run!"

Lily ran, but her mind moved even faster than her feet.

What is giving the creature its power? What was it that the man had said before this had all begun? Think! she commanded her brain as she wound through a nest of columns, the beast charging behind her.

Thankfully for our adventuress, its expanded size did not work in its favor. Its horns slammed against the ceiling as its broad shoulders struggled to fit between the pillars.

"Are you familiar with the Regent of Spain Ximénes de Cisneros? Proponent of the Crusades and one-time Grand Inquisitor?" the words of the man rang through her head as Lily panted and tried to find some piece of helpful evidence in what he'd shared.

(You remember this, right, dear reader? It's in Chapter 14, of course!)

Lily tumbled behind a pillar as the beast roared past, its great stride overtaking her. As it passed, a wide jaw tore through the air, aiming for her head and missing her by a hair's breadth.

Large pieces of the second floor were now falling like rain, crashing to the ground and sending up great clouds of dust.

"The skull," she gasped. "It was stolen, wasn't it? What had he said?"

In the center of the patio, *Le Duc* was struggling to regain his feet, the blood flow slowing, but leaving him a pale wreck nonetheless.

"His skull was stolen by priests loyal to Regent Ximénes and it was returned... here." Lily nodded, yes, but what did Ximénes have to do with it again?

A block of stone slammed against rubble beside her, forcing Lily out of her covered position and into the open. She tripped and collapsed onto the patio a few feet from where *Le Duc* knelt.

From the dusty shadows, the beast stepped, hoofed back feet casually kicking aside rocks large enough to crush a man as taloned forelegs scratched at the ground like a bull ready to charge.

"*Je crains la fin, Mademoiselle*," *Le Duc* said softly. "I did not know you well, but your bravery is unmatched. I believe this is our death. It has been an honor to—"

"Shut up!" Lily said, her mind racing. Death? Not yet.

Witches, she thought. Ximénes was a Grand Inquisitor, of course, and he spared witches and used their power and loyalty...

"They took the skull of the emperor, and using their remarkable powers they put a curse upon it."

"Yes, of course!" Lily shook her head. "The skull was *cursed*. Cursed! And he stole it. So now *he* is cursed.

And that revelation was only six chapters ago." She shook her head again. "Some memory I have! What would Hugo say if he were here to see–"

The beast charged, rubble turning to dust underfoot as it crossed the expanse of the patio towards our felled heroes.

Lily raised her eyes, and beheld their salvation.

The skull of Charles V lay against the creature's breastbone partially covered by tattered skin, revealed thanks to the not insubstantial damage she'd done with her revolver.

She put a hand to the ground to help stand and felt the unadorned tang of *Le Duc*'s lost knife beneath her palm. She closed her fingers around it.

Now, dear reader, where you and I would feel an absolute terror at the approach of such a creature's unbridled charge, Lily felt that remarkable calm once more. She knew what she had to do, and she had the tool with which to do it.

Instead of crumpling under the strain of terror, dear reader, Lily only smiled.

She took two steps towards the creature and rolled just as the first claw swiped past her. Her legs whipped over her head, her body picking up speed as she rolled. When her knife-wielding hand emerged from the precision tumble, it was perfectly aligned with the beast's chest, and with only the slightest flick her wrist, she slit through the creature's hide and pulled the skull free with a wet *slssshh*. The skull popped free like a pearl from a prize oyster and clattered to the ground.

The beast collapsed in a screaming heap.

When Lily rose, all that remained in place of the

abomination was a ruin of a man in a veritable ocean of gore.

Le Duc looked up at Lily, his face still pale but now plastered with a foolish smile.

"Generally, *Mademoiselle*, I am one who believes love has more to do with beds than hearts, but I... well, I must say, you are remarkable, *Docteur* Halifax, and I believe that my heart has now attached itself to you. I believe I am in love! I want nothing more than to–"

"That's enough, *Monsieur* Duke," Lily said. "I don't mean to interrupt–or break your heart, but I'm spoken for, and I've got my man to rescue." She slipped the bloody knife into her belt, knelt, picked up her fallen *cordobés* hat, and returned it to her head.

"Now," she said like the grand adventuress she was, "let's go."

CHAPTER 21: Two Unlikely Duos Continue Their Duo-Ness (With Split Results)

Nero was limping at an increased rate–I wouldn't quite say "running" exactly–out of the officer's building, looking over his shoulder like a child who'd just gotten something over on his Mum.

Not the worst metaphor, considering.

"What've ye gone and done, sur? Mucked up and rooned yer foine reputayshun, I would guess?" Ms. Duffy asked from where she stood by her Peugeot.

Trying unsuccessfully to stifle a smile, Nero turned to the nurse and asked, "Did you meet up with your Dr. Campbell?"

"Aye, course I did. He wan't too pleased to learn you'd done up and flown the coop, sur."

Nero pulled open the passenger door and slipped inside, forcing the small car to rock back and forth. Ms. Duffy leaned over and peered in the open driver's side window.

"But'e ded give 'is perrmitchin to discharge ye, Mr. Nerro."

"Splendid, Ms. Duffy," Nero said breathlessly. "Now, if you wouldn't mind getting in. I believe we need to be going." He looked over her shoulder. "Post haste."

The young nurse frowned. "And why would tha be, sur?"

The door to the officer's building opened and a young soldier stepped out, an officer at his heel. The former shaded his eyes from the sunshine and looked out across the small parking lot.

"Oh, no reason."

The young soldier pointed in the direction of the Peugeot, Nurse Duffy, and Nero–doing his damnedest to hide beneath the dash.

Ms. Duffy opened the door and slipped inside. The engine turned over, and as the Peugeot pulled out of the lot, a handful of soldiers stood in its exhaust wake, pointing and growling.

When they'd cleared the gate, Ms. Duffy turned to Nero.

"An' will ye be pleased to tell me the troooth now, sur?"

"I'm sorry?" he said innocently.

"I may no be an officer in her Majesty's Secret Service, but I'll no be taken for a foool."

"You are quite right, Ms. Duffy, I apologize. While you were finding Dr. Campbell, I... well, I obtained use of the radio for a short while."

"This dinna have anythin' to do with whot you said prior to sendin' me to fine Dr. Campbell, did it?"

"And what was that?"

"Borrowin' a uniform?"

Nero grinned. "Do you want the honest answer to that? I wouldn't want a fine young lass like yourself to become an accessory."

"Mr. Ne*rro*!"

Nero chuckled. "Now, now, Ms. Duffy, we're not in wartime. Those RAF boys could use a little safety check here and again."

"Well, you're no wrong 'bout tha," she said, "but I do no approove!"

"I know, Ms. Duffy, and for that I apologize."

"An whot were ya doin' tha business for? Yer liable to find yerself in quite the sticky wicket impersonatin' an officer!"

"I told you, I need to come to the aid of my friend, and in order to do that I need to contact someone in the States."

"En Am*air*ica?"

"Yes, Ms. Duffy."

"An who might thot be?"

"An old friend. I need her to get ahold of a man by the name of Quincy Max." Nero turned to her and smiled. "Don't worry, he's a Doctor, you can trust him." They rumbled over a pothole. "Now," he asked. "Do you know where a man can get a shower, a shave, and a good meal around these parts?"

Ms. Duffy, perhaps a bit taken by all the excitement, could not help herself–remember, despite being on a wretched pilot streak, Nero was quite a charming bugger–turned to Archibald and smiled, saying, "I know jus the place the twoo o'fus kin sit doown an eat. But lemme go home an git changed furst. I've enough o this bloody unifo*rr*m!"

***

Patched up as he was, *Le Duc* was just strong enough to move under his own strength. Lily had torn up *Le Duc*'s cape to use as makeshift bandages and tourniquets.

"Do not worry, *Mademoiselle*," he'd assured her gratefully, "I have plenty of capes where this one came from. *Cela ne veut pas mon premier rodéo.*"

Secretly delighted she did not have to destroy her vaquero's coat, although more than willing to do so if need be, Lily had used the royal blue cape.

Now, patched up as he was, where were we?

Ah, yes.

"What happened to him?" Lily asked.

"That savage murdered him," *Le Duc* said. "*Dieu maudit bête!*"

A body lay in the shade of a small cypress tree. Lily and *Le Duc* had encountered it on their arduous journey out of grand ol' Alhambra. A red halo circled the man's crushed head. Feeling quite the savage herself, Lily pulled a small attaché case from the dead man's grasp and flipped it open.

"I'm assuming this is the man I was *supposed* to meet."

"*Oui*, I would assume the very same, *Docteur*. The *bête* intercepted your contact and this was his fate."

Lily tried not to dwell on the dead man at her feet or the sacrifice he'd made to help her find Hugo. If she survived this mad ordeal, she promised she'd light a candle in St. Peter's Cathedral for each and everyone who'd fallen along the way.

"Lovely!" she said, pulling a pack of papers free. "The dear, he brought exactly what I'd hoped for."

She flipped through the pages, smiling and shaking her head. "I'm this much closer."

Le Duc leaned in and glanced over the pages in Lily's hands.

"*Mon Dieu!*" he said. "As if my great love for you could not grow further. *Mademoiselle*, you prove me wrong again and again!"

"What?"

"You and I are so much alike. Our minds are synched perfectly. Just imagine how our bodies would–"

"*Monsieur* Duke."

"Ah, *excusez-moi*. Apologies, *Mademoiselle*. It's just that I can't help but think of–"

"*Monsieur* Duke!"

The would-be French caped crusader sighed and shelved his amorous advances (for the moment). "Yes, of course. I see that you have gone to great lengths to find flight logs, correct?"

"Yes, *Monsieur* Duke, exactly. What I hold are flight logs going into and out of Port Harcourt during the short time I was a guest of British Nigeria."

Le Duc nodded excitely. "And what were you looking for?"

"I remember that Hugo said something about the worm used to control Archibald being Scandinavian–"

"Who are these men? I do not know these men..."

"–and being that this Scandinavian clue was one of my only clues, I used *La Tempestad*'s contact to acquire flight logs out of British Nigeria over a very narrow window."

"Because you are looking for flights originating in Nigeria?"

"Exactly."

"*Mon Dieu, je veux me enrouler autour de votre corps nu!*"

"*Monsieur* Duke!"

The Frenchman blushed. "*Mille excuses*," he said. "But I am just a man, and when I see a woman like you, with brains and a body *qui ferait un roi se mettre à genoux–*"

"*Monsieur*, if you cannot hold your tongue, this working relationship will find itself cut short prematurely."

Le Duc sighed once more. "Yes, *Mademoiselle*. Of course. I only, well. I am delighted to learn that you and I think quite similarly."

"What do you mean?"

"I have had a... well, *close* relationship with a woman once. Her name was Miette Tati and she–"

"Miette? I know Miette! She was a great friend and host to us in Tangier!"

Le Duc nodded. "Yes, indeed that is Miette. Well, I became involved when I learned that the damned devil Fang destroyed *Le Fugitif*. When I arrived, she told me much of what transpired."

"And?"

Le Duc offered a satisfied grin. "I took it upon myself to get involved in all of this. I have been following you for some time, knowing I would be a great asset in this adventure eventually. As it turns out, I did the same, *Mademoiselle*. I acquired complete flight logs in and out of the Ibn Battouta airstrip in Tangier."

"*Monsieur* Duke that is perfectly brilliant!"

The Frenchman blushed despite his blasé shrug.

"Perhaps brilliant enough to warrant a kiss?"

Lily frowned. "No. Now, where are these flight logs?"

Le Duc pointed over a baked clay wall to the east. "I have a jeep parked not far. They are within."

"All right. Then let's go."

"Can I have a moment's rest?"

Lily sighed, thinking of Hugo. "Well... just a moment. But please hurry, time is of the utmost essence!" She looked out at the sun, slowly rising in the eastern sky. "I feel like Hugo is almost within reach. Almost..."

CHAPTER 22: A Most Blessed and Inevitable Betrayal

Fang watched as Darius Dufort walked outside to smoke.

The motley crew of fascists, former madmen, and politically neutral villains had returned from the island's small cemetery not long ago just as the sun disappeared behind a mountain and the temperature dropped. The mist that had been heavy somehow increased, leaving the entire peninsula draped in clouds deeper and richer than velvet.

Through the window, Fang could barely see the lit embers burning at the end of Dufort's cigarette.

In another room, he could make out the sharp voices of Von Faust and *Der Klinge*, with Von Faust currently taking the tongue lashing he justly deserved for allowing *Der Klinge*'s plane to be taken by Brannigan's accomplice. Apparently *Herr* Von Faust would pay for Konig's failure. Fang could not decide if it was narrative sloppiness or simple moodiness that explained *Der Klinge*'s erratic behavior.

Either way, he didn't mind Von Faust receiving an earful.

Behind him, he heard the click that preceded a broadcast on the radio. With Dufort outside, the snake Lessard had taken over communications.

"Das Flugzeug verließ die Insel vor etwa zwölf

Stunden," Lessard said in rather garish and ill-accented German.

Fang listened, his mind a roiling beast. He thought of all his loyal followers, now rotting in a mass grave in the forests of British Nigeria. *All dead*, he thought. *But not this* morceau de merde. He could only shake his head.

"*Keine landungen wurden berichtet?*"

Lessard had not previously shown any faculty for the German tongue, Fang realized idly. Say what you want, *Monsieur* Delacroix, but the traitor has a penchant for languages.

"*Danke, ich erwarte ihre antwort*," Lessard said, ending his transmission. A hiss of static burst out of the small room before the radio returned to silence.

Fang rounded the corner and met the young soldier's steely gaze.

"Any luck?" he asked.

"I've contacted landing strips in Edinburgh, Aberdeen, Thurso, Elgin, Lerwick, Bergen, Oslo, Gottenburg, and Copenhagen, all with no luck, *mein herr*," Lessard said, without looking up from a pad he was quickly filling with writing. "And Berlin has no record of–"

He stopped himself when he looked up. "Oh," he said. "I thought you were someone else."

"No sign of your plane?"

Lessard scowled. "We will find the plane and *Herr* Brannigan's partner. Even a skilled pilot can only fly so far."

"True."

"And even now reinforcements are on their way from Klaksvík, their ships having arrived on Borðoy this morning."

"How many men?"

Lessard opened his mouth to speak and stopped himself. "Enough," he said. "If you have questions about particulars, you should take them up with *Der Klinge*. That is all I have to say to you."

Fang glanced out the window and caught sight of Dufort's burning cigarette. The young soldier had not moved. Fang had privacy, for the moment.

"I have to ask you a question, *Monsieur* Lessard," Fang began.

"I told you, any questions will have to be take up with *Der–*"

"No, Lessard," Fang sighed. "A more personal question."

Lessard squinted at Fang suspiciously. "And what is that?"

Fang took a step forward, approaching a mapping and drafting desk beside Lessard's radio. Spread across it was a world map and a smattering of plotting instruments. Pins, plottings, and circles marred the great map.

"What made you turn on me so quickly?"

Lessard sneered at his former leader. "You take yourself as a benevolent king," Lessard began, "when you are in fact a cruel despot, *une baise stupide*, a mad man blind to anything but your own obsession. And you would have me believe you found some ceremony in that burial today? *Vous êtes certainement fou si vous croyez que.* You are not benevolent, you are not wise, you are not dedicated to the pursuit of anything–even money; you are simply mad. I have found a purpose with *Der Klinge*, and soon the world will know our names.

And you? Now that your nemesis is cold and in the ground, I believe you have little left for which to live, *Monsieur*. Now I no longer feel anger towards you for the deaths of my compatriots, I feel only pity."

"Oh?" Fang asked.

"*Oui.*"

Fang smiled, lifted the steel divider caliper from the drafting board, and jammed it into Lessard's throat. The soldier's carotid artery burst open in a crimson fountain. Blood sprayed onto the Frenchman's new uniform and splashed onto the radio desk, a few errant gushes landing on the rug before Lessard's struggling body collapsed onto the ground. Fang followed his flailing motions, one hand clapped over Lessard's mouth to prevent an outcry. As the young Frenchman struggled in his last moments, Fang stared straight into Lessard's eyes, unblinking and without remorse.

Soon, Alain Lessard's struggling ceased.

Fang listened. Von Faust and *Der Klinge* continued their unending ripostes. Over his shoulder, Fang discovered that Dufort's cigarette still remained lit outside, even in the strong Faroese wind.

He looked at Lessard's dead body, his mind already taking him through the inevitable disposal process to come.

"You believe you are wise, *jeune homme*, but you are not wise. If you ally yourself with pigs, prepare to be slaughtered," he said. "Because I know a despot when I see one, *Herr* Lessard. And I would rather be mad then lapdog to a Nazi." He spat onto Lessard's lifeless body.

Then, ever so quietly, Fang closed the door to the radio room, for he had much to do.

CHAPTER 23: Andrew?

Being of neither the temperament nor disposition to adventure (something Andrew should have learned in the jungles of British Nigeria–or the slums of Rio de Janeiro, or the clandestine halls of the 'Iolani Palace, or barren taigas of Siberia, et al), Andrew had opted to stay with his new fickle friend Reginald Max in Sevilla rather than accompany Dr. Halifax to the Alhambra.

"I'm asking you to stay, Andrew," Lily had said rather frankly. "I'll need you to... well, be my eyes and ears here on the ground. I need you to contact Quincy and work to locate Hugo while I follow my gut, understand?"

Andrew, all too happy to oblige, had nodded. Little did he know Lily believed–and rightly so–that she could travel much faster without the young lad.

And so, Andrew remained in Sevilla. For the first few days, he traded telegrams with Quincy before locating a new fandangled long distance telephone which enabled him to *speak* with Dr. Max back in America–at no small financial setback to his brother, Reginald, but that's another story.

Andrew did not dignify Dr. Max's worries for Liliana with argument, being as he'd gotten to know a *different* side of the Doctor than the wizened old academic.

"But she is so new to this adventuresome life,"

Quincy had said over 4,000+ miles of telephone cable and a four second delay. "She is willing, but I fear not always able."

"Have faith, Dr. Max, sir," Andrew assured him. "She has changed a great deal in even the short time I have known her. She is capable of much, I know it."

With his fears almost assuaged, Quincy got on to giving Andrew as much information as he'd managed to gather–that is, not much.

"We need some luck, Andrew, because at the moment, I've no damned idea where Professor Brannigan is, or Dr. Halifax, or the Cipher of Dumuzid, or any of it. From the halls of an academic institution, thousands of miles from the action, I can't tell you how ineffectual I feel, young man. I've taken to hoping and praying that Professor Ellis Spooner stumbles out of the woods, a firearm in one hand and the answers to my prayers in the other."

"Professor Spooner, sir?" Andrew had asked skeptically.

"Yes, I know, it is foolhardy, but an old man can hope, can't he? Ellis did manage to find the Cipher, after all."

"That's true, sir, but I think that we're on our own here," Andrew said. "But don't worry, I'm going to get right to work and I'm going to find the Professor, sir. I believe I've got all I need. I travelled the world with the Professor, and I travelled from Gibraltar to Sevilla with pirates and ham smugglers. I've got some mettle myself, sir! Just you leave it to Andrew!"

That was four days previous. In mentioning Professor Ellis Spooner, Dr. Max had given Andrew an idea of how desperate the old man was. Spooner had been missing in the jungle for, well, quite some time, and to hope that the crazy ol' faculty member would stumble into the light, able to assist was nigh ludicrous. It was this realization that spurned Andrew on further.

Unfortunately, those four days were filled with one dead end after another. And now, on the fifth day, a day on which God had apparently created all the animals of the Earth, Andrew was not able to create even one fruitful lead.

And so, we find Andrew, sitting dejected in a rather dowdy conference room of the Sevilla University Central Library, a sprawl of books encircling the young man. Exhaustion weighed heavily on his narrow shoulders, but not nearly so heavy as the fates of his friends. The Professor, Dr. Halifax, even Archibald, all possibly lost to that awful band of ruffians, The Cabal. Dr. Max had expressed his feelings of ineffectuality, but Andrew believed the old man had no idea. Andrew felt so close, but he simply could not put the pieces together.

He looked out the window, hopelessly going over the meetings and discussions he'd had with Sevilla's best scientists, inquiring about the elusive worm that had turned Archibald into Zombie Nero (remember that zaniness?). *The worm is the key*, Andrew had thought countless times. *If I can just put my finger on* why *that is...*

Staring out the window at the dark clouds rolling over the Guadalquivir, Andrew did not hear his name called by the receptionist. Not the first time, and not even the second.

On the third, he looked up. "Yes?"

"*Teléfono*," the woman called. "*Señor Max está sosteniendo para usted.*"

Andrew rose and trudged to the desk, expecting nothing more than another call from Reginald, inquiring about lunch or dinner or how the research was progressing. When Andrew raised the receiver, however, he learned that while it was Reginald, it was about something quite different.

"Come back to my office immediatley, Andrew," Reginald sputtered. The old man was breathless and unequivocally rushed. "We've found something!"

"What is it? What did you find?"

"Well, in truth *we* didn't find it," Reginald said. "As a matter of fact, it found us. It's a broadcast, and it contains coordinates."

CHAPTER 24: Lies, Damn Lies, and an Old Friend

Nero, eternal optimist that he was, did feel a *tiny* bit of regret when there was a knock on the door the next morning. In truth, a part of him had hoped to have at least a few more hours of requiescence (the reasoning behind this hope being perfectly clear in just a moment).

He pulled the sheet back off his head to the tune of Scottish giggling and asked, "Did you hear something?"

Slipping a head and a pair of lovely bare shoulders from beneath the same sheet, Nurse Duffy, smiling, said, "Did I 'ear whot, Arrchay? Yooo come bock oonder 'ere an–"

A second barrage of knocks sounded on the door.

"Bloody hell," Nero muttered. "Quincy, of all the damnable times for you to be efficient..."

Nero slipped from beneath his Scottish maiden's sheets and limped across the cool wood floor, snatching at clothes from amidst a miscellany of debris.

"Whot do yoo think yer doin, Arrchay?"

"I'm sorry, Em, I'll be just a moment," he called over his shoulder.

"You bet'er hope it's not me Da," Emma Louise Duffy returned with a laugh from the bedroom. "I doo 'magine he'd have yer head now would 'e."

"I don't believe it's your father," Archibald responded, grinning. "Although it wouldn't be the first time..."

He opened the door to see a young man in a nondescript uniform frowning at him.

"Are yooo Mistah Ne*rr*o, sur?"

"Aye, laddie, that I am."

"Telegram, sur," the boy said, extended his hand and waving a paper at Nero.

"But of bloody course," Archibald sighed. He'd sent a telegram himself the day before to a contact of his in London, outlining a message to send to Quincy. But Archie never believed the blasted old man would have found him *quite* so quickly.

Nero took the telegram and shrugged at the young boy who stood expectedly waiting. "I don't even have a copper for you, laddie. You're lucky I have any pants, son. So off with you," he waved, shutting the door in the youth's face.

"Who wus it at the dooo*rr*, A*rr*chay?"

Nero unfolded the paper, saying, "It's a telegram..." as he did so. "...for me."

"For yooo? Whot do ye mean? Who wud knoow you'd be 'ere?"

"I sent word yesterday," Archibald said absently as he read the telegram, "from the base, remember? I told them to telegram me courtesy of Emma Louise Duffy at Balfour Hospital."

"Yoo *whot*?"

Nero looked up, distracted yet, but perhaps beginning to discover his *faux pas* nonetheless. "Well," he sputtered, "I was being, um—"

There was a *stomp stomp stomp* of heavy Scottish footsteps before the fiery nurse appeared in the doorway, donning a dignified sheet and scowling. "How did yoo know ye'd be wit me 'ere?"

"Uh, well... eh..." Archie stammered, caught off guard. The telegram had him right well distracted. "As I said, I was–"

"I thought this was spaycial," Emma spat. "I dinna wont to be jus another*rr* fling for yoo!"

"You weren't just another fling, dear," Archibald said, finally focusing on the matter at hand. "Believe me when I say you are quite special–"

"Perhops I *shud* call me Da," Emma continued. "He'd have a grand time putting a few pieces of pheasant shot right up yer bloomin–"

"Now, Emma!"

"Don't yoo 'now Emma' mee, A*rr*chay Ne*rr*o. Imma *rr*espectable woman, I am. I'm no cheap dock slag or stroompet, ye 'ear?"

"Of course, you aren't," Archibald said, batting his eyes. Quickly, he stepped forward and took her hand raising it to his lips and kissing it. "A thousand apologies for my rudeness, pig-headedness, foul assumptions, and bald-faced arrogance. Can you ever forgive me, my dear?"

Anger still quite evident in her eyes, the beautiful Nurse Duffy took a deep breath and let it out slowly. After a long silence, she said, "As loong as thas troo, A*rr*chay, you're foine by me."

Nero nodded. "Thank you, Emma."

Nurse Duffy took a second deep breath and let it out. "Yer bloody welcome, you eejit." She tried to quash a traitorous smile and failed. Nero reached out and wrapped an arm around her slight waist, pulling her to him and kissing her passionately.

You know, a little bit more of this and Nero was liable to lose track of Hugo and Lilly. I mean, it *is* Nero, after all.

Thankfully for our heroes, Emma pulled away and pointed at him sharply. "Thas foine," she said. "But no more lies, a'right?"

Nero nodded. "I promise."

She nodded in response before pointing at the telegram, "Now, wha's tha?"

Nero opened his mouth, preparing to say *Nothing*, when his promise (printed a scant 23 words previous) crossed his mind.

Archibald Nero? Being *honest*? Good lord, this must be love!

"Well... being honest: I've found myself embroiled in a sort of ongoing secret war involving the myriad of precious artifacts hidden around the world and our quest to keep them out of the hands of secret societies, fascist organizations, rogue nations, and arch villains, all in hopes of preventing the premature although ultimately total destruction of the world and all those who live upon it. I'd just escaped the clutches of a rather choice supervillain when I fell into your arms, dear."

He smiled his most debonair smile.

"Ye bloody feckin' liar!" Emma shouted, incensed. "I tol ye no moo*rr* lies!!"

***

We should all take a moment and reflect appreciatively on Archibald Nero's charms–significant, because if he was not so well gifted he surely would have found himself abandoned in this strange place called Kirkwall, and there is quite a high chance that if he could not have salvaged that last predicament, we would have opened this subsequent chapter section with Nero standing on a Kirkwall street corner trying to bum a ride in his damn skivvies.

Instead, we'll open on the placid azure expanse of the Scapa Flow.

The Scapa Flow, a great bay nestled in the center of the Orkney Islands, was busy with ships on that brisk morning. The wind was blowing something fierce, and in the distance, a fog horn moaned.

"Me Da brought me 'ere back in '28 to see Cox's boys *rr*aise the *Seydlitz* and tow et en ta sho*rr*," Emma said, pulling a tam lower over her fiery red hair. "Quite a scene tha wos, I'll sey."

Archibald was distracted, pulling a borrowed peacoat tighter around his body to protect it from the wind off the bay. Beside him, Emma retied a long scarf around her neck and glanced at him.

"Why are we 'ere again, A*rr*chay? Lookin' fer bloody aliens while we're at it?"

Archibald smiled slightly and shook his head. "Not aliens, dear, no. When the ship arrives, you'll see that I'm not crazy."

Emma leaned against him for warmth, her face red from the cold, and smiled. "I don think yer crazy, A*rr*chay," she said. "Well, I hope yer no crazy."

"I'm not, Emma, I promise."

"Careful, A*rr*chay," she replied. "Don't ye make too many p*rr*omises, ye hear?"

Nero smiled despite himself. "Don't worry, I won't. I'll make just the right amount. I'll–"

He stopped.

"Whot es et?" Emma asked.

Nero squinted against the morning light at an incoming skiff puttering towards the dock from a small freighter anchored in the bay. A shape was standing at the prow, eyes shaded to the morning light not unlike Nero himself. There was something familiar about that person...

Nero squinted. "Is that...?"

The skiff thudded against the dock, and Nero could not help but smile.

"Great Scott," Nero laughed, "why it's–"

"Hold your tongue, you English *cochon*," Miette Tati said from the boat, a long-barreled pistol aimed at Nero. "You are the man *Monsieur* Max sent to meet me? *Ce qui la baise*? *Il doit être fou*. The last time I saw you–"

"Miette, I can only apologize. I was, you see, under the control of Delacroix through the intrepid employment of a rare type of worm that took away my control of myself."

Miette–standing at attention and with pistol cocked–raised an eyebrow. "*Oui*?"

Archibald nodded. "*Oui*."

After a long moment, she shrugged. "I trust *Monsieur* Max enough to trust you–for now. But I caution you, if you are lying..."

"I am not, I promise."

Miette lowered her pistol, and as she did, Emma

slipped out from behind Archibald, her eyes wide.

"An 'ere I thought I was brave?" Emma laughed nervously. "Noo bloody chonce a tha," she said. "Ess everythin' safe now?"

Nero took her hand and led her out from behind him. "Everything is fine, Emma. This is a friend of mine. Emma Duffy, this is Miette Tati," Archibald introduced. "And Miette–"

"*Il est un plaisir de vous rencontrer*," Miette said, bowing her head slightly. "My name is Mignonette Tati. You may call me Miette."

"*Enchanté de faire votre connaissance*," Emma said, with a slight bow, her Scotch brogue replaced by perfect French pronunciation. "*S'il vous plaît appelez-moi* Emma."

"You speak French?" Nero asked the nurse skeptically.

"Aye, I learnt it in schoool," Emma said.

"*Votre français est très bon*," Miette said. "*Je espère que votre goût chez les hommes est tout aussi bon.*"

Emma smiled. "A*rrchay il prétend être un imbécile, mais il est un homme bon. Et il est remarquablement bon amant.*"

A look crossed Miette's face that can only be described as extreme skepticism. "*Cela me surprend.*"

Emma laughed. "It surprised me, too!"

The two women shared a good laugh at that. Nero simply looked at them, confused.

"Remind me to learn a language eventually, will you, dear?" Nero asked Emma.

"Aye. An I'll help ye," Emma said. Nero turned to her and smiled warmly.

Miette looked at them and shook her head. "*Je ne aurais jamais imaginé...*" she said softly.

"Well, Miette," Nero said finally, "I got Quincy's telegram that someone would be here to meet me this morning, but I know little else. Tell me you are not the only help I can expect."

"You need more help, *Monsieur*?" Miette asked. "Do not insult. *Vous pouvez être si ridicule*. Yes, I am all the help. And I am all the help you will require."

"What is the plan?"

Miette pointed back over her shoulder at the small freighter from which she had departed. "*Monsieur* Max charted that vessel, and I sailed yesterday from Wick after flying from London via Aberdeen."

"But what is the plan?" he asked.

"We are to board that ship once more," Miette said. "And we are to sail north by northwest."

"No*rr*th?" Emma asked. "But whot is northwest o 'ere, A*rr*chay?"

Nero turned to his Scottish lass. "The Faroe Islands," he said ominously. "It's where I came from. I told you I had to leave my friend there. I hope he is still alive..."

"In'nt tha dangerous?" she asked.

"Aye, it will be."

Despite her cold-reddened face, Emma blanched. Ah, young love.

"But..."

Nero, steeling himself with a deep breath, turned to Miette. "We're going to need guns," he said. "A lot of guns."

Miette, as you can imagine, smiled quite broadly. "Oh, *Monsieur*, guns I have. Do you know me at all?"

CHAPTER 25: Arrivals, Investigations, and Introspections

A host of men disembarked from a long, narrow cutter anchored not for from the rocky shore, leaping down into the water and trudging towards the makeshift base of operations.

Heinrich Von Faust stood waiting, Darius Dufort a few steps behind him.

"Danke für das Kommen, meine Herren. Wir haben viel zu tun und wenig Zeit, es zu tun."

A few guttural responses were muttered back in a smattering of languages (had Von Faust been a language expert, he would have recognized Portuguese, Swiss French, Tagalog, Mandarin, Russian, Bengali, Xhosa, and... Hmong?).

"Excuse me, *meine Herr*," Dufort asked mutedly from behind Von Faust. "I'm sorry sir, but why are we allying ourselves with these men? They look like pirates, sir."

And look like pirates they did. They were not in uniform, the only common denominator among them seemed to be guns and scars and layers of dirt. The term "rogues gallery" comes to mind–and feels quite fitting, to be honest.

"They'll get done what needs to get done, Dufort,"

Von Faust said sourly. "Do not trouble yourself with the thinking. Leave that to me."

"But why are they here, sir?"

"The artifacts, you fool," Von Faust growled. "We need experienced hands to move the artifacts and to be prepared when Brannigan's woman–"

"Von Faust," a voice called from the cabin.

Dufort and Von Faust turned to see Mr. Shindo standing in the doorway, frowning.

"Where have you been?" Von Faust shouted. "I haven't seen you since Chapter 15! I thought you were dead. We could have used your *verdammt* help searching the island for Brannigan's *verflucht* partner prior to his *vermaledeit* escape!"

"I *was* searching the island for Brannigan's partner prior to his escape," Shindo said, shaking his head. "It's a bigger island than you think."

Von Faust shrugged. "Fine. What do you want?"

"Neither Konig nor myself have located Lessard. Have you any more information regarding his whereabouts?"

"As I already told *Der Klinge*, the last I saw of Lessard was yesterday evening. I haven't seen the *dummkopf* since! But he must be here somewhere. That ship is the only way off the island now," he said, pointing at the recent arrival.

Dufort didn't need to know Von Faust well to see that the man was fraying. One foul up after another had brought him to quite a desperate place. Dark circles ringed his bloodshot eyes and his hands had taken on a demented shake.

Shindo turned his back on the Nazi and slipped inside

the house.

"That fool *amerikanisch* could not find a–"

He stopped himself when *Der Klinge* stepped outside, a customary scowl carved into his wrinkled face.

"What are you doing, Von Faust? Shouldn't you be helping Konig and Shindo search for this deserter of yours?"

"Of *mine*? He is one of Fang's men," Von Faust whined.

"And *you* recruited him, yes?"

Von Faust opened his mouth to respond, but nothing came out.

"I thought so," *Der Klinge* correctly concluded. "We need to find Lessard and be prepared to depart. I will not wait for this failed plan to resolve. *Herr* Brannigan is dead. We will have to locate this Halifax woman and take the Cipher from her. I no longer believe she will stumble upon us here. I have already radioed for a plane and it has been dispatched. Before we leave, we will destroy the house and the landing strip and the jeep– even the graveyard. Destroy it all. I want to leave nothing behind. Not a trace."

"And what would you have me do, *mein Herr*?"

Der Klinge sighed dramatically and shook his head. "*Durchsuchen sie die insel und finden sie das verdammte mann!*"

Softly, Dufort asked, "What did he say, sir?"

Von Faust, face red with anger and worry, turned to Dufort and shouted, "Lessard is missing, yes? SO FIND HIM!"

***

Sitting on a small outcropping of rock and watching the sea, Black Fang Delacroix smoked a strong *Gauloises* cigarette and thought about his past and his future.

Now, I know Fang is French, but he's not terribly existential. In this case, I mean his *immediate* past and his *immediate* future.

He did not regret killing Lessard, not for a minute. He had his reasons. But what was Fang's endgame? He may have been press-ganged into service to the Cabal, but once part of their legion, he'd done little to extricate himself from their clutches. And now he was trapped. He'd witnessed the arrival of the rogue ship with no small amount of concern. He also understood that in addition to everything else falling apart, it was only a matter of time before the ambiguous *THEY* located Lessard's body.

Those rogues are here to take the relics from the cottage, he thought. *Once that is done, Der Klinge will want to abandon this place, perhaps then return to Germany*. The thought shook Fang. As a Frenchman who had lived through the Great War, he had no great love in his heart for Germany, and certainly no burning desire to visit Berlin. Frankly, it had occurred to him that it was quite possible he would not be welcomed on the passenger manifest to Berlin, either.

Intelligent man that he was, Fang understood that his death lurked not far away, and it would certainly close on him if given the chance.

And now he'd taken what some may describe as "desperate" measures. Well, desperation was something Fang understood all too well. But what was his next move? He smoked his *Gauloises* and watched the tide rise, thinking.

He'd made his move, and as in any good game of chess, now he had to wait. Yes, he had to be patient and see how things were to play out. And Black Fang Delacroix, sensing that the end of his character arc could quite possibly be near, had no intention of dying without a fight.

CHAPTER 26: Lily and *Le Duc* Travel the Remaining Miles To Where All of Our Heroes Will Find Themselves Neck-Deep in Peril (aka The Last Slow Chapter, I Promise)

The great Quincy Max had, at this point in our twisted tale, made contact with a number of characters including Archibald Nero (in Scotland), Mignonette Tati (in Tangier), Andrew the intrepid assistant (in Sevilla), and perhaps some others who will, at this juncture, go unnamed. He had not made contact with our dear Dr. Liliana Halifax or her mysterious masked compatriot, *Le Duc*.

Not until now, I should say.

When the small single prop Cessna DC-6 touched down on the private landing strip outside of the Faroe Island's capital city of Tórshavn, a mustachioed courier was waiting.

The door opened and out came Lily and *Le Duc*, mid-argument. The howling western wind was not enough to cease their bickering.

"If I've told you once, *Monsieur*, I've told you a thousand times, I am *spoken for*. Do you not understand this simple sentiment?"

Apparently, *Le Duc* did not. Frankly, dear reader, I believe both *Le Duc* and Archibald need to be presented with a good lecture on gender equality and women's rights, as they can be rather overbearing, but alas.

"But *mon chérie*, you are not married. I do not understand, no."

Lily sighed, something that she was beginning to find quite exhausting. However, before she could begin an umpteenth tirade, our silent courier made himself known with a slight wave of his hand.

Lily, grateful for a diversion, trotted away from *Le Duc* as the Cessna's engine returned to life. Slowly, the wheels started rolling and the chartered single engine craft began to pull away, leaving our adventurers at their chosen destination.

"*Mon chérie?*" *Le Duc* asked.

As Lily approached, the courier said, in a deep, nordic accented voice, "Dr. Halifax?"

"Yes?"

The courier extended a clipboard. "Sign here please."

Lily scrawled her name across a paper with a borrowed pen. "What is this–"

Before she could finish, the courier handed her a sealed envelope and turned away, making a silent exit. Little did Dr. Halifax know, but the poor man had stood sentinel for nearly fourteen hours awaiting her arrival.

She opened the envelope. "Good lord!" she laughed. "It's from Dr. Max?"

"Who?" *Le Duc* asked.

"Quincy," she continued, smiling. "He found me. And that means–"

"We've come to the right place," *Le Duc* finished for her, grinning himself. "*Dieu seul aurait pu deviner*. What luck! And so our deductions were correct! Bless those *foutu* flight plans!"

"Archibald is here, and Miette, as well," she continued reading. "Quincy says he knew in his heart I would find this place. Oh bless him." She turned her attention back at the telegram. "It seems Archibald escaped the Cabal's clutches, but was forced to leave Hugo behind." Her face paled as she looked up. "Left him behind...?" she said aloud. "I don't..."

Le Duc took a step towards her, her obvious concern bringing out a different side of him. "Do not fear, *mon chérie*, I am sure that if he is all you describe him to be, he is quite safe."

She swallowed and struggled to meet his eye. "I just..."

"You have faith in him and his abilities, do you not?"

"Yes, of course."

"Then, Liliana, do not fear."

She took a deep breath and nodded. "You're right. I know Hugo. And I believe in my heart that he is safe. He is alive."

"*C'est ça*!" he said. "You have it now. What else does your friend say?"

Lily continued reading silently. After a moment, she said, "Quincy says a nearby station received a strange radio broadcast with coordinates."

"Coordinates?"

Lily nodded. "Quincy had the porter waiting here with the telegram because this is the Faroe Islands most heavily used private strip, but we should be north of here."

"*Au nord d'ici*?" *Le Duc* asked. He turned his attention skyward just as the Cessna disappeared behind a dark cloud. "But our plane is... gone."

Lily lamented letting their pilot leave so quickly, but their charter terminated at Tórshavn, which is where they now stood.

"We'll need to find an alternative means of transportation," Lily said, folding the telegram and slipping it into her vaquera's coat. She still wore her long coat and *cordobés* hat, both quite strange for her current clime. In the cool northern air, she shivered. "And perhaps some new clothes."

Le Duc, shelving his more lascivious comments (at least for the moment), turned his attention to the sprawling village arranged down the rocky plateau from where they stood.

Nestled around the rocky coastline was a village dominated by brightly colored and blockish two-story houses framing a harbor crowded with a multitude of ships, both large and small. As the wind continued from the west, a wet fog began to creep in off the ocean.

"What do you know of this place, *Monsieur*?" Lily asked, reflexively tightening the strap to Brick's nigh forgotten bag, still safely containing the Cipher of Dumuzid and the Eye of Aja.

"Very little," *Le Duc* said. "And there is but one way I know to become acquainted with a place," he said. "Go there."

With that, he started down a curving roadway leading into the heart of Tórshavn, capital city of the Faroe Islands.

***

Restless as you and I both grow, dear reader, let us fast forward beyond the compulsory exploration bit and the requisite selling of jewels for Faroese currency, to say nothing of the clothes shopping, failed flirtations of the Frenchman, or eating of Faroese cuisine–including whale meat, potatoes, puffin, skerpikjøt, and Föroya Bjór pilsner–and move straight to what we're waiting for:

"Curse this ridiculous land," *Le Duc* spat. *"Si je voulais être piégé avec des moutons, j'irais à l'Ecosse!"*

"Stop complaining," Lily said as they passed over a bump in the road. "This was the first ride I could find."

Lily and *Le Duc* sat huddled in the back of a rusted lorry, sharing minimal space in the bed with white-faced Faroe sheep, their woolen coats wet and pungent.

"Je suis Français, et je crois que je mérite la dignité!" he grumbled.

"Yes, *Monsieur*, I know!" Lily grumbled right back. She'd been with the Frenchman for too long, discovering that he seemed to vascillate between two distinct moods: amorous and fussy.

Of the two, she would choose the latter, if pressed, but only just.

Traveling north by road was slow and arduous, and our adventurers had already been trundling through the cold, green Faroese hills for nearly two hours, the lorry winding around big curves and crossing between flat-topped mountains. Before departing Tórshavn, they'd acquired a map, marking out in pencil the coordinates that Quincy had sent. The dot was in the hills of the island of Borðoy, north of the main island Streymoy onto which they'd arrived. The coordinates came up near an abandoned settlement called Strond, not far from the large settlement Klaksvík. Yes, it's confusing; Lily thought so too. She was, however, gladdened to see that the distance between Tórshavn and Klaksvík was a scant 15 miles as the crow flies. By road, however, it was almost 50 demanding miles and one stretch of rough, cold water.

"Will we ever arrive?" *Le Duc* moaned as they rumbled over another bump in the road. Beside him, a sheep bleated *BAAAAAA*, apparently in response.

Before *Le Duc* could manage a quippy response, the lorry hissed to a stop.

Slowly, our adventurers stood, raising themselves on sore legs above the sheep heads to discover a vista overlooking the snowcapped mountains of Kunoy and Kalsoy, in the distance the high peak of Enniberg stood, casting a shadow over the settlement of Klaksvík, nestled deep and hidden by the surrounding moutains.

The only thing standing in their way was a hair less than three miles worth of frigid ocean.

"We need to get over there," Lily said, pointing.

"No," *Le Duc* said, smiling. "We just need to get down there."

They were stopped at a curve in a road. If you continued down the hill from the steep curve, there lay at the ocean's edge, a tiny settlement, almost lost in the emerald green of the fields.

"That is Leirvík," the driver said from his open window, pointing. "Boat is down there."

"Thank you, Nóa!" Lily called. She turned to *Le Duc*. "Up and over," she said, as she climbed out of the truck's bed and leapt to the ground. *Le Duc* was one step behind her.

As they started down the hill towards Leirvík, the

lorry rumbled off, leaving them to the last leg of their journey. Walking silently, Lily checked her bag, found the Cipher and Eye still where they belonged. She checked her hip and found the pistol, fully loaded. Briefly, the image of the dead Nigerian chap flitted through her mind and she shivered. Was she willing to kill again? Was she able?

It was almost time.

In the quiet harbor of Leirvík, *Le Duc* paid a man named Rókur 2000 kroner–the remainder of their money–in exchange for his services. They gave him their map, pointing at the small pencil dot. In broken English, Rókur promised them one way passage to which they agreed.

Weathering a brief rainstorm as they crossed the channel on Rókur's small fishing trawler and winding their way through an ever-narrowing passage between the hulking mountain of Kunoy and approaching hills of Borðoy, everything seemed to be working out well. Quite well, in fact.

Things changed when they heard the gunfire. It rolled off the foggy, green hills of Borðoy like peals of thunder.

They had arrived.

CHAPTER 27: Boom Boom Boom Boom

Gunfire.

Black Fang Delacroix was on his fourth *Gauloises* when the first hammer struck the first firing pin, igniting a little bit of powder and firing the bullet (for the record, the very first fired was a .455 from a Webley Mk VI–if you're curious) into the air. The echo from that first shot echoed endlessly through the fjord. The round in question was fired by one of the rogues at one of our intrepid heroes–who? we will probably never know.

Dropping his *Gauloises*, Fang stood and bolted across a narrow expanse of green towards the cottage and blackened remains of the barn Brannigan and Nero had burned down so many pages previous. The gunfire was coming from the beach a few hundred yards to his left, and Fang could hear a smattering of languages through the fog–a hail of German rising above the rest.

Automatic fire came next, a fierce hurricane of fire from an apparent phalanx of soldiers, followed by the deep *BAROOOOM* of a double-barrel shotgun. Somewhere in the fog, someone laughed.

Someone else screamed.

How many men are besetting this island? Fang asked himself as he crossed over a ridge and came within sight of the Cabal's cottage. However many there were, it sounded like a bloody army.

The machine gun fire returned, and Fang would have sworn there were at least 10-12 men. He kicked open a side door and rushed into the small house, blinking his eyes to adjust to the darkness.

"*Aufhören!*" a voice shouted.

Fang skidded to a halt. "It is me," he said. "It's Fang."

"*Dumm Franzose!*" *Der Klinge* cursed, lowering a Luger. "I should kill you where you stand. Where is your weapon?"

Fang scowled at the old man. "I am here to arm myself," he said. "Where are the guns?"

"Most are gone," *Der Klinge* said as he stuffed a bundle of papers into an attaché case. "Almost everything is loaded onto the ship. It's moored around the coast," he waved his hand nebulously to the southeast. "If you can find a pistol, it's yours."

Fang looked around the cottage as his eyes adjusted to the dim interior. The room seemed stripped, the radio was smashed, the maps and cache of weaponry gone. On the floor beside *Der Klinge*, a trapdoor was open, exposing a square of darkness below.

"Where you are going?" Fang asked, scouring the floor for a pistol.

Der Klinge sealed the case and made for the rear doors as a rapid *tatatatatat* of gunfire raked across the front of the house, shattering glass.

"To the cutter, fool! We're sailing for Viðareiði. The last transmission warned of a possible incursion from the south. With this," *Der Klinge* continued, slipping the attaché over his shoulder, "the plane will not land. It is too risky."

"There is a second landing strip in Viðareiði?"

Der Klinge nodded. "If you're not on the ship by the time I get there, you'll be left behind." The old man relished that last bit a little more than necessary. "Understand?"

Fang nodded. "And what of–"

"Von Faust!" *Der Klinge* interrupted, unknowingly completing Fang's question.

From the open hatch, Von Faust's head appeared. Sweat ran down his bald head. "Almost ready, *mein Herr*," he said. "Shindo is almost–"

"Leave that *amerikanisch* to complete it. Take this," he said, extending the attaché to Von Faust. "I trust he can complete it competently!" He scowled at Von Faust, the frown rife with meaning.

"Sir, I–"

"What of the landing strip? And the jeep?"

"Rigged to explode, sir. I put enough dynamite inside the frame to leave a crater the size of–"

"Then let's go."

"But what of the invading forces, sir. Dufort and Konig and the pirates are fighting them, but I believe we should offer assistance before–"

"The cutter is loaded, Von Faust. *Zur Hölle mit den anderen*! They should not have turned their backs. As I told Fang," *Der Klinge* pointed. "If you are not on the ship, you will be left behind."

Shindo emerged from the dark basement, a devious smile on his face. "The fuse is set for about fifteen minutes," he said. "But I wouldn't push it."

"Thank you, Mr. Shino," *Der Klinge* said. "Now... let's go."

***

On her arrival, Lily did that which never would have occurred to her prior to becoming a formidable adventuress: she ran *towards* the gunfire.

Le Duc had trouble keeping up, his replacement royal blue cape flapping in the wind as Rókur's trawler disappeared into the mist behind them.

"Wait, *Mademoiselle*! We must proceed with caution if we–"

"I'm too close now!" Lily shouted back at him. "Hugo is close by, I know it!"

Climbing a steep hill, Lily leapt over a low rock wall only to crash into a young red headed woman, toppling her and tumbling to the ground in a heap.

"'ELP ME A*RR*CHAY!" the redhead hollered, her skinny arms and legs flailing beneath Lily.

"What? Who are–"

"Liliana!"

Lily looked up to see Nero stumbling towards her, a 30.06 rifle held across his chest.

"Archibald! You're safe!" Lily called, beginning to pick herself up.

The Brit smiled. "Reasonably so! I was more worried about you, frankly. Getting left behind back at Gibraltar after I'd gone bloody mad from that worm–"

"Git offa me, if ye please!" Emma shouted from beneath Lily.

"Oh, I'm so sorry," Lily said, pulling herself upright.

"I see you've met Emma," Nero smiled. "Emma, this is my friend, Dr. Liliana Halifax."

"Please, call me Lily–"

"Oh, hallo, I'm Emma–"

"–you've lovely hair, Emma–"

"–an ye've got a grand–"

A volley of gunfire ripped through the casual meeting of friends, reminding our collection of heroes that they were still in a damned war zone.

Lily and Emma knelt as Archibald turned and fired a pair of shots from his rifle, ratcheting the bolt after each shot.

From behind them, *Le Duc* spilled over the wall in one of his less graceful maneuvers, landing prone on the grass beside the Scottish nurse.

He raised himself to his knees and looked at Emma. "*Oh, mon amour, vos yeux sont une merveille. Qu'est-ce que je donnerais pour vous emmener au lit et déguster vos lèvres et le corps.*"

Without pause, Emma unleashed an open handed slap that crossed *Le Duc*'s face like a frying pan and sent him tipping back into the stone wall.

"I speak bloody French ye feckin pig!" she said. Turning to Lily, she asked, "An who's thess masked buffoon, anyway?"

Lily could not help but smile. "An acquaintance," she said. "But don't hold it against me."

"Onward," a voice called from over a low rise. "We need to take the cottage. I believe I have *les sales voleurs* on their heels."

Lily turned to see Miette–loaded for bear and weighed down with perhaps a dozen firearms of miscellaneous sizes and calibers–waving them on.

"Miette!" Lily called.

"*Bonjour, Doctor!*" she said, smiling. "Would you like a weapon?"

***

(00:14:44 until Shindo's detonation)

Miette, now three guns lighter but not an ounce less determined, led our motley crew of heroes up an embankment towards the cottage. She carried her customary pair of machine guns, heavy calibre canons a 300 pound ruffian would have trouble handling. Miette, on the other hand, handled them with aplomb. She emptied round after round through the fog-thickened air, scattering the band of rogues like cockroaches.

Behind her, Nero fired his 30.06 occasionally while Lily and *Le Duc* wielded small arms. Emma, regretting more every moment her presence on the island, carried a satchel of ammunition and grenades.

"*Je ne peux pas croire que vous êtes ici!*" Miette admonished *Le Duc*. "What did you hope would happen? I would kiss your feet?"

"*Je ai pensé que peut-être que vous me pardonner?*"

"*Après avoir baisé cette femme de Suède, je ne vais pas jamais vous pardonner!* You will die alone, *Duc*, and you will never be in my bed again!"

"Don't say that, *mon chérie, Je te aime beaucoup!*"

A pale skinned rogue with a claw-like scar lancing across his face burst from the mist with a pair of long knives in hand. Miette, closest to the man, lowered one machine gun and swung it at the rogue like a bat, catching him across the face, crushing his nose. He collapsed to the ground in a burst of blood. She leveled a machine

226

gun at his face, preparing to introduce him personally to the .45 round.

"Не убивайте меня!" the man said.

"*Je ne parle pas russe*," Miette said before pulling the trigger.

"Good lord," Lily said, taken aback.

"Well, does anyone speak Russian?" Miette asked the group.

No one responded.

"No, I thought not. We have no time for prisoners. We must find Hugo and leave this island."

"Remember, Quincy also said to be mindful of relics," Nero said. "If we find any relics–"

"I do not do this for relics," Miette interrupted. "I do this for my friend Hugo. I owe him my life. If you want relics, *Monsieur* Nero, you find them." She stepped over the rogue's body and continued on.

Miette's a cold fish, remember, dear reader?

When she turned back to the mist-entombed cottage, a muzzle flashed from one of the broken windows and a round slashed through Miette's shoulder.

"*Fils de pute!*" she shouted, reeling onto her back foot.

Le Duc rushed to her aid as a tripod-mounted Browning machine gun opened fire from beside the cottage.

The rogues had finally mounted a proper defense.

The rapid *BOOMBOOMBOOMBOOMBOOM* of the browning sent our heroes running in all directions. Nero grabbed Emma's arm and pulled her to the right, away from the cottage towards a large lichen-covered boulder about twenty yards away. *Le Duc* backpedaled with

Miette, pulling her towards the rock wall from which he and Lily had emerged previously.

Lily, alone, sprinted to the left, crossing in front of the cottage and running towards a faded red shed for cover. Behind her, 7.62mm bullets tore into the turf after her every step. She fired ineffectually over her shoulder until she reached the shed, crashing into the door and collapsing inside. Desperately, she kicked the door shut behind her.

Bullets ripped through the clapboard shack, kicking up splinters and dirt as rounds zipped over her head.

As the Browning ceased fire–perhaps, she hoped, to reload–she pulled herself up off the ground and ran towards the shed's back wall, pocked with enough quarter-sized bullet holes as to become porous, and kicked a hole through it. She raced through, turning a sharp corner to try and come around behind the Browning when she ran into a wall.

No, it wasn't a wall.

It was Konig. Remember him?

CHAPTER 28: A Few More Shots Are Fired

(00:13:02 until Shindo's detonation)

Nero collapsed onto Emma after the twenty-yard scramble to the boulder. Bullets tore through the air behind them, a few rounds *ping*ing off the huge rock. Panting, Nero looked down at Emma.

"Are you all right?" he asked. "You're not hit are you?"

The young Scottish lass was crying. "No I'm no shot," she said. "I'm jes no cut oot fer this. I'm so*rr*y, Archay, I came because you were kind and exciting, but I–"

Another volley of gunfire bounced off the boulder, spraying stone fragments and lichen into the air and down on our heroes.

She shook her head. "I jes... I made a mistake comin 'ere."

Nero felt something tug at his heart. This wasn't [just] a primal thing, he realized. He softly put one hand to her cheek. "I'm sorry, Emma. Terribly sorry. I should have known better than to bring you here. I was selfish. I asked you because I didn't want to be away from you."

"Es tha rully troo?"

"I'm sorry. Yes, it is true. And this is not like me! Not

like me at all!" Despite all the awful things happening (of which there were many) he laughed. "Bloody hell, no, it's not like me!"

"Can I go bock?" she asked. "I don belong 'ere, truly. Amma nurse!"

"No," Nero agreed, "you don't belong here. I'm grateful you came, but you're right, you don't belong here."

The young lass shook her head, terrified as the Browning returned to life. *BOOMBOOMBOOMBOOM*.

"I could go bock to–"

"There is no where to go," Nero said over the sound of the Browning. "The freighter dropped us here and will come back when we radio for it. There should be a radio in the cottage, but until we call for help, it's gone."

Emma closed her eyes, a lonesome tear running down her red cheek.

"I'll take care of you, I promise."

"Will ye now?"

"Aye," Nero smiled. "I will."

"I have to be strong now, don't I?"

Nero nodded. "You do. And we'll make it out of this. This is how adventures are written, don't you know?"

Emma laughed. "I dinna think of tha," she said. "I jus hoped it'd be a bet easier, is all."

Nero smiled. "Nothing involving bullets is ever easy," he said. "Nor should it be."

He lifted himself off her and into a kneeling position. With one hand, he helped her up and peered over the boulder, his 30.06 still handy.

"Why not slip a hand in there and give me a grenade,

love?"

"A whot?"

"A grenade."

She slipped her hand inside and pulled an oblong, pineapple-reminiscent object from her satchel and passed it to him.

"This is a Mills bomb," Nero said. "It's a fragmentation grenade, and it should buy us some time to get closer to the cottage. I just pull this pin..." he pulled it free with a *clink*, and peered over the boulder once more, holding down the explosive's safety lever with one hand.

From his vantage behind the boulder, Nero could see the cottage about forty yards to his left. The pirates had marshaled their forces and currently swam across the front of the cottage like gnats. With Miette wounded and *Le Duc* tending to her, their major source of return fire was currently silent.

It was time for Nero to get involved. He'd been a spectator long enough.

He pulled his arm back, preparing to throw the Mills bomb at the cottage when he stopped. Something was moving through the mist, slowly and stealthily away from the cottage.

"What the bloody hell...?"

"Whot es et?"

"Do you see that?"

Emma took a breath, building her courage, and rose up, just enough to peek over the rock.

"Whot?"

"Over there, to the right."

Emma turned her head. At first, there was nothing.

After a moment, however...

"Aye, I see et," she said. "It's a g*rr*oup of men slippin 'way through the fog, es it."

Nero frowned. "That's what I thought, too, but there are at least four people. And it's not Brick. It's that old German bastard and the torturer, Shindo."

Emma squinted. "There's another t*rr*io, as'well. A bald one... and... I canna see the otha.s"

Nero snuck a peek once more. "Well I'll be dipped in treacle and fried in Colman's, it's bloody Fang." He shook his head. "That sneaky bastard is still alive. Now where in the name of Mad King George is Brick??"

"We'll find hem," Emma said, touching Nero's arm. She was calming, slowly coming to terms with the extreme situation into which she'd been dropped. "Whot do ye wont to doo?"

Eyes locked on Fang, Nero said, "THIS!" just as he released the lever and launched the Mills bomb in the Frenchman's direction.

The grenade bounced through the emerald grass and rolled to a stop about four feet from the sneaking group (or in this case: *Der Klinge*, Von Faust, Shindo, Dufort, and Black Fang).

"*Granate*! *Bewegen*! *Schnell*!" Von Faust shouted, turning away from the grenade and leaping for cover.

His compatriots followed suit as the small explosive detonated, spraying shrapnel across the field.

A moment later, screams cut through the gunfire. Nero looked up to see bodies scattering. Von Faust had raced uphill, away from the smoldering crater and the old man. *Der Klinge* was on all fours, crawling away from the cottage in the general direction they had been going.

Fang was prostrate on the ground, blood covering his face. Beside him lay what remained of Dufort.

"Where the bloody hell is Shi–"

As if conjuring the American torturer, Mr. Shindo jumped over the rock, one hand holding a knife, one clutching for Nero's throat. The two collided and tumbled backwards. Nero shouted something unintelligible as he dropped his rifle and Shindo closed his hand over Nero's windpipe.

"You??" Shindo rasped. "I cannot believe you have returned, you filthy dog Englishman. You survived me once, but *you will not survive me again*!"

He lowered the serrated edge to Nero's jugular and pressed down, the blade cutting through the top layer of skin and unleashing a long, thin rivulet of blood.

Now, these are the kinds of situations that truly do test a person's mettle. And Emma Louise Duffy, loyal nurse of Balfour's Hospital in Kirkwall, Scotland UK, did not shy away.

From the long grass at her feet, Emma lifted Nero's rifle and aimed it at Shindo.

"Have you ever imagined this moment?" Shindo asked. "The minute of your death? I almost envy you! This is a once in a lifetime experience!"

Nero, his face quickly turning blue, grappled ineffectually at Shindo.

Emma leveled off and aimed at Shindo, her pale hands shaking like a leaf. In this moment before pulling the trigger, when so many novices freeze up, Emma did something remarkably smart (for which Nero would later thank her endlessly). She did not fire.

She was no fool. She'd never fired a gun in her life. If she even managed to muster the courage to pull the trigger, there was only the slimmest chance in hell that she would hit Shindo.

So she lowered the rifle, turned it butt-out in her hand, and swung it, cracking the gun against Shindo's temple like a baseball bat.

The torture artist's eyes rolled back in his head. As his grip loosened, Emma jumped at him, knocking him off Nero before his weight could push the knife downward, finishing the job.

As Shindo collapsed in the grass, she raised the rifle again and gave him a few more good whacks just for posterity.

That was the end of Mr. Shindo. Goodbye, sir.

Coughing, Archie caught her hand on the fourth or fifth swing.

"Wait," he coughed, "Emma, it's all right. He's done for!"

She turned to him, eyes wide, struggling to catch her breath. "Oh, aye... I jus wonted to make sure!"

Nero smiled. "I am–" he coughed. "–grateful!"

"Course I wud doo somethin," she said. "Didja think I'd jes watch ye die?"

"Well, no–"

"Bloody 'ell, he cut ye dinnae he?"

Nero ran a hand across his neck, feeling blood running freely. "It's not deep," he said. "I don't think..."

"Es not," Emma agreed. "But we need to be careful, eh? No more surprises!"

Nero nodded. "Speaking of..." he peered over the rock once more.

Other than a smoking crater, Von Faust, *Der Klinge*, and the bloodied Fang were gone.

***

(00:11:14 until Shindo's detonation)

"Let me go, damnit!" Lily said, struggling against tightly bound ropes on her wrists and ankles. "Or I swear Hugo will have your–"

"Shut up!" a scar-faced rogue shouted, tying a tourniquet around his thigh. Blood was streaming out of a bullet wound Lily imagined Miette had caused.

She was inside the cottage, bound and deposited in a corner. She couldn't see much from her vantage, but she could hear the gunfire waning. Considering there were at least four rogues in the cottage along with the German giant, that was a bad sign.

Where is Miette? she wondered. *Where is Nero?*

"*Precisamos voltar para o navio!*" one of the pirates said from the shadows by a front window. "*Eles vão nos deixar para–*"

"I speak not Portuguese!" the scar-faced rogue shouted in broken English. "I do not understand your words."

The Portuguese pirate looked out the window, a long-barreled machine gun in his hands. "We need to go to the boat," he said. "I think they leave us."

"The hell they will," a third pirate said, from the back of the room. He was tall, almost as tall as the German giant who stood silently at the front door, blood smeared across his face from a wound at his hairline. "They aren't going anywhere without me."

"Without *us*, you mean," a fourth pirate said. He was short and had braided blonde hair. "They won't leave without *us*."

"You can do what you want, I don't care for you," the bloody pirate said. "I know I won't be left to die on this frozen mountain." He turned his attention to Lily. "Search the woman."

She shook against her restraints, all too aware of the bag around her shoulder and the artifacts that it contained. "If you touch me–"

Moving with surprising speed, the giant Konig was upon her, slapping her across the face with a huge hand.

Lily cursed him, scowling up at his huge, looming form.

"You will pay for that," she growled.

In response, the giant tore the strap on Hugo's bag, lifting it from her shoulder and ripping it open.

Even in the darkness, she could see the giant's eyes open in wonder at what he'd found.

"You give that to me or I'll–"

A single shot rang out, cutting through the quiet that had fallen, and a bullet ripped through the cottage in a spray of blood.

The blonde pirate collapsed to the ground, dead.

The men inside scattered for cover.

Lily uncharacteristically laughed. "Let me go and you will be spared," she said. "Because outside there's a Frenchwoman prepared to destroy this whole island..."

The scar-faced rogue opened fire through the window, but from her vantage on the ground, Lily could see that the fog was rolling in, thicker than ever. Wind was blowing off the ocean, carrying with it a blanket of the purest white, both cold and wet, reducing visibility to almost nil.

"*Eu não posso ver uma coisa maldita...*" the Portuguese pirate muttered, aiming his rifle at nothing. "*Eu não podia ver um–*"

A second shot from outside traveled through the *pirata*'s eye and out the back of his head.

Lily turned her face away as he collapsed onto the ground. "I warned you," she said finally. "You may want to give up."

Scar-face turned to her in all his ugly glory. "You do not suggest anything, woman," he said. "We have you, and we have your treasure," he said, gesturing at the bag still in the giant's hands. "I do not understand where your courage comes from, but–"

"I have courage because I know we will win and you will lose. Such is the faith instilled by a man named Brick Brannigan. We have come this far for him, and we will not leave without him."

The scar-face rogue screwed up his face and said, "Who the hell is Brick Brannigan?"

Before Lily could answer, Konig turned to Lily, and in his deep, nigh inaudible voice, he moaned, "Brick... Brannigan... is... *DEAD*."

Lily's mouth hung open as all the blood drained from her face. She tried to speak and couldn't. She could barely breathe.

"What did you say?" she whispered.

CHAPTER 29: Miette Does What Miette Does; Tick Tock Tick Tock

(00:09:57 until Shindo's detonation)

Before any of the ruffians could answer Lily's desperate question, there came a shout from outside.

"Lily! Lily, are you there? Are you all right?"

It was Nero. Brought out of a daze by a distant familiar sound, Lily turned towards the shattered bungalow's windows. "Y-y-yes..." she said softly.

"Lily?"

"Y-yes!" a little louder this time.

"Have they hurt you?" he continued.

"N-n-n-no," she replied, her mind still a flurry of horrible images. "A-A-Arch... they say H-Hugo is... *dead.*"

As she called through the windows, the diminished number of rogues moved around the blown out remains of the cottage's front study while Konig stood over Lily, contemplating his own next move. Behind him, the scar-faced rogue and the bloody pirate limped from window to window, checking their ammunition and trying to get a bead on Nero.

"And you believed them?" he asked.

"W-w-why would they lie?" she asked, her lower lip beginning to quiver slightly as the impact of Konig's news began to resonate deep in her core.

"If I believed every salty dog who promised Brick's death, the old bastard Yank would be dead twenty times over, dear," he called, a jaunty laugh in his voice. "Remember hope? Where is that adventuress' spirit?"

Lily took in a deep breath and looked around. Here she was, tied up in a burned out cottage on the rocky coastline of a faraway land, surrounding by pirates and a murderous giant–to say nothing of the priceless, volatile artifacts that were under her protection (until very recently). If there was one thing she'd learned, it was never to write off anyone or anything.

This world is infinitely stranger and more mysterious that I'd ever imagined, she thought. *Why stop believing that now?*

"You're right, Arch!" she called. She looked up at Konig, then over at scar-face and the bloody pirate. "There are three of them in here," she said. "Come and get me out of here. Then we can go save Hugo."

Nero's laugh echoed through the fjord like a witch's cackle. Konig turned to the sound, wary, as though he knew what it heralded: a villain's doom.

When Nero finally stopped laughing, he called, "It's not me they need to worry about, Lily!"

Even before he'd finished speaking, the back door to the cottage exploded open, revealing Miette in all her French glory. Two Tommy guns were leveled straight ahead, a spattering of blood staining an otherwise impeccable ensemble (what else would you expect?).

"*Je suis désolé, mais je suis ici pour vous tuer tous*," she said simply before pulling both triggers.

The guns roared to life. In the small space, they

sounded like the very core of the Earth was splitting in two. Scar-face and the bloody pirate were dead within a heartbeat, Miette's smoking barrels mowing them down before they could turn their guns in her direction.

Konig was a different story.

A barrage of bullets ripped across his massive frame, but seemed to do little more than break the skin before the giant tucked Lily's bag beneath his arm, took off across the room, and crashed through the far wall. Miette turned, aiming her guns to follow the behemoth as he ran.

When the guns clicked empty, the stink of cordite filled the small room, overwhelming even the salt air from the ocean.

"*Crétins*," she said, shaking her head at the felled pirates. "I was hoping to be challenged." She spat on the nearest body. "*Si vous nuire mes amis, vous paierez en pintes de sang.*"

Rounding a pile of steaming carnage, Miette peered through the remains of the cottage's north wall.

"*Jésus-Christ*," she muttered. "He passed straight through. *C'est un géant.*" She turned back to Lily. "I hit him, no?"

Lily nodded. "I could've sworn you hit him."

Miette lowered her guns and rested them on the empty drafting table that had once held the Cabal's maps. She ran her hand along the smashed wall. When she took her hand away, it was wet with blood.

"*Oui*," she said. "I hit him."

"Are we okay to come in now?" Archibald called from out front.

"*Oui!*" Miette responded as she loaded fresh

magazines into her guns.

(00:07:43 until Shindo's detonation)

Archibald, Emma, and *Le Duc* stepped into the ruins of the cottage as Miette finished cutting through Lily's bonds.

"Thank you," Lily said, as Miette helped her to her feet.

"*Soyez le bienvenu,*" the Frenchwoman replied. She turned to Nero. "*Où est* Hugo?"

"What?" Nero asked.

"She wonts to know whe*rr* Hugo es," Emma translated.

Miette nodded.

"He does not appear to be here," *Le Duc* added unhelpfully.

"I... uh, well..." Nero made a cursory search of the cottage, finding nothing but blood and bullet holes. He returned empty-handed. "I... I don't know."

"Miette," Lily said, digging into her inside coat pocket. "How good are you at maps?"

"I am not," the Frenchwoman said honestly. "But he is," she nodded at *Le Duc* begrudgingly.

"I am," *Le Duc* smiled.

"Did we ever figure out why he wears that mask?" Archibald asked Emma, his voice low.

"Ummm, noo, I don believe we ded," she said, equally low.

"Why?" Miette asked Lily.

"Because... I don't think we are where we're supposed to be. The coordinates..."

Nero chuckled. "Do you think we got into a gunfight

with the *wrong* villains?"

"No," she shook her head patiently. "We're in the right place to find the Cabal, but we're not quite at the right place for these coordinates."

From her coat, she'd pulled the same map she and *Le Duc* had used to get to the island of Borðoy. They'd marked on the map where Quincy's coordinates were supposed to be. They appeared to be much farther inland than where they currently stood.

"Where did we get these coordinates again?" Nero asked. "Quincy gave them to me, too, but I don't know where he got them."

"They were broadcast," Miette said. "A mysterious radio signal sent the coordinates to a nearby station and was recorded. The transmission included the name Q. MAX and a set of coordinates, nothing else."

"How do you know this again?" Nero asked.

"Quincy told me, of course."

"But who sent the transmission?" Lily asked.

"We do not know," Miette said.

(00:05:02 until Shindo's detonation)

"Let me see the map again," Nero said, taking the creased paper from Lily.

As he did, a deep and roaring blast echoed from nearby, sending shockwaves through the ground. Pieces of shot-up plaster fell from the eaves as the heroes stumbled around the blown out cottage.

"*Qu'est-ce au nom du diable était-ce?*" Miette gasped, steadying herself against a desk.

"Hey, what the hell was that!?" Nero sputtered redundantly.

"An explosion, not far away," *Le Duc* said. "Do you

242

think these men are erasing their tracks?"

"Maybe," Lily said. "If so, we need to get *here*," she pointed at the map coordinates, "quickly. Can you lead me?"

Le Duc nodded. "I think I can."

"Let me come, too," Nero said.

"An me as'well," Emma added.

"No, Em, stay here with Miette," Nero said. "Wait to make sure no one comes back, and take care of Miette. She's been injured, after all. Just remember, Von Faust, Fang, and that old bastard are still missing, so be careful."

"You do not need me to go?" Miette asked.

Nero shook his head. "We'll be all right, just keep an eye on her," he said. He looked into Emma's eyes. "I promised I'd keep her safe."

(00:03:22 until Shindo's detonation)

Miette nodded. "You can count on me, *cochon*."

Nero nodded. He kissed Emma briefly, saying "I'll be back in a flash, love. You'll be safe here, I promise," before slipping out the back door with *Le Duc* and Lily.

"Come back soon, A*rr*chay," Emma called. "I'll be waitin fer ye."

Outside, Lily, Nero, and *Le Duc* believed themselves quite lucky to find a jeep parked near the back door, keys in the ignition.

CHAPTER 30: The First Breath of a Dead Man

The ride was short–only a few minutes. Lily chose to sit in the back, despite Nero's protestations, losing herself in the fog. She did believe that Hugo was alive and well, and there was a wellspring of hope that she'd almost forgotten, still reminding her that the two of them had a long life left to spend together.

The pair of dirt-covered shovels lying in the back seat stared up at her, perhaps questioning her sanity, but she paid them no mind.

When the jeep rolled to a stop, Lily stood, pulling herself upright using the backrests in front of her, her fellow passengers eerily silent. "Well," she said. "Shall we–"

Her voice caught in her throat. Both Nero and *Le Duc*'s silence was much more understandable.

Spread out before the idling jeep was a mist shrouded graveyard, dark, dreary, and dreamy enough to put those recent Universal Studios horror pictures to shame.

"We can't be..." Lily muttered. "This isn't the right place. Is it?"

Le Duc consulted the map and a military compass that dangled from the jeep's rearview mirror.

"It..." he trailed off. "I..."

Lily looked once more at the shovels. *Dead?* she thought. *Is that correct? Can it really be?*

While not one to suffer superstitions, Lily found herself searching her heart, looking for some sign of the truth. *What feels right?* she asked herself. *Trust yourself, Liliana. Is this right? Is Hugo really... gone?*

The answer came like a divine bolt of lightning...

...in the form of a bolt of lightning (perhaps divine? if you're curious, dear reader, ask a holy man somewhere else; ain't no holy men here).

From the fog swallowed sky, a lance of pure white light shrieked through the air, splitting a short willow straight through the trunk from the highest branches to the muddy ground. The smoking halves fell to the ground with a muffled *fwwsshh.*

"Great Scott!" Nero said. "Where did that–"

"Let's go!" Lily said, leaping out of the jeep, shovels in hand. "Trees aren't exactly prevalent on these islands," she said. "And there was no storm here a minute ago. What were the odds of that happening? I'm not one to say such things–as I find them somewhat ridiculous, frankly–but if there was ever a sign–"

"That was it, *mon cher*?" *Le Duc* asked, a faint twinkle in his eye. "I must say, Lily, I admire your faith. But–"

"No room for doubt, Duke," Lily interrupted. "It's not about faith. I know it. I just..." She looked up at him. "You'll see. If you choose not to, stay here."

Nero stepped onto the wet grass. "I'm with you, Lily. Like I said, if I wrote off Brannigan every time someone told me the bastard was dead, I would've lost my friend years ago." He took one shovel from her. "As you said, let's go."

(It should be noted, dear reader, that at this point, Mr. Shindo's countdown had entered extra innings, as it were. Old fashioned fuses, after all, are an imperfect science)

Winding their way through headstones, our adventurers carried themselves with the utmost respect through this village of the dead, the menagerie of gravestones worn and beaten by countless seasons of wind and snow and rain. They were silent, neither Nero nor *Le Duc* certain what they were searching for, but like Lily, hoping beyond hope that if there was something to be found, they would know it when they saw it.

And it was Lily who saw it.

"Here," she said.

She stood between a pair of graves, looking at a six-foot long mound of mud, piled from a recent dig.

Nero and *Le Duc* walked over to her. "Do you think–"

"No, Arch," Lily interrupted. "I *know*."

"But you cannot possibly–" *Le Duc* stopped, concern creasing his face. "If this is–"

Lily silenced him but pushing her shovel deep into the wet earth.

"*Madame,*" *Le Duc* said. "This is just... morbid."

Nero stood watching for a moment as shovel after shovel of damp soil tumbled in a pile beside the gravestone of Kaspar Mikkelsen. The Englishman opened his mouth, perhaps to comfort her, perhaps to admonish her, perhaps to ease her obvious pain, but he was unable. *Surely this is madness, isn't it?*

It's not madness, Nero realized. It's Brannigan.

Le Duc nearly spat when Nero took his place beside Lily and pushed his shovel into the ground.

Together, they dug. When Lily began to tire, *Le Duc* took her place, a pair of fresh hands to blister on the cracked, wooden handle. Slowly, the earth was moved, the pile beside Kaspar Mikkelsen growing taller as the breathing of Nero and *Le Duc* became increasingly labored.

Sweat poring off his face, Nero finally switched off with Lily, taking a break beside the still smoldering willow. In the cool air, steam rose off him as he wiped his wet face with his sleeve.

When *Le Duc* hit something hard, there was a moment of terror. What was it? A rock? A casket? Hugo's skull?

They proceeded with caution, Nero joining them in the pit.

Together, they uncovered a canvas sack.

"*Mère de Dieu...*" *Le Duc* whispered, making the sign of the cross.

Nero looked at Lily, unable to believe what they were doing. "Is that..." he could not even finish the sentence. Was that his friend? Were they really *doing* this? Has this tale really become so macabre?!?

Lily knelt, grabbing the canvas and pulling. She grunted, barely moving it.

"Help me," she said.

"...Liliana," Nero said.

"Help me!"

Regretting it immediately, Nero knelt beside her. Together, the three heroes lifted the canvas sack from the grave, lying it beside the muddy pit in the grass.

Together, they climbed free.

"Liliana, I don't think you should–"

She shook her head. "I know it's going to be all right," she said, although not so sure herself anymore. Was there some sort of divine knowledge at play, or had she become unhinged? She looked at her friend. "I know it."

Kneeling once more, she loosened the knot tied at the top of the bag and yanked it open, realizing how cold the cloth was.

"It's waxed canvas," she said. "It wouldn't have let in any water. It would have kept him dry..."

She pulled it down to reveal... Hugo. Dead.

Lying longways across his body was the shiny metal shape of a curved blade, Fang's scimitar. *Le Duc* had struck it while digging. It was laid over his body *à la* a viking burial, the blade creating a sort of pocket within Brannigan's canvas coffin. She pulled the heavy blade free and lay it on the grass beside her, finally exposing the face of her love.

Hugo was pale and frigid, eyes closed, mouth slightly open. It was, dear reader, terribly morbid (what? I'm just being honest).

Lily shook her head. "There's something..."

Nero knelt beside her. "Liliana..." he said.

"He's not bloating, Archibald," she said. "There are usually signs of death and decay, one of the earliest being bloating, but in this case–"

"It's cold here," he said, shaking his head. "Even colder underground. It wouldn't happen in this climate!"

"What about this?" she asked, touching what looked like dried spit or even foam on his chin. "What is this? Is this the cause of death? Was he poisoned? There are no obvious signs of trauma..."

"Death is a terrible and mysterious passage," *Le Duc* said. "Let us lay your friend to rest and return to–"

"No, damnit!" Lily said, the emotional half of her brain so terribly overloaded that it began to shut off, the curious and stubborn scientist half taking over. She pulled his mouth open, remembering what he'd said to her in Nigeria. "Tetrodotoxin...?" she muttered. "Bufo-toxin... that could explain it..."

His mouth open, she pushed two fingers inside, probing for something.

"Liliana, what are you–? Oh, oh no, please," Nero turned away, shaking his head. "That's just... oh, that's bloody awful."

She shook her head, her actions becoming more and more urgent. "Something's strange," she said. "Someone chose the waxed canvas because it would prevent him from drowning in muck–"

"Drowning?" Nero asked. "He's *dead*, Liliana!"

"–someone put the sword in here and it created a sort of space in the grave, preventing the dirt from crushing down on him. Like an air pocket–"

"–dead, I said," Nero continued. "He's dead!"

"–and here, here is the *coup de grâce*," she said, fingers ceasing their probing, as though they'd located exactly what they'd been searching for.

"–I'm sorry, Liliana, but Hugo is–"

She pulled her hand out, two fingers wet, stained with an off-white colored foam.

"–dead," Nero finished. As he said the final word, his eyes came to rest on her fingers. Mouth open, he cocked his head to the side before asking, "What is that?"

"His back molar is broken," Lily said, her breathing increasing. "I believe he did this on purpose. I believe this is a toxin, the same toxin that saved *our lives* in Nigeria. Have you forgotten?"

"Tetro-what-do-you-call-it?" he asked.

Lily nodded. "Give me something hard. A metal pen or a–"

"Here," *Le Duc* said, pulling a metal lighter from inside his coat. "Will this do, *mon cher*?"

She took it from him. "Let's find out."

Prying his mouth as far open as she could, she slipped her hand inside, the silver lighter tightly in her grasp.

"I'm just guessing," she said, "and *hoping*, but it would make sense if it was the molar opposite..."

She twisted her hand and spun it, slapping the lighter against his back molar as hard as her wrist could manage in the tiny space. Nothing. She tried again. Still nothing.

The third twist cracked the enamel, spilling suspiciously warm liquid into the back of his mouth.

"Oh," she said. "Oh my, it worked." She pulled her hand free, dropped the lighter, as she took his head in her hands, leaning it forward. "Don't aspirate it, darling," she said. "Down your esophagus," she said, her hands moving quickly, "not your trachea."

After a moment, the liquid seemed to have drained out of his mouth. Still, no pulse, no breathing, no nothing. Brick Brannigan was still dead.

"Now what?" Nero asked, a part of him beginning to buy this mad scheme.

"I... well, I don't know," Lily admitted. "I've never

250

done this before."

Le Duc sighed. "I'm sorry, Lily, I fear it is for naught. You had me believing for a moment, but–"

Not thirty feet behind them, one fuse finally defeated the wet weather and did its job as the jeep exploded in a red and orange fireball, launching burning metal and rubber and shrapnel through the graveyard. At the same instant, the explosion fired a burning hot shockwave across row after row of tombstones, scorching the grass and setting the felled willow aflame.

Brick Brannigan, still wrapped in his cold death shroud, sat up with a deep gasp and opened his eyes.

Le Duc, mid-reproach, screamed like a nine year old girl.

Nero burst out in mad, jubilant laughing, the sound carried away by an ember-filled gust of wind.

Lily, eyes wide, hair blowing wildly in the burning rush of air, could only manage to whisper, "Hugo!"

He wrapped his sluggish, half-dead arms around her, pulling her to him as he said, "By the branches of Yggdrasil, I knew you would come for me, my love!"

Nero's laughter was interrupted by a second explosion as the cottage by the shore disappeared in a dynamite borne inferno.

CHAPTER 31: Brick Brannigan Is Not The Only Walking Dead These Islands Have To Offer...

Waiting neither to offer an explanation nor greet his recently resuscitated friend, Nero rose and took off, knowing all too well what that detonation heralded.

Le Duc, his scream silenced by the blast, was only a step behind.

"Wha? Where? Wha?" The Professor shook his head. "I don't know which questions to ask first, my love," he said, grinning like a fool.

"At times like this, I'm almost afraid to ask questions. Questions at times like this only conjure doubt," she said, grinning like quite the fool, herself.

"Well said," Brannigan nodded. "And so you've found me. Am I still on the Faroe Islands?"

Lily nodded, kissing him for the second or perhaps third time. "This island is called Borðoy," she said before kissing him again. "If we weren't here for such an awful reason, I think I'd quite like it!"

"You know," Brick said, sitting in a burial bag not two feet from his previously occupied early grave, "it really is quite a nice place. Downright picturesque!" Lily laughed and kissed him again.

***

Unfortunately, not everything was as joyous.

The cottage was gone, in its place a roaring conflagration erupting from a shallow basement and a debris field that was fifty yards wide. Above the ruins, a column of black smoke rose high into the sky.

Nero collapsed twenty feet from the blaze, the wall of heat too strong to approach further. *Le Duc* met up with him a moment later, breathing heavily, his eyes wet.

"*J'ai été un imbécile, mon amour, ai pris cet avantage de vous,*" *Le Duc* said, finally pulling off his cowl and revealing a face as debonair and handsome as would befit a man like *Le Duc*. He wiped at a tear as it rolled down his face. "I will not see you again. I am a failure of a hero."

Nero sat in the wet grass, his face that of a statue. "I can't... I don't..." He had nothing to say. Something inside was broken. He had promised, after all, hadn't he? And now this.

This wasn't right, was it?

"*Arrête de pleurer, vous chatte. Pensez-vous que je veux baiser un homme qui pleure?*" a voice asked from deep in the fog.

Le Duc turned towards it, eyes wide. "Only my Miette would be so filthy and honest!" he said.

From the mist, two shapes emerged. Yes, of course they were alive.

Nero's breath caught in his throat. "E-Emma?" he asked. "Are you all right?" Quickly, he scrambled to his feet. "Is that you, lass? Tell me that's you!"

"Es me, ye fool eejit!" she said, running towards him.

They embraced, their bodies folding into one as he kissed her gratefully and she let him.

Le Duc ran to Miette, but she turned her chin up at him. "Did you even hear what I said?" she asked, looking down her long aquiline nose at his tears as she straightened her beret.

"But how?" Nero asked. "Why did you leave the cottage? How did you know? It exploded and I thought you were... no, I *knew* you were–"

Miette interrupted him with a sextet of words that truly baffled Archibald Nero:

"It was Fang," she said. "He saved us."

***

They were sitting on a rock wall a few hundred yards from the remains of the cottage, all six of them, each living and breathing and healthy and safe.

The Professor had taken some time to make the trek from the cemetery, even with Lily to help. By the time he'd arrived, Archibald disentangled himself from Emma while Miette had started and ended an argument with *Le Duc* (ah, love). And now here they sat, regrouping as the fires of the island burned.

"Why did he help you?" Lily asked.

"I've noo cloo," Emma said, shaking her head. "He came runnin en an said et was woired to bloow."

"I know why," Miette said simply.

"If there is a reason for Fang's mercy," Brannigan said, "my mind is too death-addled to grab it."

"I don't know if you know this, Hugo," Miette said, "but Fang knew my father. They fought together in the

Great War."

The Professor shook his head. "I didn't know that."

Miette nodded. "Afterwards, they became enemies, as any sane man would of Delacroix. But when my father died, Delacroix... he acted very strangely. It seems he valued his rivalry with my father a great deal. I did not know it until the funeral, but he looked on my father as a close friend. He told me that his struggle with *père* gave him... purpose. It gave him meaning."

"He did it to save you," *Le Duc* said.

"Yes, of course," Miette replied. "Are you not listening, *amoureux*?"

Nero was shaking his head. "I thought I'd killed him. Emma, you saw me throw the grenade–"

"Oh, aye, I ded. He was damned bloody 'e was," she said. "You ded him damage, fer sure."

Miette agreed.

"But he still came back," Brick said, staring off into space, his mind racing.

"Are you all right?" Lily asked, quietly.

"Of course," he said, turning to her. "It's just been, well, quite a day."

"What now?" Nero asked.

"You need to get to the airfield at Viðareiði," an accented voice said from a distance, mangling an already baffling pronunciation. "There is still time."

"What?" Nero asked, turning to face the fog.

"Who said that?" Lily asked.

But Brannigan knew all too well, his hand went reflexively to his hip, finding only an empty holster. It was the immediate and obvious reaction.

Fang strode out of the fog, dried blood smeared across his shrapnel sliced face, grim smile pulling back his lips to reveal his namesake teeth.

"Relax, Hugo," Fang said, "I come not to fight–not now, only to take back that which belongs to me."

The group was silent. Miette raised one of her Thompson .45s from the ground and rested it across her lap.

"Is a wicked man scorned even after saving a pair of innocents?" he asked.

"What do you want, Fang?" the Professor asked, genuinely confused.

"I come to take something, and leave something."

"Take, Fang?"

Fang raised a hand and pointed. "That," he said.

Everyone turned to Lily, who in her right hand absently held the scimitar she'd taken from Brick's burial shroud. She looked down at it, almost as surprised as everyone else to discover its presence.

"This is... yours?" she asked.

Fang nodded. "Can I have it back, please?"

Brannigan took it from Lily and, moving ever so cautiously, passed it back to Black Fang Delacroix, tang first.

"Thank you," he said, returning it to his empty sheath.

"And to leave us?"

"A piece of information," the French villain said. "*Der Klinge* and whatever Cabal stooges yet live will make for the airfield at Viðareiði where they hope to escape." He looked around at the filthy, bloody faces of those he would gladly call his enemies–perhaps Fang's best compliment. "If you hurry, you may still catch them. There is a cutter moored around the island to the southeast."

After a long pause, Brannigan asked, "Why are you helping us, Fang?"

"The whims of a mad man are never to be known, Brick," he said, smiling. (Like, dear reader, why did this French Madman send those coordinates to our friends? Or save the lives of Miette and Emma?) He continued, "But never let it be said that our doings are random or without reason. Now, I will make my exit, for subsequent volumes will surely lack something profound if cursed by my absence."

He smiled, bowing slightly, before turning and disappearing into the fog.

The only sound to accompany his exit was the crackling of fire and the crashing of waves on the shore.

CHAPTER 32: The Last Transitional Chapter Of This Post-Inaugural And Aptly Titled *Volume 2*

Ah, the fog.

In this case, it acted in the same capacity as education did to Horace Mann: it was the great equalizer.

Why, you ask? Because less than two miles away, *Der Klinge*–high-ranking Cabal mastermind and general pain in the tukas for heroes of every ilk–was lost.

He'd been wandering, cursing a *Deutsch* storm, expecting that beyond each outcropping, over each stone wall, around each lichen-stained cliff lay the cutter, loaded to the brim with pilfered artifacts from around the globe.

Unfortunately for him (but fortunately for us, dear reader), the cutter eluded him. The only solace the terrible old man found in his meandering journey was the distant sound of Shindo's dynamite detonating.

And now, standing on a sharp incline, he stopped. He was not tired, much to the contrary, but he did need to marshal his senses. *Der Klinge* had wandered for so long that he'd begun to doubt his own judgment.

"Damn that Fang," he spat. "And Von Faust, useless *idioten. Alles, was sie tun musste, war zu töten* Brannigan *und sein freund*!" He cursed, shaking his head. "It is this fate that we are met with when forced to collude with fools."

Yes, *Der Klinge* was the man who'd first press-ganged Black Fang Delacroix into the service of the Cabal, but don't remind him of that. The same can be said for Von Faust's promotion-laden career. *Der Klinge* had seen something in Heinrich–lord knows why.

"*Meister*?" a low voice seemed to groan through the mist, interrupting *Der Klinge*'s ranting and catching his attention.

He looked up. "*Bist du da, mein kind*?" he asked. "*Sind Sie der einzige gläubige, der noch lebt*?" The old man stood, his black heart beginning to beat faster.

"Come," he said. "Come to me. Follow the sound of my voice!" he called.

From the mist emerged Konig, blood staining his uniform, a bag clenched in one of his massive hands.

Der Klinge gasped, a new feeling of hope beginning to bloom in his chest. Konig had himself visited the cutter earlier that very day, assisting those *nutzlos verdammt piraten*.

Shaking his head, the old man reached out and touched the wounds that peppered the giant's body, dried blood caked against his skin.

"What did they do to you?" he asked.

Konig only whimpered a wordless response.

When *Der Klinge* opened the bag in Konig's hand, his concern fell away.

"Konig, my son," he purred, "you have done well. You have done very, very well..."

***

The crew of heroes stood on the shore, waves crashing against the rocks. They'd gone through the introductions–many, and the expository background tales–ditto, and now they were left to decide what came next.

"What's the plan now, eh Brannigan?" Nero asked, one arm wrapped around Emma's waist. "Find this ship? Get to... what's the place Fang said? Viðareiði?"

"That was an example of poor Faroese pronunciation, Arch. But aye, we must," Brick said, stretching his muscular arms, trying to fight off the stiffness that had set in since, you know, *his death*.

Le Duc leaned over a wide, flat rock, and opened the same map he'd used to locate the Professor's tomb across the stone face as though it were a tabletop.

"*Ici*," he pointed at a tiny dot on one of the northern most islands in the archipelago.

"Bloody hell," Nero said.

"And where are we again?" Lily asked.

"Here, love," Brick pointed.

"Thas bloody far, es et," Emma said, shaking her head. "How doo we git the*rr*?"

It was indeed far, and not a straight shot, either. The Faroe Islands are a twisted mass of jagged, uneven slivers of land, many of them less than a mile wide at their narrowest points. The frigid North Atlantic wound its way between the eighteen islands, creating narrow canals with strong, sometimes violent currents. To complicate matters, a number of the passages curved and bent unexpectedly, often terminating in dead end inlets.

"Oddly enough, it's not that far," Brannigan said, pointing to the map's legend. "It's only maybe fifteen or twenty miles, but as the young lass pointed out: it's no straight shot."

"And, I don't mean to be a wet blanket," Lily said, "but we've got no ship, ourselves. We can't walk there, can we?"

"Whot uhboot yer boat?" Emma asked Lily.

"We paid a man for the trip," she said. "But only one way. What about you?"

"We need th'reydio," Emma said. "The one thot es bock the*rr*," she pointed at the remains of the cottage, still burning heartily.

Everyone looked at each other, a bit... dumbfounded?

And is this how it ends? With our heroes *stuck*? How simplistically anti-climactic! How anti-climactically simple! What a trash literature cop out! How ridiculously–wait! What's that?

"*Regardez ce*," Miette said, pointing. "It seems fate is on our side."

Our hero collective looked southeast and saw the prow of a ship cut through the fog.

"Is the*rr* anythen that *won't* come ootta this fog??" Emma asked.

Brannigan smiled. "Apparently not," he said. "You have to admit, luck does seem to be on our side."

Luck, Brick Brannigan, had nothing to do with it in this case. This was a voyage of *good will*, and a promise made long, long ago (well, Chapter 8), when a Spaniard told Dr. Liliana Halifax that he would take care of her.

Lily laughed, shaking her head in disbelief as the ship's prow turned, revealing its starboard side with the name *Barco Jamón* painted across it.

"Aurelio!" Lily shouted, waving to the Spanish

smuggler.

He stood at the starboard railing, smiling and waving back. His loyal assistant Capo stood at the wheel, grimacing against the wind.

"The salvation of Prospero!" the Professor laughed. "*Mi querido amigo Aurelio, cómo te perdiste...*"

"*Yo no dejaría que usted congela, lo haría?*" Reyes shouted, his hands cupped around his mouth. He rested one hand on his great belly and leaned back, barking a laugh that crossed the expanse of water.

"Who the bloody hell is that chap?" Nero asked. "And why is he *here*?"

"A friend," Lily and Brick said simultaneously.

"*Je ne aime pas que,*" Miette said suspiciously. "He seems so... happy." She frowned.

***

"A man found me in *La Coruña* and told me he was working for a man named... Max something?"

The *Barco Jamón* had anchored at the end of a rocky outcropping, allowing the rotund Aurelio Reyes to make landfall without dampening his trousers. He stood beside our hero gang, trying to explain his rather fortuitous appearance.

"Quincy Max?" Nero asked.

"Reginald Max?" Lily asked.

"*Était-ce* Mortimer Max?" Miette asked.

Aurelio glanced at each person as they spoke. When each had finished he thought for a moment before saying, "No."

"It was Alphonse Max, wasn't it?" Brick said, nodding.

"*Sí, sí, ese es su nombre*," Aurelio replied. "How did you know, *amigo*?"

"Because he is one of the Maxes involved with international shipping, but that is another matter. Anyway, what did this man say?"

"He told me he was looking for a man he could trust. He got my name from Raúl in Gibraltar. I must say, Hugo, there are many people trying to help you–and your lovely assistant." He smiled at Lily.

"*Assistant*??" Lily choked out, agog.

"She's, uh, not my assistant, Aurelio," Brick said. "And yes, the Max brothers are doing a great deal to help us all. They are good and loyal men. Most of them."

"Well, once Raúl gave this Alphonse Max my name, they tracked me to *La Coruña* where they enlisted my help."

"Could they not have located someone... closer?" *Le Duc* asked.

Aurelio shrugged. "For what I am being paid, I would sail to the Galapagos," he smiled. "Not that this is just about money..."

"Oh, of course not," the Professor said. "But how did you know where to find us?"

"I was told to come to these islands. But looking for Brick Brannigan?" Aurelio smiled. "Just follow the smoke and flames." He laughed, and it was hard to argue.

"Now, that's enough of this unnecessary explanation– who really cares, anyway," he said. "So, where are we sailing?"

The fog-adorned ghost of the sun was slipping towards the horizon by the time *Der Klinge* and Konig finally located the cutter. It was moored in a narrow inlet, bobbing up and down on the tide, and it only took *Der Klinge* a moment to notice that the ship was in preparations to set sail. The mainsail had been hoisted, the anchor raised. *Der Klinge* could see Von Faust on deck, shouting orders to one remaining rogue to cleat the halyard and get the ship pointed into the wind, which was now blowing substantially.

Der Klinge pointed Konig forward, and in one deft grab, the giant locked onto the cutter's rail and pulled it towards the jutting rock on which the two Cabal agents stood.

The port side bow slammed against the rocks, forcing the ship to lurch wildly in the water.

"Be careful, you fool! Do you mean to sink us??" Von Faust screamed at the rogue, turning towards the coastline to inspect supposed damage.

When his eyes fell on *Der Klinge* and Konig, the duo climbing over the rail and boarding the cutter, Von Faust froze.

"*Herr* Von Faust," *Der Klinge* said. "Are you preparing to depart?"

"I... uh, no, sir," Von Faust stuttered. "I was simply awaiting your arrival. I believe that–"

"Stop, Heinrich," *Der Klinge* said. "That is enough."

"But, sir–"

"No, Heinrich, you must stop talking now. I am afraid your luck has bounced its last check."

"What?"

Der Klinge scowled. "Where were you after the grenade detonated? You ran like a whipped dog. You should have helped me. Your duty is to secure my safety and the safety of the artifacts. Instead, you only worried about yourself!"

"Sir–"

"Do you not believe I am worth *more* than you, Heinrich?"

"No, *Herr*–"

"Because you are not, Von Faust. You are worth nothing. *Sie sind ein stück scheiße.* I am all that matters."

"Sir, I didn't–"

"Enough!" *Der Klinge* shouted. "That is simply enough."

Von Faust opened his mouth to respond, but out of fear of retribution, he said nothing. Admittedly, he had made many mistakes, yes, but not for lack of effort, nor lack of desire to do right by the old man. This was certainly no different, was it?

"Father," he said after a long silence. "I apologize. Once again, I–"

"You shame me, Heinrich," *Der Kling* said. "Your failures are omnipresent, your presence a curse. You remind me why I hate children."

"–didn't want to–"

Der Klinge turned to Konig, waving nonchalantly with one hand.

"–let you down, but–"

Konig grabbed Von Faust by the neck, and with one deft twist, broke his neck.

Von Faust's body hung lifelessly in the giant's fist, feet dangling a foot above the listing deck.

"Into the water, Konig," *Der Klinge* gestured. "We have much to do, and we cannot be delayed any longer by... him." He waved again. "Get rid of it."

Konig tossed Von Faust's body into the water with all the ceremony of a cigarette butt disposal.

Der Klinge turned to the lone rogue and said, "Now we may go. I want to be at Viðareiði as quickly as possible."

The rogue stared at him, eyes wide.

"I said LET'S GO!"

CHAPTER 33: Take Me To Church

If the Faroe Islands were a pile–and let me tell you, dear reader, this metaphor isn't really *that* bad–Borðoy would be the island fourth from the top. The island just above it, Viðoy, shadows Borðoy closely, so much so that at one point the two land masses are a scant 500 or so feet apart.

But being so near the top of this proverbial pile, Viðoy is one of the least populous of the large islands, one of its few villages being Viðareiði, a small collection of homes on a narrow isthmus between two oppressively large mountains.

By the time the *Barco Jamón* entered Viðareiði's quaint harbor, the sun was beginning to rise on a new day. It was, perhaps, a small number of miles to be traveled, but traversing the winding waterways of the islands proved no small task. And now, with a new day dawning, our adventurers hoped only that *Der Klinge* had faced more delays than they had.

With Nero remanding Emma to the boat (and then refusing to leave her side), our band of six slimmed down to a chubby four as they disembarked at the dock, leaving Nero and Emma in the capable hands of Aurelio and Capo.

"Guns," Miette said, lifting her trusty Tommy guns and making sure they were loaded.

"I'm sorry?" Lily asked.

"We will need guns, no?" She turned to Aurelio. "You have guns?"

The ham smuggler shuffled his feet. "I don't much like guns..." he began.

"...but?" Miette asked.

"I have a pair of pistols and a shotgun. You can take them."

Brick opened his mouth, preparing to volunteer when Lily said, "I'll take the shotgun." She caught Brick's inquiring eye and shrugged. "I went hunting once with my father. I trust myself with a shotgun more than a pistol."

Le Duc just shook his head. "I have my knives," he said, gesturing to his would-be utility belt. "I prefer these when given the choice." That left Brannigan with two pistols and Miette with two .45 Tommy guns. With that, they set off.

The last thing Brannigan heard before the boat fell away behind him was Aurelio ask someone onboard, "Have you ever tried *jamón ibérico*?"

The harbormaster, a tall, gaunt man named Bjarke, knew about fourteen words in English. Luckily, one of them was "plane," and it was only a moment before he was pointing due north towards the looming shape of Mount Villingdalsfjall.

They made slow progress across town, stopping twice to catch their breath.

By 9AM they had made their way through the collections of buildings, coming out the other side to face Villingdalsfjall, its southern face beginning to rise only a few hundred yards away.

"We can stop here," Brannigan said.

"What? Why?" Lily asked.

"Look," he pointed.

There, parked on a narrow strip of land tucked into the mountain's east face, was a plane. It was a duel prop cargo transport, and both props were unmoving in the cold, morning air.

"I'm assuming it's been here for a while, no?" Miette asked.

"It doesn't look as though it's just arrived," Brannigan agreed.

"Which means we arrived prior to this *fasciste*," Le Duc added. "*Il regrettera nous rencontrer!*"

"Exactly," Brannigan smiled. "And by the hammer of Thor, we'll make sure that plane doesn't *ever* take off, no sir. I have no trouble believing that–"

"Hugo, look!" Lily pointed.

On the eastern edge of the isthmus was an old white-steepled church overlooking the bay from a jagged cliff, perhaps a half-mile north of the harbor where *Barco Jamón* was currently moored. Bobbing up and down in the surf just off the coast was a cutter, its black sails unmistakable.

"Damnable poltroons!" Brick shouted. "Of course they would not come into the harbor! They hope to slip past us unawares!"

"There they are now," Miette smirked, ratcheting back the slide on one of her .45s. "I believe I'd like to meet this old man who has caused so much destruction."

"No, Miette," the Professor said. "I will take care of him. I must get the Cipher back. The Cipher is the most important thing now."

Lily groaned. "I'm sorry I lost it, darling. I was captured and–"

"It's not your fault, of course," Brick said. "You cannot be held responsible for the actions of a murderous ruffian. But what's done is done, and we need to make sure that we don't leave without the Cipher, all right?"

Lily raised her double-barrel shotgun. "I'll get it back, love. And like Miette said, I'd like to meet the old man who's caused all this *death* and destruction."

"Death and destruction, a'plenty," Brick said, smiling. "And here they come now."

Over the jagged stone edges of the cliff, Konig's huge paw rose, locking onto an unseen handhold and pulling him up and over the lip. In a moment he was standing on the edge, helping *Der Klinge* pull himself up.

"We must hurry," Brannigan said. "We're positioned equidistant between them and the plane. We must split up!"

Miette looked at him. "I believe splitting up is always the worst option, Hugo. Truly, the worst."

"*Oui, je suis d'accord avec* Miette," *Le Duc* said, nodding.

"Have you noticed you always agree with her?" Brannigan asked the Frenchman. "Also, why do you wear that dreadfully silly mask and cape? Really?"

Before *Le Duc* could respond, the Professor continued, "So it's decided! We split up!"

"But Hugo–" Lily began.

"Miette and *Le Duc*, you take care of the plane," he pointed. "Incapacitate it. Make it useless. But be careful, as it may contain precious artifacts, all right?"

"And you will fight the giant and the old man?" *Le Duc* asked incredulously. "Alone?"

Lily smiled despite her fear and misgivings. "Oh, he won't be alone, *Monsieur*."

***

The Viðareiði church is a small, white structure, standing near the village's placid eastern coast and overlooking a rocky Atlantic inlet. It was young for such a church, having been erected just prior to the turn of the century, and it was well-kept by a young priest named Díðrikur.

On this morning, Father Díðrikur was nowhere to be found–bully for him!

The heavy wooden front doors were ripped open and slammed against the church's front face. It was dim inside, and the visible silhouettes of two men against the ocean could not have been more different.

One was old and stooped, one was massive.

"They will be by the altar," *Der Klinge* said, pointing. "Hurry."

Much like a decision made by a few other notable characters, *Der Klinge*, Konig, and the rogue had split up, with the Cabalists sending the rogue on ahead to prepare the plane while they made a short detour to the church.

Konig's jackboots sounded heavily on the cool, stone floor as he tromped up the aisle to the altar.

"They're not here," he said, turning in the multi-colored light of the stained glass and facing *Der Klinge*. "There is no silver."

"No," a man's voice said from the shadows. "It isn't there. I removed it. I knew you couldn't resist a few pieces of silver."

Der Klinge stepped into the church. "That voice..." he said.

"And we didn't want you pilfering anything else," a woman's voice added.

"Who...?"

Stepping into the light, Brick Brannigan and Liliana Halifax smiled.

"*You,*" *Der Klinge* hissed. "*Meine verfickte Sohn ist nutzlos,*" he shook his head. "So Heinrich could not even secure *your* death, *Herr* Brannigan? Then I most assuredly made the right decision in removing him from our ranks."

"Don't blame Von Faust," the Professor said. "He couldn't fathom my ingenuity. I faked my own death. Why give you the satisfaction of killing me when I could do it myself?"

Der Klinge nodded. "A good point," he conceded.

"Anyway, it's done now. Your plane has been seized, along with all the stolen relics. All that's left is for you to surrender and allow us to take you to the Peace Palace in The Hague to face the Permanent Court of International Justice and your inevitable conviction!"

Der Klinge laughed. "The Hague? The Peace Palace? The Permanent Court of International Justice? Who names these things?"

"Why you–"

"And what makes you think, *Herr* Brannigan, that the Cabal does not *own* the World Court?"

The Professor opened his mouth to quip a response.

"Uh," he said. "I... Oh, damn. Quips have been hard since coming back from the dead!"

"I see that," Lily said. "Now what?"

"I was hoping to do this easily," Brick sighed. "But oh, well. You take the old man."

"And you're going to get the giant?"

"Looks like it."

"Be careful, I met a man in Spain who had been *changed* by relics," Lily said softly.

"Changed? What do you mean–?"

All 350+ pounds of Konig charged, overturning a pew or two along the way, roaring like a possessed rhinoceros every step of the way.

Lily sidestepped the giant and dashed towards *Der Klinge*, double-barrel shotgun raised. Behind her, the two titans impacted with all the delicacy and grace you would imagine from that much uncut masculinity. The sound was atrocious.

"Hands up, sir," Lily said, proceeding the final few feet to *Der Klinge* slowly and cautiously.

"What was it I heard you say about Spain, my dear?" *Der Klinge* asked.

"It's not important," Lily said. "Put your hands up, please."

"Hands up? Why? You have seen too many of those crime pictures from your country, *fräulein*. I have no weapon. What are you afraid of?"

Lily swallowed, pulling back one of the two hammers on the shotgun. "Just put your hands up, please."

Behind her, someone was groaning in the melee, and a substantial piece of wood cracked.

"You see, I believe you said something about a man in Spain who had been changed by the relics. Is this correct, *fräulein*? It's so hard for me, frail old man that I am."

"Hands up, sir." She gestured with the barrel.

"Were you in Granada, *fräulein*?"

Lily stopped. "Yes, I was. How did you–"

"Because Rainer was well known for his... abilities."

"Rainer? Was that his–"

Der Klinge frowned. "If you crossed paths with him and live to tell the tale, then you are formidable, indeed, *fräulein*. My respect for you grows. Even if you are a weak woman."

"Don't underestimate me," Lily growled. "You will not like what I am capable of."

Der Klinge laughed. "*Fräulein*, it is *you* who will not like what *I* am capable of. You see, the relics cursed Rainer. He stole the skull and was remanded to the Alhambra. He could not leave and maintain his powers, and so he stayed." The old man smiled. "Fortunately, not all relics are quite so... restrictive."

"What do you–"

"Have you wondered *why* we were here? The Faroe Islands? Such a remote and desolate place? For a reason, I assure you. We were searching for something. And we found it."

Lily's stomach was beginning to swirl, a good signifier that she was in over her head. "Hugo–" she began.

Behind her, the fracas continued. The church would be lucky if it still stood when that battle had ceased.

"There is a mythological creature spoken of in all

Scandinavia called the Nøkken. It is a shapeshifter who is able to become that which is desirable–an attractive man, or woman, or what have you–and lure people to their deaths by drowning. You see, we came to these islands searching for something, something we *found*."

"Hugo–!"

"The blood of the Nøkken," *Der Klinge* said. "And I *drank it*."

Lily raised the shotgun.

"I'd really hoped to save my energy, but," he shrugged. "What the hell?"

Lily pulled the trigger. But it was too late.

CHAPTER 34: One Last Battle
To The Death

The blast erupted like an explosion in the small church, shaking the simple hanging chandeliers and rattling the stained glass.

But *Der Klinge* was gone.

"What the bloody hell?" Lily said, channeling her best Nero.

She knelt, searching the floor, looking under the pews on all fours for any sign of where the old man had gone, but there was no trace.

Finally, she turned, resolved to help the Professor.

"Good lord!" she cried.

The first four rows of pews were smashed, little more than splinters remaining. The two men stood, locked together, hands around each other's throats, battling for control.

"Let... go... you... *bastard*!" Brick said, his face beet red, veins pulsing.

Konig, face slightly pink, grit his teeth and pulled back for a punch. "*Ich werde dich zu vernichten, kleiner mann*!" he said.

Lily swung the shotgun, raking the mahogany stock against the giant's head. It sounded like a 2x4 impacting a cinder block and elicited no response whatsoever.

Konig unleashed his punch, catching Brannigan square in the cheek.

Stars filled the Professor's eyes as he coughed, struggling to catch a breath. He swung his own fist, barely slapping the huge man.

Desperate, Lily raised the shotgun. She had one round in the barrel and a few shells stuffed into her pockets.

"It's... buck... shot..." the Professor gasped.

"Oh, damn!"

On the ground at her feet was one of Aurelio's pistols. Lily snatched it up and raised it to Konig's temple.

"Are you bullet proof, *jüngling*," Lily said, cocking the pistol.

"Yes," Konig said, punching Brick again.

"Oh. Um." Lily lowered the pistol, looking at Brick–now with a bloody nose–and shrugging.

"I was not the only one to be changed, *fräulein*," an inhuman voice said from behind Lily. "Konig is my son, but not of woman born..."

Lily turned and gasped at the abomination that stood looming over her.

Behind her, Konig released Brannigan and knelt, bowing his head. "*Gepriesen sei der Vater! Ich verneige mich vor ihm!*"

Brannigan fell to the ground, coughing. "I've woken up in a horrorshow!" he sputtered. "What the *hell* is going on? Is this the Faroe Islands? or the *Grand Guignol*?!"

Der Klinge–The Sword if you haven't Googled it yet–had become *Die Spinne*–The Spider. He stood on six long, black arachnoid legs, giving way to a hairy, muscle-ripped and vaguely reptilian torso. In place of his two arms were long, razor-like blades, droplets of venom falling from a pair of ferocious, barbed points.

His face–mercy me, dear reader–was far from human. Scaled and hideous, the mouth was too large for the head, and so it stretched around past where the man's ears would have been. Fangs filled the gaping maw, above which two crimson eyes glowed.

"*Steigen, mein sohn,*" *Die Spinne* said. "We have much murder to do. I believe this town has seen far too much of us, no?"

Now able to breathe once again, Brannigan stood, two fists clenched at his sides. "Not today, you over-grown insect!"

As Konig rose, Brannigan lashed out, connecting one vicious kick to *Die Spinne*'s knee–or one of them, the leg buckling under the creature's weight as one of its razor arms lashed out for our hero.

Brannigan rolled beneath it, snatching up the shotgun as he did so. Lily fired the pistol into Konig's body, pulling the trigger repeatedly until it *click*ed against an empty chamber. Droplets of fresh blood appeared on Konig's already bloody shirtfront, but very little else seemed to be accomplished.

"Worry about this spider thing!" Brick called to Lily. "The giant is... well, too much to handle right now!"

He raised the shotgun and fired it into the *Die Spinne*'s body. Green blood sprayed across the church floor.

Die Spinne swung again, cutting through a chandelier chain, severing it and sending the heavy iron frame plummeting to the floor. A second swing cut through a pew, reducing it to kindling. As *Die Spinne* stalked towards them, Brannigan and Lily backpedaled, avoiding *Die Spinne*'s errant swings as they struggled to reload the shotgun.

"More shells, dear," Brannigan said. "Empty your–" he ducked to avoid the blade arm thing, "pockets!"

Lily pulled a handful of shells out of her jacket pocket as *Die Spinne* smashed into a plaster wall and shrieked, a grand stained-glass window shattering beside it.

"Through the window? Good idea!" the Professor said, turning to a stained-glass window opposite *Die Spinne* as he grabbed Lily's arm. "Let's go!"

Running full-speed at the window, Brannigan raced across the narrow chapel and leapt through the beautiful old glass, pulling his love behind him.

They rolled to a bloody stop in the grass, covered in cuts and panting as shattered remnants of the window rained over them.

Behind them, *Die Spinne* was demolishing the church, struggling to escape the confines of the building as Konig climbed through the ruins of the window after them.

"Back up, love," Brannigan said, moving back towards the cliff. "I think it's high time we used our surroundings in our favor."

Lily and Hugo ran for the front of the church a scant few yards from the cliff's edge. Konig tramped after them, bloody and bloody angry.

He caught them at the front of the church, lashing both arms around Brannigan's neck and lifting the hero off the ground. The giant tensed his huge arms against Brannigan's neck and twisted cruelly, hoping to crack the Professor's spine just as he had Von Faust's.

Lily snatched the shotgun from Brick's hands and turned it on Konig.

"Sorry, my love," she said. "We'll have to take our chances with the buckshot!"

As she spoke, *Die Spinne* finally discovered how to escape the church: piece by piece.

Behind Lily, the facade of the church was ripped down, one brick at a time, green blood-speckled stones rolling towards Konig and the Professor as *Die Spinne* climbed from the church ruins. Behind it, the roof of the church collapsed with a creaking sigh.

The Professor's eyes began to close, the strong flow of blood to his brain ceasing beneath the strain of the giant's incredible strength. Lily stood, finger tightening on the shotgun's trigger, praying the buckshot was enough to slow Konig without taking Hugo's life.

"Goodbye, Brannigan!" *Die Spinne* screeched, swinging a razor arm at Konig and Brannigan in hopes of a double-beheading (sorry, Konig).

Eyes wide, Brannigan had nothing he could do.

It occurred like another bolt of epiphanic lightning: rather than firing the gun, Lily turned it in her hands and swung it, connecting the shotgun's stock with the Professor's knee. He collapsed, straining *just* enough against Konig's grasp to slip downward.

Q: How far down did he slip? **A:** Enough!

Die Spinne's razor passed through Konig's–and only Konig's–head, just about eye-level.

Brannigan only lost a few wisps of hair.

Blood erupted everywhere as Konig's grasp released and Brannigan collapsed to the ground.

On witnessing the giant's end, *Die Spinne* roared, "*Noooooooooo!*"

"Damn it all, I can't seem to catch my breath today!" Brick huffed and puffed. "Or do anything right, for that matter! Who'll save me next?"

"I volunteer, *le héros*," Miette said, rushing towards them, guns at the ready.

Lily ducked as Miette's double .45s roared to life, round after round of the Tommies slicing through *Die Spinne* in a storm of his weird green blood.

The creature stumbled towards the cliff, baying and clawing at the ground, dragging its massive body *towards* the precipice.

"Don't let it escape!" Brannigan shouted. "We didn't get the Cipher back! It still has the Cipher and we need it!"

He rose to his feet and stumbled towards it as Miette finally ceased fire. He grabbed one of *Die Spinne*'s legs, closing both hands over it and pulling back with all his might.

Behind him, *Le Duc* finally arrived, panting. "What– *ce que le putain que c'est*??"

"Come here, damn you!" Brannigan shouted to *Le Duc* as he pulled. "We... can't... let... it... get... away!"

In a flash, the French superhero was at his side, grabbing another leg and adding his own not insubstantial power.

Die Spinne's progress just about ceased, its powerful forearms not enough to conterract our duo of adventurers.

Unfortunately, our two tugging heroes hit a wet patch of mud and their footing gave way. Hugo fell to the ground, releasing his grasp as he did so. Beside him, *Le Duc* held tight as he flopped to his belly, legs kicking behind him.

Die Spinne had reached the edge and had traction to burn. Miette opened fire with her Tommies once more, round after round tearing into *Die Spinne*, but it was too late.

"Let go!" Brick said. "*Duc*, let go!"

Eyes wide, *Le Duc* shouted "*Aidez moi*! Help me! I am going to–" as *Die Spinne* tumbled over the edge with the Professor's battle-scarred bag.

Brick, Lily, and Miette watched as *Le Duc* was pulled over with it.

CHAPTER 35: This Is The End
(Though The Story Is Not Quite Over)

"Tu es fou, tu es mort pour une énorme araignée?" Miette said from her knees, her smoking .45s lying defeated on the grass beside her.

Brannigan, sprawled in the mud beside the cliff, crawled to the very edge.

"...Hugo?" Lily asked. "Is he...?"

Brick shook his head. "I don't... I hope not, but..."

The Professor, at the edge, looked over. Miette and Lily could only hear the crash of waves on the rocks below.

The first thing Brick saw was the black and bloody body of *Die Spinne* slip below the tide in a bubbling mass of green water.

The second thing Brick saw was *Le Duc*, dangling by a tiny handhold, feet peddling against nothing, cape flapping in the wind.

"A hand, *mon ami*?" he asked with a smile.

***

Heroes returning to Aurelio's smuggling vessel, they– and *we*, dear reader–are left pondering: What comes next? Their trip back was arduous, considering they needed to make it a number of times to carry the liberated relics from *Der Klinge*'s second plane at the base of Mount Villingdalsfjall, leaving them plenty of time to mull this question over. Miette and *Le Duc* may have left the plane intact, albeit unable to fly. Unfortunately for the nameless rogue and pilot, there were no survivors.

That is all well and good, dear reader, but once more: What comes next? What of the Cipher of Dumuzid? What of the Eye of Aja? What of *Der Klinge*, I mean *Die Spinne*? Gone. Such is the only word applicable to far too many of these difficult questions. Did *Die Spinne* carry the Cipher and Eye to his death? Were they lost to the sea? Is that freaky weird *Die Spinne* thing alive or dead?

And what of the Cabal? Lest we forget *Der Klinge*'s threat regarding the World Court. Was their influence and power *so* far reaching? As I'm sure you remember, dear reader, *Der Klinge* was far from the only agent of the Cabal. There are more supervillains and more relics in more magnificent places in even more remote corners of this miraculous place we call Earth.

Something tells me that, although the Professor has recaptured a planeload full of relics, the threat of the Cabal is anything but finished.

We will be left to wonder, indeed, but in the wake of bodies that now litter these islands, there is one that left with a beating heart and a poisoned mind full of stratagems: Black Fang Delacroix.

He departed the Faroe Islands healthy and rejuvenated, filled with a new black-hearted passion and shiny, invigorated agenda, already scheming on how to rebuild his felled army of madmen and cut a fresh swath of destruction across the very face of the globe.

Who will stand for us, protecting the innocent and battling the legions of evil?

No, not *Le Duc*–although granted, he is a superhero.

Think harder.

Yes, I expect you know, dear reader, that Brick Brannigan is the only man for the job–with the assistance of his true love Liliana Halifax and that uncanny band of remarkable heroes, to boot.

And that is why...

Brick Brannigan (et al) Will Return in

BRICK BRANNIGAN IS SEARCHING FOR A NEW TITLE!

FOR THE BRAVE EXPLORER IN US ALL:

EUROPA POINT LIGHTHOUSE, GIBRALTAR
PICTURE BY PAUL HANDLEY, USED WITH PERMISSION

THE CITY OF CÀDIZ
PICTURE BY ANDREA
VERDELLI, USED
WITH PERMISSION

THE TRIANA BRIDGE IN SEVILLA, SPAIN.
PICTURE BY GREGORY ZEIER. USED WITH PERMISSION.

LA GIRALDA
IN SEVILLA, SPAIN

PICTURE BY
WIKIERNST
USED WITH PERMISSION.

CATHEDRAL DE SEVILLA
PICTURE BY PEPIJNTJE, USED WITH PERMISSION

THE ALHAMBRA'S
COURT OF THE LIONS,
PAINTING BY ADOLF SEEL
(1892)

THE PALACE OF CHARLES V IN THE ALHAMBRA
PICTURE BY HISMATTNESS, USED WITH PERMISSION

TÒRSHAVN, THE FAROE ISLANDS
PICTURE BY STIG NYGAARD, USED WITH PERMISSION

THE VILLAGE OF KLAKSVÍK, FAROE ISLANDS
PICTURE BY VINCENT VAN ZEIJST
USED WITH PERMISSION

CHAPEL,
THE VILLAGE OF
VIÐAREIÐI, 1899

IMAGE IN PUBLIC DOMAIN

About The Author:

Eric Bonkowski lives in Delaware. While he is not a brave explorer, he finds inspiration daily in Saturday afternoon cliffhanger serials, classic comics and comic strips, and horror films of the '30s and '40s–to say nothing of mystery, fantasy, and science fiction pulp writings of every age.

He spends his time reading, watching campy movies, and writing, supported all the while by his remarkable wife and family. During the rare quieter moments, he can be found listening to jazz and falling asleep well before bedtime.

In addition to Brick Brannigan, he is also the author of the *Gil's Grimoire* series.

Visit him at:

http://www.GilsGrimoire.com

http://www.BrickBrannigan.com

www.ingramcontent.com/pod-product-compliance
Lightning Source LLC
Chambersburg PA
CBHW030030180626
46810CB00001B/299